Black Eye

Black Eye
A Johnny Black Mystery

Neville Steed

St. Martin's Press
New York

Library of Congress Cataloging-in-Publication Data

Steed, Neville.
      Black eye / Neville Steed.
          p. cm.
      ISBN 0-312-03797-X
      I. Title.
      PR6069.T387B55   1990
      823′.914—dc20   89-24167
                                                  CIP

First published in Great Britain by George Weidenfeld & Nicolson Limited.

First U.S. Edition
10 9 8 7 6 5 4 3 2 1

To Lily
with love

Introduction

Around two years ago, a considerable collection of old, hand-written manuscripts were discovered hidden in the attic of a most attractive thatched house situated near the small village of Staverton in South Devon.

On inspection, these papers were seen to be the intriguing personal record of a certain John Black, né Smith, who in 1937 had started a small detective agency in the fashionable resort of Torquay on Britain's Riviera coast.

The papers had been neatly divided into sections, boxed and labelled. Each box contained John Black's personal account of a particular case his detective agency, called, aptly enough, Black Eye, had undertaken. The following memoir details the first of many involved and very often dangerous assignments undertaken by this extraordinary man, who went to such pains to record his own feats and feelings, yet, seemingly, had no intention of releasing his dramatic and absorbing record to the outside world. Or, maybe, as has happened to others, successive British governments have actively prevented publication for reasons of their own.

Despite extensive enquiries, it has proved impossible to trace John Black's whereabouts or history after October 1950, when he apparently left South Devon suddenly and without explanation. It was assumed then that he went to live abroad. However, there is considerable speculation that he could be the John Smith whose knighthood was announced in the 1955 New Year's Honours List. The citation at the time ran, 'For distinguished service on behalf of Her Majesty's Foreign Office', which some commentaters have since read as a useful cover for secret service activities on behalf of M15 or M16.

However, no known public record reveals Mr Smith having actually received his knighthood at the hands of the Queen. For, as already stated, all positive records of John Black/Smith seem to have terminated abruptly in the autumn of 1950. Where he might be now, whether he is still alive, whether he was, for reasons only perhaps to be found in the most holy of files of Britain's secret services, forced to adopt a whole new identity, will probably never be known.

John Black, né Smith
Only known facts

Born John Smith, 1910, in Croydon, Surrey. Middle-class, suburban background. His father was an assistant secretary in the Board of Education and his mother, according to some letters from one who knew her, 'was a colossal snob' and 'affected a life-style way above her husband's means'. Prep school education, followed by minor public school.

Father was knocked down and killed by a get-away car driven by robbers raiding the Croydon branch of Barclays Bank. The tragedy seems to have been one of the triggers for John Smith's interest in crime detection. A subsequent flying friend of his has described how John Smith was an avid reader of all crime fiction, from Hammett and Chandler to Christie, Sayers, Conan-Doyle, A.E.W. Mason, et al. Also great fan of private eye films in the cinema.

It would seem that lack of money on his father's death forced John to leave school at just seventeen. His mother arranged for him to be articled to her brother, who was an accountant in Torquay, Devon. But he quit after only eighteen months, hating the dreariness of the world of accountancy, but loving the countryside of Devon.

His mother then despatched him to her late husband's brother in Kenya, where one who remembers his four years there recounts he discovered girls and flying, but developed a strong dislike for the colonial way of life.

Then twenty-two, John Smith returned to England a qualified pilot. He became a flying instructor at Denham, but some time later he was badly injured in a plane crash caused by a careless student. Inevitably, his injuries caused him to lose his pilot's licence and for the next three years, he seems to have tried his hand at a variety of jobs. These range from flying club administration, to helping out an old school friend, the Hon. Peter Courtenay, who raced at Brooklands, to playing odd roles on the provincial stage, and acting as an extra in several Korda films being made at Denham.

Ultimately, he seems at the age of twenty-seven to have changed both his name and his life style. With some money he had won on the Grand National, he moved back to Devon, became John Black (according to one source, it was originally Black-Smith, but he soon dropped the Smith), bought a dilapidated cottage in Dartington, and set up a modest detective agency called Black Eye in Torquay.

The fortunes and misfortunes of this agency form the substance of the many manuscripts discovered in the attic in Staverton, and cover the ten years 1937 – 1947.

One
May 1937

I heard it coming even above the rattle, tinkle and phut of my Austin Seven. And, hell's bells, it was low. The black shadow of its tapering wings licked across my hands on the steering wheel, as if asking why I wasn't up there, at the controls of a sleek DH96, instead of a battered Austin Chummy.

I cocked a covetous eye at its biplane beauty, as it winged its way on towards its undoubted destination – Plymouth. At the head-skimming height the Railway Air Services airliner was flying, it must have made a request stop at Haldon; quite a common occurrence these days on its regular route from the North via Cardiff. I guess there will come a time when British airlines will get so big, they just won't bother to make request stops any more. They will get like the railways who own them – as cold and impersonal as the steel rails on which their stock runs. Roll back the day.

The thick Austin Seven wheel shuddered in my hand, as if to jerk my head down out of the clouds and back to reality, which was that I was well and truly pegged to the ground these days. All thanks to a dear pupil of mine who, after only two hours of instruction, had decided that flying was a doddle and the guy in the rear cockpit was only there for ballast. Well, he doddled himself down into an instant grave and me into the lingering death of never again being able to pass a pilot's medical. For some crazy reason, the quacks didn't go for a damaged eye, a slightly shortened leg and collapsed lung. And they closed their earth-bound ears to my impassioned pleas that I could still fly an aeroplane with under half the physical equipment the crash had left intact. The dreaded truth is that they would rather pass an A1 twit, who has less feeling for flying than your average mole, than a C3 guy, even though he may have aviation fuel for blood and still be able to fly a Puss Moth between his girlfriend's legs without either wingtip laddering her stockings. Hey ho.

I corrected the shimmy on the steering and rattled on. The day was hot. Soon my radiator cap started to steam like the Riviera Express and spewed spots of rusty water back onto the windscreen like measles. I calculated that I would just make the car dump before every drop of H_2O was red hot dust. I was right.

Bobby Briggs' head popped up from the greasy entrails of a terminal Ford Model A. From the hiss of steam from my Austin, I guess he must have thought a traction engine had just pulled in. All he said was, 'Oh, it's only you.'

I scissored out of the Chummy without opening the door. The steam was a bad enough advertisement for my car, without the scrap-dealer knowing the body was so rotten that once the door was opened, the rest of the coachwork seemed to want to close over the hole.

Briggs put down his spanner and strode over.

'That it?'

I nodded. "29 model.'

A mischievous grin came over his bulldog features, which always looked as if he had just slammed into a wall.

'Didn't know they made cars in 1829.'

'It's the only one,' I offered. Well, what else could I say over the hiss of still escaping steam?

He walked right round the car, seemingly in two strides, then kicked a front wheel. It gave some fifteen degrees but I noticed the steering wheel didn't turn an iota. Needless to say he spotted it too.

'How many days' notice d'you 'ave to give it to change direction?'

'Depends if it's raining,' I said.

He put a greasy bulldog paw on my shoulder and laughed. 'All right, Johnny. Tell you what, I won't charge you a penny to take if off you.'

'Thanks for nothing, Bobby.' I extended my arm towards the drunkenly leaning stacks of junked and half dismembered cars that stretched almost as far as the eye could see. 'Whatever you say, my Austin's better than ninety-nine per cent of the rubbish you've got here.'

'Ah, but you're forgetting something. Not much pickings on an Austin Seven. Not enough to it.'

He steered me over to the lopsided hulk of a 1932 Humber Snipe that looked as if it had been hit by a train.

'Now, a nice big car like this, there's plenty of pickings, ain't there?

Makes me money on the pickings, not on the carcase.'

He dug me in the ribs. 'Car-case,' he repeated, his grin displaying his disdain of dentists. 'Good, that. Car-case – pickings . . .'

I forced a grin. I didn't want to upset Bobby Briggs. And not just because we hadn't, as yet, clinched any deal. For the good will and knowledge of people like the scrap dealer I recognized might be of untold value in my newly minted profession. But no. That wasn't really the reason either. I just sort of liked the man, rogue though he might be. I'd liked his blunt manner and even excused his appalling sense of humour, from the very first moment I'd met him via the barman in Torquay's Imperial Hotel. That's why I had come all the way over to his yard that morning. Better the devil you know, horns and all.

'Okay,' I said. 'Forget my Austin for a second and let me see *your* offering.'

I looked around the chaos of the yard, but could not see anything approaching the streamlined contours of my quest. I looked round at him sharply.

'You haven't sold it, have you?'

He patted my back reassuringly. That would be some more grease marks for the cleaners.

'What d'you think? I'd get Johnny Black out here on a wild goose chase?' He winked his eye as subtly as he slammed a bonnet and propelled me further into the mangled maze of machines.

'Wouldn't dare disappoint you now, Johnny, case I might need your services one day.' He sniffed and went on, 'Never know in my business. Get some queer customers sometimes. That's why I let my dogs loose when I lock up at night. Sometimes I think I need them in the ruddy daytime too.'

I looked round nervously, but to my relief there was no sign of the meanest brace of curs this side of Jack London's imagination.

But there was still no sign of the voluptuous curves I had come to appraise, though we were now back from the road by at least ten ranks of tangled transport towers. He read my concern.

'Not far now. Just behind the concertina-ed Airflow and that big Morris on its side. Daren't have put it in sight of the road. Be 'alf-inched, even if I had a million dogs.'

He stopped, blocking my path.

'Looks a million dollars now.' Smiling gleefully, like a child, he went on, 'Even got its original whitewalls. Never know it had been out of the showroom, let alone in a pile-up.'

I returned his smile. 'Going to let me see it now?'

He hesitated, as if he were afraid I might not match his excitement. 'If you don't want it, I'll keep it for myself.'

I waved my hand. He led on. And there it was. Just like on the silver screen. Only better – it was in full glorious colour. Cream to be exact. A deep, rich cream, which the whitewall tyres only high-lighted. Red leather glinted richly through a window. Biplane bumper blades dazzled in the sun. Bullet shaped headlights hugged the slimmest of slim grilles. The only thing missing was William Powell as the Thin Man, suavely at the wheel.

I took a deep breath. I was in love. Madly in love with a lady called La Salle.

Briggs waved a current copy of *Autocar* at me.

'Look for yourself, Johnny. Going rate for a '29 Tourer is twelve to fourteen oncers. And that's in good nick, mind you. One like yours outside can't fetch more than a tenner of anybody's ruddy money.'

I looked around his so-called office – a wooden hut nestling amidst the metal mountains – to give me time to think. My recent win on the Grand National, after I had paid the first three months' rent on my tiny office in Torquay, kitted it out and bought an eighth-hand typewriter, did not really stretch to big American cars, even if they were at knock down prices because they had been insurance write-offs. But I knew, somehow, I just had to have that La Salle, even if I had to give up eating to get it. I turned back to him.

'Look, Bob, impressive as it looks now, you can't get away from the fact that the La Salle has made love to a tree on the A303 and nearly killed its Cuban owner. You've bent it back into pretty good shape, I'll admit, but a write-off is still a write-off and not everyone's idea of motoring heaven.'

He sat back in his seat, that I recognized as from an old Austin 12-4. He steepled his fingers and lifted his small but all-seeing eyes to the ceiling.

'Knew that before you came, didn't you, Johnny Boy?'

'Granted. But I did not know what you'd be asking for it. I too flipped through the pages of *Autocar* and *Motor* in Smith's before I came. Going price for a non-crashed '34 La Salle is around £285–£300. So your £250 is a mite steep.'

14

He leaned forward towards me with a 'Tell you what' expression on his face.

'Tell you what,' he said, 'I'll do myself an injury just for you, Johnny. Straight deal. Two hundred nicker, it's yours. You'd be mad to turn it down. That La Salle will do more for your new private eye business than any ruddy office or eye fluttering secretary. Admit it, Johnny. '34 model it may be, but its lines. . .' His hands outlined the shape, as if he were describing a Hollywood starlet. 'Why, it still makes other motors look as if Noah ruddy made 'em. Admit it, Johnny. That La Salle is the next best thing to flying.'

Briggs had tried the sucker punch and struck home. The test run in the La Salle had been almost as smooth as flight and the sense of power. . . I did some mental arithmetic yet again. It still came out the same way. I was at least fifty pounds short, even without eating, drinking, switching on a light or wearing shoes.

I sighed a sepulchral sigh.

'I'll take it,' I said, but then added quickly, 'Hundred down, fifty in a month, ten bob a week for six months.'

He sucked on a greasy knuckle. 'Still leaves twenty five.'

'Credit note. A Black Eye credit note for twenty-five-pounds worth of investigative services, that can be taken in dribs and drabs or all at once and, what's more, credit with no time limit attached.'

He plucked his knuckle from his mouth to point a finger at me.

'Hundred down, fifty in a month, fifteen bob a week for six months and a tenner's worth of services.'

I gave his proposition deep thought and it was at least one and a half seconds before I replied.

'Done,' I said.

We shook on it and he held onto my hand, whilst he added, 'Won't let me down, will you Johnny?'

I shook my head. Not really in reply, but in desperation. I could hardly afford to run the Austin Seven, let alone an eight-cylinder La Salle coupe the length of a tennis court.

Briggs looked at his watch.

'Well, I'd better be off,' he said, 'seeing as how I need a nice motor for myself now that I'm not keeping that beauty of yours.'

He opened the door of the hut for me. I blinked against the sun.

'Got one in mind?'

'Yeah. Nice sporting number. Almost no mileage neither.'

'MG?'

'No. Frazer-Nash.'

I raised my eyebrows. Frazer-Nashes were not exactly thick on the ground. In fact, I had only heard of one in the whole area and that one. . . I suddenly whirled round to face him.

'You don't mean – ?' I began, but he cut me off.

'I do, Johnny, I do. Knew he'd be bound to sell it, once the inquest was over. No one likes to keep a car that's gone and killed a nearest and dearest, now do they?'

Two

A rap at my door startled me. I looked up from my *Aeroplane* magazine and was about to stow it away in my desk, when I recognized the silhouette behind the glass door. I relaxed.

'Come in, Babs.'

She came in. Her baby blue eyes shone with excitement.

'Have you seen what's outside?' she breathed, and ran over to the window.

'Torquay harbour,' I offered. 'A Guernsey freighter, two trawlers, twenty-two smaller craft and the tip of a mast sticking out of the water. I've counted them three times already.'

She double-took, then her Cupid's bow mouth untied itself into a grin.

'No, Johnny, no. I mean, have you seen what's outside?'

'Torq –' I began again, but she cut in.

'No, I mean it could be your first client. And important, too, by the size of his car. Come and have a look. I spotted it just now from my own window. Wow! I just had to come and tell you.'

Before I went to look, I knew precisely what I was going to see. However, Babs was the kind of girl you couldn't disappoint.

I peered down.

'See?' she went on. 'He's probably on his way up here now.' She went to straighten my old Triptonian tie. I held my hand to my collar.

'Too late,' I said. 'He's been up.'

She looked as disappointed as Alice would have been with a solid looking glass.

'You mean . . . he's been . . . and gone?'

'No, just been,' I smiled.

She frowned. At least, I think she did. Her bubbly blond curls hid most of her less than generous forehead. Then she looked slowly round the room. I'd have been an utter cad to have teased her any

17

further.

'The "he" is me, Babs. Me. Johnny Black.'

'"He" is you?'

'Me.' I put a hand on her shoulder. The crêpe de Chine of her dress was charged with static. I removed my hand from her shoulder.

'It's not a client's car, more's the pity. It's my car, Babs. I picked it up yesterday.'

She looked at me in complete disbelief, as if I'd said I was the Duke of Windsor. I sat her down in my chair.

'You . . . own . . . that . . . car?'

'I . . . own . . . that . . . car,' I repeated. 'Least, I own about half of it. The rest I'm paying off in. . .'

I did not bother to finish the sentence, but switched to others that explained how I had come to own such a large streamlined two-passenger overture to bankruptcy.

'Wow!' was all I got when I had finished. More than I deserved, I guess.

'Don't get any wrong ideas, Babs,' I felt I had to say. 'I can't afford a car like that. Or any car really. It's just that an Austin Chummy doesn't exactly impress clients. The clients I haven't got.'

She got up from my chair and stood by me. She was almost a foot shorter than my six feet one and I felt a trifle embarrassed.

'You'll get clients, Johnny, just you wait and see.'

'I'm waiting,' I grinned, 'but not seeing too much.'

'I had better get back, otherwise Mr Ling will get mad again.'

I stood aside for her. 'Mustn't annoy Mr Ling.'

'No. I don't mind so much for me. But I don't want him to. . .' She hesitated so I helped her.

'. . .throw me out because I'm too disruptive?'

She nodded sheepishly. 'I like Black Eye having its office here. You don't know how boring it is working for Mr Ling. All I do all day is type invoices, answer the phone and pack and unpack those silly novelties he imports from Hong Kong. The tin ones cut your fingers, the celluloid ones often smell something awful. So having you here, a real detective and all – well,' she blushed, 'well, it brightens up the day a bit.'

She made for the door, then looked back.

'Don't forget, if you want any typing done or phones answered while you're out on a case. . .'

'I won't forget,' I smiled. 'When I've got a case to go out on.'

'Yes, well. . .' She bumped into the door knob, then let herself out.

I went back and looked out the window, just in time to see a rag-and-bone man's horse relieving itself as it passed my La Salle.

The rest of the morning was a long drawn out yawn, unless you deem the Guernsey freighter leaving harbour of scintillating interest. At this rate, Bobby Briggs would be having his La Salle back in double quick tempo.

I cursed the *Torbay Express*. The tiny advertisement I had placed in the current issue had not even pulled a single tinkle on the old telephone or caused a rattle of my letterbox. Surely somebody somewhere needed somebody to look into something for some reason sometime. Maybe they didn't. Maybe Torquay, Torbay, nay the whole of South Devon was too law-abiding and caring, courteous and careful ever to need the services of someone like me. Maybe I should have opened Black Eye in London's Dockland or in a Birmingham back street, or even in the sinful suburbia of Croydon, where I was born, raised and almost ruined.

But glorious Devon was where I wanted to live and breathe. My love affair had begun upon my father's death, when my mother had packed me off to be articled to her brother, my uncle's, accountancy business, which was then situated in Torquay – her widow's income being insufficient for me to be incarcerated further at my minor public school of Tripton. And though I speedily grew to hate everything to do with the plodding pulse of accountancy and those who practised the profession, I did find enormous satisfaction in my geographical surroundings and took every opportunity to be out and about in them, rather than in the pokey office. So much so, my uncle constantly had to remind me of the dreaded 'articles' by which I was bound; which, to me, seemed the most indefinite of articles and not to be taken too seriously, as my main duties seemed to be as delivery and tea boy extraordinary. I survived for just eighteen months before I turned it all in for a Colonial alternative in Kenya's Happy Valley – sufficient time for the British Riviera to have chosen me as its own.

With no calls, by lunchtime I knew the contents of that week's *Aeroplane* magazine backwards, forwards, downwards and upwards. And every soaring photograph seemed to rub salt in the wound of the loss of my pilot's licence. I had just tossed the issue into the bucket I used as my waste-paper basket when, glory be, the phone rang. I took the receiver off the hook with a quivering hand and had to hold onto the daffodil-shaped body of the instrument to steady myself.

I needn't have sweated. It was only Bobby Briggs, asking how I liked the La Salle now I'd got it home. I reassured him that I was still a satisfied, if penniless, customer, then asked him in turn about the Frazer-Nash he had gone to see.

'Got it, Johnny. Goes like a bird. Ruddy noisy one, mind you, but a bird all the same.'

'Good. Remember not to wear a scarf when you're at the wheel, won't you?'

He gave a guttural guffaw.

'Don't remind me, old son. Still, mustn't grumble. That's the reason I got it for more or less a song. That Seagrave fella wasn't 'alf keen to unload it. Accepted my first ruddy offer. Still, can't blame him, can you?'

'No,' I agreed. 'I bet Isadora Duncan's friend got shot of his Bugatti quickly too.'

'Pardon?'

I instantly regretted my reference.

'Oh nothing. It's just that it's not the first time someone has been strangled by her scarf catching in the chain drive of a car. They brought up the previous case at the Seagrave inquest. Didn't you read about it?'

'Suppose I did. Some high-falutin' dancer, wasn't she? No better than she should have been, wouldn't wonder. Did the dance of the veils, didn't she?'

'Something like that. Anyway, so you like the car?'

'Sure thing. Chain drive and all. I reckon I can run it for a year and still sell it for more than I had to cough up for it. Ship it to London. The name Seagrave on the log book won't mean so much there.' He cleared his throat and I suddenly realized that it was most unlike old Bobby Briggs to bother to ring up just about one of his sales. He was more the kind of car shark who changed his address and telephone number every time he conned another customer.

I interrupted his phlegm clearance. 'Out with it, Bobby. You haven't rung me just to find if I'm still cock-a-hoop about the La Salle, have you?'

'Er, well . . . not exactly.'

'So what is "exactly"? Let me guess. You want to cash in some of your Black Eye credit. That it?'

'In a manner of speaking, er, yes,' he conceded.

I laughed. 'You want me to sleep nights with those wolves you call Alsatians in case they miss a prowler?'

'Come off it, Johnny. You said I could have a bit of your time, didn't you? Part of the deal, it was.'

His normal gravel voice became face powder soft. 'It's my wife, Johnny. I – er, think I may have a bit of a problem with her, like.'

My heart sank. That my first case should be free and on account was bad enough, but for it to be a sordid marital fidelity enquiry was the last straw. I prayed fervently before my next question.

'What kind of a problem, Bobby?'

Someone up there did not like me, for the scrap dealer replied, 'I've reason to believe she may be seeing some other ruddy fella. I can't follow her around myself, now can I? Wondered if you might like to work off some of what you owe me – say, for a couple of weeks.'

I sighed – but out of range of the phone's mouthpiece.

'All right, Bobby. Tell me where you live and I'll see what I can do. It's probably nothing, you know.'

'Yeah. Maybe. Maybe not. Anyway . . .' he cleared his throat once more, 'glad you still like the La Salle. She won't let you down.'

Now it was my turn to clear my throat. And I took down his address and his wife's description, with a somewhat heavy Conway-Stewart. It was a hell of a way to open up the files of the Black Eye Detective Agency. My only consolation was that I wasn't the hero of my cinematic imagination – William Powell in the *Thin Man* series. For I had, as yet, no Myrna Loy to wag her beautiful but disapproving head at me.

'Stick 'em up!'

I dropped my door key. I'd never get used to it.

'Stick 'em up. Drop 'em,' the raucous voice commanded.

'Oh, shut up,' I growled. 'I don't need you after a hard day watching a lady who did nothing but hang her washing out.'

Still, I only had myself to blame. After all, I'd taught him every word he knew.

In my temper, I hit my head against a beam as I made my way through my small sitting-room to the even smaller kitchen.

Groucho – that's my parrot – fell back on the clichés he had been taught before I'd bought him, some eighteen months back: 'Pretty Polly,' and 'Who's a pretty boy, then?' – the last being a damn fool phrase as an old girlfriend of mine, who was adept at sexing everything, had concluded that Groucho was actually a girl.

I lit the oil stove to brew myself some tea, then flopped down in one of my junk shop easy chairs near the sitting-room grate. I felt a hundred years old instead of twenty-seven. For four days now I had been watching a woman who seemed to do nothing but walk down to the local store and back, drub her washing on a washboard in an outside scullery, hang it out, take it in, chat to the milkman, pat the milkman's horse, hob-nob over the fence with her balloon-faced neighbour (who had to be at least twenty stone in her non-stockinged feet) and iron endlessly in her front room.

The rest of her domestic activities were not visible from outside the house, but unless she had got some Don Juan held captive under a bed, in a wardrobe or in a broom cupboard (all places I would have thought Bobby Briggs might have checked before ringing me) she seemed as faithful as the day is long. At least, so far. I still had ten days of my credit to go, but Mrs Briggs just didn't really look the part of a cuckolding siren. Like her husband, she was built like a bulldog and the way she took it out on her washing sent shivers down my spine. Maybe, if she ever met her lover, it was only on visiting days at St Dunstan's.

The kettle duly boiled and I made some tea, a far cry from the extra Dry Martini I am sure William Powell would have downed after a hard day's sleuthing. But in the present parlous state of my finances, I could hardly afford even Lyons' cheapest tea. As I put the cup to my lips, Groucho shrieked out, as yet another loose piece of hairy plaster fell onto his cage. This was a fairly familiar occurrence in my cottage. Not just downstairs, but everywhere. I often wake up at night, plastered, so to speak. That's what comes of shelling out only twenty pounds more for my home than I had for my new car. Still, as the house agent so fervently pointed out to me, 'This cottage, Mr Black, is full of potential.' He omitted to add that it was also full of rot, wet and dry, death-watch beetles, competitive woodworm, degenerative plaster, spiders as big as Hispano-Suizas and rats in what was left of the thatch.

I bought it because: (a) it was dirt cheap (quite literally) and all my winnings on the Grand National would allow, considering I still had to buy a car to impress my clients; (b) it was actually charming – if you didn't have to live in it, that is. All exposed beams and rickety windows like you see in the cartoon films they show when the cinema organist has disappeared down again into the bowels of the auditorium; (c) it was in an equally charming area near Dartington, only half a gallon's drive from the room I rented from Mr Ling in Torquay (used to be about a sixth of a gallon's ride in the Chummy); (d) the house agent had been right. It was full of potential. Now the only problem was whether I was too – and could make enough money to spare a little for the renovations and extensions I planned and the acre of land allowed.

Just as I opened Groucho's cage to prevent him swallowing the length of horse hair he had pecked out of his plaster shower, we were both startled by the unmistakable 'da-da' of *Colonel Bogey* being played on a set of car horns. I looked across to the window. Behind the cream bulk of my La Salle on the track was now the slippery blue of a Bugatti 57 – the nearest you can get to a Grand Prix car that the law will allow on His Majesty's highways.

Hair retrieved, I went to the front door and opened it. The familiar sight of the white leather flying suit and goggles did me a power of good and the problem of Mrs Briggs and Black Eye faded at the sight of this dazzling figure. With a boyish leap, my visitor was out of the doorless cockpit and striding up the muddy track that served as a path.

'So this is the Black hideaway, old boy.'

He doffed his goggles and extended a powerful hand. I shook it. He pointed to the La Salle.

'Got visitors, old boy?' He winked. 'Can always call back later, you know, when she's vamoosed.'

I grinned. 'No, PC, would you believe that's my car?'

He pulled a face. But the Honourable Peter Courtenay (known to all his closest chums as PC) is so damned clean cut and debonair looking that even when he pulls a face, he's still handsomer than ninety-nine per cent of the male population. Isn't quite fair, is it? Silver spoon. Title. Oodles of spondulicks. Motor racing stable. Lap record at Brooklands. House in Belgrave Square, mansion and estates near Staverton, not far up the road from my cottage. And a girlfriend, Prissy Wagstaff, who makes the likes of Margaret Lockwood, Sally Gray and Valerie Hobson seem like kitchen maids.

23

'Your car? That La Salle?' he queried, then clapped me on the shoulder. 'You've had another win on the races.'

I ushered him indoors. 'No, that's not the gamble I've taken.'

The beams in my sitting-room made his six feet four frame droop like a heron at feeding time. He looked round the room, as I took his leather gear from him.

'Nice and cosy,' he said. 'Not like my draughty halls. They strike cold even if the sun's cracking the hedges.'

'Trade you half my cosiness for half your draught ridden space,' I grinned, as I cleared some back issues of *Flight* and *Aeroplane* off the only other chair. He sat down and his long legs almost reached into the kitchen. Before I could offer him anything, he had pulled a silver monogrammed hip flask from his jacket pocket.

'Got any glasses?'

I went to the old walnut sideboard my mother had given me, when she had moved to a smaller house after father's death. I took out two of my four glasses and soon the Scotch was burning my throat beautifully.

'Old times,' he beamed, raising his glass.

'Old times,' I repeated.

'Miss 'em, you know,' he said.

'So do I.'

'Not the same at Brooklands without you around.'

'Nice of you to say so,' I said, 'but I wasn't much use to your racing team really. I was no mechanic, as you well knew. It was good of you to give me a job at all – certainly tided me over a bad patch.'

'Any friend of Prissy's is a friend of mine, old boy. Miss your friendly face around.'

I think I blushed. 'Was with you under a year, you know.'

He kicked my foot. 'Seemed like a lifetime,' he laughed, then poured us both the last from his flask. 'Don't worry. Got more in the Bug.'

I was intrigued as to why he had called on me so unexpectedly. PC projected the image of a playboy, but in reality, was anything but. He organized his life with the immaculate precision with which he drove his racing ERA. What chances he took were always calculated to the nth degree.

'Down here for the weekend?' I tried.

'Not really. Got to go back in the morning. Trying out Bira's ERA.

24

Want to see what makes the crafty Prince faster round the tight banking.'

'So you came all the way down to Devon just to see my tumbledown home? I'm honoured.'

'Glad I did,' he smirked. 'Could never have imagined it.' He drained his glass at a gulp and went on, 'By the way, how's your new venture going – Black Eye?'

I parried. 'Oh, early days yet.'

'Not snowed under?'

'Wrong time of year.'

He pointed out the window.

'Bet your clients are impressed by the La Salle.'

'All of them are,' I smiled. 'That's why I lashed out. Can't afford it really.'

'Nice job.'

'Nice job.'

Now ensued one of those silences that dares the first one to break it. I broke it.

'Come on, PC, why've you really motored two hundred and fifty miles to see me? You've got something on your mind, haven't you?'

He folded his legs up and leaned forward.

'Not my mind, old chap. Someone else's, to be honest. Someone you know.'

I shrugged. 'Can't think. . .'

'Lady. Good sport. Lives near here. Soft spot for you.'

'Leggy? Lovely? And I taught her to fly?' I added.

'Very same, old boy. The gorgeous Tracy.'

This time I leaned forward.

'Now, what kind of thing can the delectable Tracy Spencer-King have on her mind that she can't come straight to me about it? Rather than getting a mutual friend to motor the breadth of Britain on her behalf. I'm not a hairy ogre, you know?'

He cleared his throat.

'No, of course not. It's just that. . .' He ran his long fingers through his lazy blond hair. '. . . well, old boy, she's a bit embarrassed.'

'About what?'

'About asking you.'

'About what?'

'About a friend of hers.'

'What about a friend of hers?'

'Well, this friend of Tracy's is in a bit of a fix.'

'What kind of a fix? Marital fix, boy-friend fix, financial fix? There are a million kind of fixes.'

'None of those.'

'What then?'

'Well, you see, Johnny, you might call it a frightened fix.'

'Frightened?'

'Sort of.'

'Frightened of what?'

He unfolded himself from the chair and went over to my pokey window, hitting his head on the beam as he did so.

'It's like this, Johnny. She came round last night, apparently, to see Tracy. And she was in a hell of a state. Now it sounds a bit far-fetched the way it was told to me. But she thinks her sister was murdered.'

'Murdered?'

He nodded. 'Sounds like something out of Agatha Christie, doesn't it?'

'She lives round here,' I said needlessly.

'Anyway, Tracy believes there might be something in this girl's suspicions and she immediately thought of you. I mean, you know, your Black Eye Agency. Bit embarrassed to approach you direct, you know being a friend . . . all that. Business and friendship. Best kept separate. Rang me this morning. Asked me if I thought you would be interested. Said I thought you might. Apparently, this friend of Tracy's seems willing to pay quite a bit to have her suspicions investigated.'

I thought for a moment.

'Why doesn't she go to the police? Murder is their province, surely?'

'Bit late, apparently, old chap. Police been and gone. Inquest over. Everyone quite happy that her sister's death was accidental.'

'Know Tracy's friend's name?'

'Travers, I believe. Diana Travers.'

'And her sister? What Travers?'

'Nothing Travers. She was married, you see. Name's on the tip of my tongue. Now what did Tracy say? Hell. . . Ah, yes, I remember. It reminded me of that guy who broke the World Land Speed Record in

Golden Arrow in 1929. Seagrave. That's the name. Seagrave.'

Groucho suddenly summed it all up for me. 'Hello, baby,' he squawked out of the blue.

Well said, Groucho. 'Hello', indeed.

Three

Tracy came to pick me up, but I said it might be better to go in my car, rather than her brand new SS100 Jaguar. She slid into the red leather of the La Salle, looking as cool and elegant as Mrs Simpson, sorry, the Duchess of Windsor, but a thousand times more feminine. I was kind of glad Edward VIII hadn't seen her first.

I reversed out of my track and headed for Ashburton, where this Diana Travers, apparently, lived in a rambling old house on the edge of Dartmoor. Tracy turned to me.

'Sure you're happy about taking it on, Johnny?'

I nodded, but did not say anything. To tell the truth, happiness was hardly the word for my feelings. Whilst, of course, I was relieved to get a case with some financial reward attached to it, I was, nevertheless, distinctly nervous about plunging into the deep end of the detective pool at the baby stage of my career. For, if Diana Travers' suspicions were correct and her sister had been murdered, then I might be swimming in some very shark infested water indeed. After all, I hadn't even passed the water-wing stage of my new profession – the finding of lost pets, the tracing of lost relatives, the trailing after lost souls, the provision of evidence of lust and illicit loving for Divorce Court judges. Murder, it seemed to me, was high-dive stuff and I hadn't even paddled yet. For you could hardly call spying on Mrs Briggs getting your feet wet, let alone your body.

After a while, Tracy said, 'You drive a car the way you fly a plane, Johnny. Like you're part of it, instead of just the driver or pilot.'

I wished she hadn't said that. I put my foot down and swooshed past a Morris Eight that was making heavy weather of the incline.

'Flew a plane,' I observed quietly. 'Not fly.' I looked at her. 'You still fly?'

'Yes.'

'Often?'

'As often as I can. Got my own little plane now.'

'Oh, what type?'

'Puss Moth. Got it a week ago. Cream and green. Sun-ray design on the wings.' She patted the seat. 'Lovely leather inside, like this. Only green.'

'I'll look out for it flying over,' I smiled weakly. Hell, I hoped that one day the pain would grow less. It was one of the reasons I had started up Black Eye, to give back to my life a little of the excitement I had lost through being grounded. Not the only reason though. The way my father died had a deal to do with it. I still had a debt or two to collect from the criminal fraternity for his needless death under the wheels of a get-away car.

The La Salle whisked us in smooth silence to Ashburton before we really knew it.

'You go out of the town, as if going up on the Moor. And then in about a mile, take a left, ' Tracy directed. 'I'll tell you where. Then about a hundred yards down there's a drive on the right. That's Diana's place. It's got a big mirror on the fence opposite so that you can see what's coming before you launch yourself onto the road.'

I duly followed her directions and soon saw the mirror ahead, round and shining, atop a post on my left. I slowed.

'Tell me again, Tracy. Are you sure your friend isn't just being hysterical about her sister's death? I mean the shock might have rattled her temporarily.'

'Diana Travers is not the hysterical type,' Tracy replied firmly. 'She gets intense about things sometimes. Feels things deeply, I think. But she's not a nut-case, if that's what you're thinking. If I'd thought that, I would hardly have bothered you with her worries, would I?'

I guessed she wouldn't. And Tracy was nobody's fool. Some people make the error of mistaking her somewhat languorous manner as a product of a languorous mind. And thinking that besides its big blue eyes, its generous mouth, high cheek bones and cascades of chestnut hair, there is very little else to that glamorous head. They are riding for the shock of their lives. Tracy's languorous manner is like a Venus fly-trap and I'm sure it amuses her to see fools wriggle and squirm as they discover their misjudgment. For Tracy's mind is as sharp as a razor. I should know. We got quite close when I was teaching her to fly. And she went solo quicker than any pupil I had ever had. Off the airfield, we went round as a duet for quite some time. And now it was her turn to teach me quite a bit. And I loved the learning. But ultimately, we realized that each of us needed a little more solo experience of life before settling for a permanent two-seater. So now we've settled for seeing each other, when we feel the need, the desire. No rules, no pack-drill. She's marvellous. A lover *and* a friend. Pretty rare combination, I'm told.

I accelerated again and was just swinging the La Salle's long and elegant bonnet towards the entrance of the drive, when Tracy gave a shout. Mesmerized by the mirror, I guess, I hadn't seen what was tearing up the drive towards me at a rate of knots. I slammed on the anchors and slewed to a halt just before the gate posts. A red Alvis flashed past me, its driver, in the open cockpit, fighting to keep control as he swung the long, low car hard to the left. He only just made it. The big wire wheels mounted the bank on the far side of the road and the rear wheels slammed hard against the turf before, in a snaking, juddering curve, and a scream of tortured rubber, the Alvis regained its balance and sped on up the road and out of sight.

Tracy and I looked at each other. Certainly, she was two shades paler than when she'd started out. I felt three shades. After a moment's breath-catching, I said, 'Didn't know they'd moved Brooklands down Dartmoor way.'

'They haven't,' she said with a frown. 'It's more worrying than that.'

'What do you mean?'

She took a deep breath.

'Do you know who that was?'

'Other than a suicidal or murderous maniac, no.'

'You may be right about the last,' she grimaced.' That was Diana's sister's husband – Michael Seagrave.'

I guess Diana Travers was around twenty-eight. But it was difficult to tell, as she was one of those ladies whose brows were knitted at birth. Not that she was bad looking. Far from it. Raven black hair, a flawless, yet pale complexion, a sensuous mouth, a five-foot-six figure that undulated exactly where it should, was very fair issue from Life's store-house. And her eyes were large and appealing – but appealing for help and relief from pain rather than male or female approbation or interest. I could see what Tracy meant about her being intense and feeling things deeply.

After the standard, if slightly stiff, greetings, we repaired to her drawing-room, which was all chintz and rather strange oil paintings. Pictures that I learned later were actually all her own work, painting being her hobby – dabbling with brushes being a fairly common pastime for those who live so near the moor.

Directly we were seated, she offered us both a drink, which we declined. We just sat and watched her pour a gin and lime for herself. Her hand was shaking. I wondered whether from the visit of the red Alvis.

'Thank you for coming, Mr Black. And thank you, Tracy, for the introduction.'

We smiled self-consciously and she went on.

'I expect your time is precious, Mr Black. . .' Little did she know, thank the Lord. '. . .so I'll get down right away to why I need your help. You may remember the tragic event that occurred on Bigbury Sands two months or so back?'

I interrupted to save her further pain.

'Yes, I read all about it in the papers. I'm very sorry.'

She closed her eyes. 'So I don't need to go over horrifying details. Suffice it to say that my sister was riding with her husband, Michael Seagrave, in his new Frazer-Nash sports car whilst he was attempting to achieve a run on the sands of a hundred miles an hour. It was early in the morning. There was no one else on the beach.'

'Any reason for making the attempt so early?' I asked.

She waved her slender hand dismissively.

'Oh, Michael – Mr Seagrave – claimed the engine would develop more power the cooler and damper the atmosphere. Besides, at that time there would be no one in the way.'

'Okay. Sorry to interrupt.'

'Ask away, Mr Black, as you see fit.' She more than sipped her gin and lime. 'Anyway, it is said that during the early stages of the run, my sister's long scarf became entangled in the Nash's wire wheels and then in the chain drive. As a result, her neck was dislocated and her husband found her to be dead immediately upon bringing the car to a stop.'

'So it wasn't quite like the Isadora Duncan case? I believe she was strangled by her scarf.'

Her hand trembled more than somewhat and she put down her glass.

'So it would seem. The post-mortem clearly showed that my sister

31

had died from, in effect, a broken neck. She had not been strangled.'

She looked at me in case I had any further queries.

'No, please go on,' I nodded.

'Well, naturally, the police inspected the car and the remains of the scarf and came to the rapid conclusion – too rapid in my view – that what Michael Seagrave had claimed had occurred was actually what had taken place. As you know, the inquest only followed the police evidence and came up with a verdict of accidental death. The case, therefore, in police eyes is closed.' She picked up her glass once more. 'That's why I have no resort but to come to somebody like you, Mr Black. Someone who is impartial. Can look at all the evidence from a fresh stand-point. Carry out more elaborate enquiries than the constabulary ever bothered to do. And come up with the *real* facts. Facts that I'm sure will prove that my sister was murdered in cold blood. And the whole accident was a stage show to throw everyone off the scent.'

I hesitated for a moment before asking my next question. Diana Travers filled in time by reaching in her handbag for her silver and gilt cigarette case. I lit her black Sobranie for her, whilst I plucked up the courage.

'I gather you reckon you know the murderer?'

She exhaled as she nodded.

'Of course. Who else would it be but her ever loving husband, Michael Seagrave.'

'You seem very certain, Diana,' Tracy interceded. 'Not only that it was a murder and not an accident, but also who committed it.'

Diana Travers suddenly rose from her chair, her dark eyes flashing both impatience and irritation.

'Come on, Tracy. Who else could it have been but Michael? He had the motive. He had the opportunity.'

She stopped abruptly and flashed a look at me.

'Oh, I'm sorry, Mr Black. Perhaps I'm running ahead of myself. You see, Tracy knows some of the background and I'm forgetting that you don't.'

I smiled. 'That's all right, Miss Travers. Take it as it comes.'

She inhaled deeply and the cigarette smoke did not reissue until well into her next statement. I was starting to get worried.

'Let me explain. My sister, Deborah, was the beneficiary of quite a considerable fortune left to her by her eccentric godparent, a William Trubshaw, who emigrated years ago to Australia and was fortunate

32

enough to strike gold on his claim. He had no relatives he trusted, so he left his estate to Deborah. He died when she was sixteen and she came into the money when she was twenty-one. Deborah tried to confine news of her luck to close members of our family, but somehow word soon got around and she, naturally, started to attract suitors like there was no tomorrow.'

She stopped to stub out her cigarette. Her fingers seemed to be punishing, rather than putting out a fire. Even the gold tip ended up bent.

Tracy and I exchanged glances.

'Michael Seagrave was the last of a long line, then?' I said.

She nodded. 'She should never have married him. She might have known an out of work actor was only after her for her money.'

'Seagrave was an actor?'

'A minor one. Rep, that kind of thing. But I think he "rested" – isn't that how they term it? – rather more than he worked, from all accounts.'

'His accounts?' I asked.

She hesitated. 'Oh. . .all accounts.'

I wondered whether now was the time to ask about the red Alvis, but decided it wasn't.

'Michael Seagrave might have actually been in love with your sister, Diana,' Tracy tried. 'After all, she was quite a beautiful girl.'

'She was beautiful,' she reflected. 'People were always wanting to take photographs of her. That's how she and Michael met. In a photographer's studio in Torquay. She was having a twenty-first-birthday picture taken. He was sitting for some new portrait shots for his agent. Snap, bang, wallop. Within a couple of months, they were engaged.'

She reached for her cigarette case and this time offered it round to us. We both declined. (I don't go for Turkish or gold tips.) I flicked my lighter and Diana Travers continued, but now her tone was anything but reflective.

'But no, Tracy. You can be quite sure her looks were only a bonus to her bank balance, as far as Michael was concerned. You've only got to know him a short while to realize that. He's about as sentimental as a train.'

It was pretty clear by now that Diana Travers did not want me to discover the truth about her sister's death unless it provided confirmation of her suspicions against Seagrave. I wondered if she hated him as much before the tragedy on the sands.

'So you think Michael Seagrave staged your sister's death to get his hands on her money?' I asked.

She shrugged. 'Of course. He was in the acting profession. He would have known all about the way Isadora Duncan died. Much more than the average man. So all he had to do to reproduce the accident was buy a car with chain drive.'

'How long had he had the Frazer-Nash?'

'He took delivery only six weeks before her death.'

'Is Seagrave interested in cars? I mean, the Frazer-Nash is a fairly esoteric, enthusiast's choice.'

'Not as far as I know. I've never heard him talking about them. And he only had an ancient Austin Seven when he first met Deborah. Nobody interested in cars would go around in one of those, now would they?'

I smiled inwardly. Diana Travers' upper middle-class mind had, typically, not equated choice with available means. But I notched up one for my money guzzling La Salle. I'd seen her eyes appraise its motoring status, when she had opened her front door to us. Now, a private eye in an Austin Seven. . .

'So you think Seagrave bought the Frazer-Nash for one reason and one reason only: like Isadora Duncan's Bugatti, it had chain drive.'

'Exactly. Why else? I've been out in it. It's a draughty, rattly, noisy, hard-sprung affair. Maybe all right for the race track, but hardly for Devon lanes.'

'So you've been out in the Frazer-Nash? Does this mean you and Michael Seagrave were, before your sister's death, on good terms? After all, the Nash is strictly a two-seater. No room for three.'

I instantly regretted my question. The look in her eyes spoke of cancelled assignments for loose-tongued detectives. I was learning.

'He was my sister's husband, Mr Black. If I was to continue to see my sister after her marriage, I had, at least, to be civil to her husband – whatever my private feelings.'

'Of course,' I blandished. Tracy came to my aid and, to my surprise, asked the very question I had been postponing.

'Was that Michael's Alvis we saw leaving just as we turned into your drive?'

Diana Travers turned towards the French windows. I regretted not being able to see her face.

34

'Yes, it was,' was her staccato reply. She turned, but now, being back-lit against the windows, her expression was still hard to discern.

'He just came to . . . er . . . let me have some of Deborah's more personal things. Nothing of value, of course. Childhood stuff, mainly: her old teddy bear, a black-faced doll. . .School examination certificates, a leather bound Grimm's Fairy tales she had won as a prize.'

I surrepticiously glanced round the room. I could see no obvious sign of the items she had mentioned, yet she could hardly have had much time to stow them all away before our own arrival. Maybe she had stuffed them somewhere in the hall or under the stairs.

'I didn't know he was coming,' she went on, looking now at Tracy, 'otherwise I would have stopped him and arranged to have the things picked up. I have no wish to see Michael Seagrave ever again. Except, perhaps, in the dock of the Old Bailey.'

A quarter of an hour later and we were sweeping back out of her drive. For there had been little more to learn – except practical bits and pieces, such as the address and telephone number of her sister's lawyer and the name of the Chief Inspector who had been in charge of the police investigations into Deborah's Seagrave's death. Plus, I'd been given a wedding photograph of the then seemingly happy couple.

Oh, and of course, there was the little matter of my fee. To my immense relief, Diana Travers had circumvented all discussion over its size by offering me a retainer so much more than I'd been willing to settle for, that bargaining would have been highly indecent. One hundred pounds to engage my services (she gave me the cash there and then. I almost fainted) and fifteen pounds a week plus reasonable expenses for four weeks, the situation to be reviewed after that date. Upon a successful conclusion to my enquiries – which I took to mean proof of Seagrave's hand in her sister's death – I would be given a further one hundred pounds. I wondered what I'd get if I came up with proof that the whole thing was, in fact, a genuine accident. Beyond a thick ear, that is.

Tracy and I discussed it on our way back home. She defended her friend from the worst of my suspicions, which, I suppose, was only natural.

'You mustn't assume that Diana is always as edgy and icy as she was today. Don't forget that Seagrave had only just left and she was obviously still upset. From what I've seen of Diana, she can be quite a generous girl.'

She saw my expression and chided me. 'And I don't just mean with money, you bounder.'

I swung the La Salle down Ashburton's main street, being careful not to frighten the dray-horses champing at the bit outside a local hostelry.

'What have you seen of Diana? I mean, how long have you actually known her?'

'A couple of years. Not long. I met her at a house party one weekend. Turned out we were both bored with our respective escorts, so we got chin-wagging. Discovered we had quite a few things in common.'

'Like what?'

'Oh, going to the theatre. Not that Torquay is quite like the West End. But we sometimes make up parties to go when there's anything decent playing. Been to the pictures with her on the odd occasion and even tried *thé dansant*, unescorted. Diana's got quite a knack for catching the eye of young men, without it seeming like a wanton invitation. Whenever I've tried to get a dancing partner on occasions like that, I've been taken for a girl of more than easy virtue. You'd be surprised at how many hands young men can prove to own on a dance floor, when they have misinterpreted the glint in your eye as a hint in your eye. Whilst Diana. . .'

'. . . keeps her man under control, once she's got him?'

She laughed. 'I suppose she does. She certainly does not get pestered the way I do. Must be something to do with the difference in our personalities. It doesn't say much for yours truly, does it?'

I reached across and took her hand. 'You and Diana are chalk and cheese. I know which I prefer.'

She squeezed back. 'I'm not sure I like being likened to a cheese, if that's what you mean. I'm hard and yellow, if I'm Cheddar, and soft and gooey if I'm Camembert.'

I leant across and kissed her cheek. Her face powder smelt good enough to eat.

'Sorry, I made a mistake. It's chalk and peaches and cream.'

She slid up closer to me on the bench seat.

'It seems ages,' she said quietly.

'For me too,' I returned. 'Anyway, thanks a million for recommending me to Diana. You will never know how it's just in time to save my bacon.'

She rested her head on my shoulder. 'I like your bacon, Johnny. Breakfast hasn't seemed the same without you.'

'A rasher statement you've never made,' I oinked back, with a grimace.

She chuckled, bless her. 'I take it all back. I'd forgotten the jokes.'

Her delicious bodily warmth was getting through to me. I opened my quarterlight a little more to lower my emotional temperature. It was just too easy to pick up where we had left off all those months ago. Wonderfully and wickedly easy. Besides, I now had some work to do. work in which Tracy might well want to dabble her elegant fingers and I didn't want her to get involved. Not because I wanted all the kudos (if there was any to be had), or that Diana Travers was her friend. It was just that I had a funny feeling that this Black Eye's first case might well turn out to be not so much a can of worms as a basket brimful of vipers. And I preferred that Tracy kept well clear of their fangs.

Neither of us spoke for a while and we were almost back at my cottage before I took the plunge.

'Tracy, do you mind if I go straight on into Torquay, directly I've dropped you? I want to open a file on this assignment, whilst all the facts are fresh in my mind.'

Instead of appearing disappointed, her languorous look changed into one of excitement.

'Mind? Course not. I'll come into Torquay with you. Then afterwards, you can treat me to a nice dry cocktail at the Imperial as a kind of thank you.' She winked. 'After all, you can always charge it to Diana on expenses.'

I argued until the cows, and we, came home, but to no avail. And Tracy had a point. Without her, I wouldn't have got wind of the case and therefore, she insisted, she had no intention of getting excluded on the very first day.

'Besides,' she grinned, 'I've never sat in a private eye's offices before.'

'Office,' I corrected her, 'not offices. One room. Desk, filing cabinet, bucket for waste-paper, typewriter I'll swear that Churchill fellow used in the Boer War and two chairs, one with horsehair on the inside and my own, that is rapidly becoming the reverse.'

She raised a pencilled eyebrow and ran her fingers over the red leather of the La Salle's seat. 'Sounds wonderful. Maybe you should hold all your meetings in your car.'

'One day, I may have to,' I grinned. 'That's why I bought it.'

The grin soon came off my face when I arrived at the Ling offices and went to my room. I had hardly got the key in the door when a worried Babs fussed up to me.

'Johnny, the phone has been ringing all morning. You have to ring back.'

She suddenly realized I was not alone and put her fingers to her mouth.

'Oh, I'm sorry, I didn't know – '

'That's all right, Babs,' I said, letting us all in. 'This isn't a client. She's an old friend of mine. Tracy Spencer-King. Tracy meet Babs. Babs meet Tracy.'

Blushing wildly, Babs almost curtsied as she shook hands with Tracy.

'Now, calm down, Babs. D'you know who it was who was ringing?'

'Yes. I popped in and answered every time. Luckily, Mr Ling has been out this morning.'

'So who was it?'

'Mr Briggs. He sounded crosser and crosser each time he rang. He said he'd noticed you weren't parked at the usual cross-roads.'

I caught my breath and looked at Tracy. 'Oh, hell's bells, I'd forgotten all about Mrs Briggs.'

'Mrs Briggs?' she queried.

'Yes. Her husband was my first and only client, until Diana came along.'

I mimed keeping two balls in the air at once, then went to the phone.

'He suspects his wife's two-timing him. I'm supposed to watch her. I'd better ring him back.'

Which I did. I just hoped his shouted expletives did not reach the delicate ears of my two female companions. However, I managed to calm him down, albeit with a lie – that I had been making discreet enquiries about her movements in and around the neighbouring villages and that I would be back on the regular beat on the morrow.

Once I'd hung the receiver back on its hook, I asked, 'Anything else, Babs?'

She shook her head.

'Not really.'

'What do you mean, "not really"?'

'Well er – a Mr Shilling from the Imperial Hotel. He said to give you a message.'

I raised my eyebrows and asked the question to which, unfortunately, I already knew the answer.

'Which was?'

'Would you pop into the bar, soon, as it's some time since he's seen you.'

Tracy laughed. 'We're going to, the second Johnny has finished opening up a file on his big new client.'

Bab's blue eyes doubled their size.

'You've got a big new client, Johnny?'

I nodded.

'Er, really big?' she queried excitedly.

'Well, the lady isn't, but the case might be and the fee. . .Well, let's say it will more than pay my rent.'

Had Tracy not been there, I'm sure Babs would have jumped up and down like a kid with a new toy.

'Oh, well – that's nice,' she faltered, then sidled towards the door. 'Well, let me know if you need me to type. . . or anything.'

'I will.'

She performed her usual trick of bumping into the door knob and exited.

Tracy took my hand. 'You know she's madly in love with you, don't you?'

'Who? *Babs?*' I said, incredulously.

She kissed my cheek softly.

'Amongst others,' she breathed.

'Fancy seeing you, Johnny,' Ted Shilling grunted with a wry smile.

I reached in my pocket, took out two crisp pound notes and laid them on the bar.

'In answer to your call.'

He covered the notes with his big hand.

'I didn't mean you to – ' he began, but I cut in.

'Yes, you did. And you were right, Ted, to phone to remind me. A debt's a debt.'

He more than glanced at the notes before he stowed them away in his pocket. Ted was reputed to be able to tell a counterfeit from a hundred paces. Not that he would ever think I would pass one off on him deliberately. He pushed his thick, horn frames back up his podgy nose, which was really too diminutive to deal with their spectacular bulk. His glasses had more than once taken a swim in the beer he was pulling.

'You know it's too much, don't you? Or are you building up credit?'

'No, I'm also paying for a Scotch and splash for myself and. . .' I turned to greet Tracy as she returned from the powder room, '. . . and an extra dry Martini for my old buddy.'

Ted guffawed, his double chins wobbling like a jelly fish.

'Hello, Tracy,' he said, wiping his hand on a bar towel before extending it to her.

'Hello, Ted. How's life?'

He winked. 'Better now I've seen you two.'

When we were settled at the bar with our drinks, and Ted had served a colonial-type figure with a long gin concoction that was his own speciality – aptly called a Count Shaker, after Ted's nickname, The Count, which he had earned for his rather imperious manner with the rest of the staff and the meticulous way he counted out change – I answered Ted's masked but imminent question about where the filthy lucre had suddenly come from. For normally, he knew me as poor as a church mouse, unless the horses were running strong. Hence the need to sub me occasionally, bless his hide.

'My first ship's come in,' I said.

He glanced out the window towards the harbour.

'You mean Black Eye has got its first customer?'

'Not customers, Ted. They're called clients in my game.'

'Oh,' he said. 'Big ship?'

'Do for the time being,' I said and raised my glass. We all clinked.

'Would I know the captain of yer ship?'

I shrugged, then reached into my jacket pocket and brought out the wedding photograph Diana Travers had given me of her sister.

'Don't know.' I put the photograph down on the bar. 'But you might have seen one or other of these two. The Imperial is just the kind of place the man, especially, might have frequented.'

Ted picked up the picture and peered closely at it through the pebbles in his horn-rims. After a moment, he said, 'I've seen this

40

picture before, haven't I?'

'You may have done,' Tracy jumped in. 'A similar one was published recently in the *Torbay Express*, when it all happened.'

Ted scratched at his slick, Brylcreemed hair that fitted his head like a black bathing cap.

'Don't tell me. I know,' he muttered, then he looked across at us, saving his glasses sliding off at the very last moment. 'She was killed, wasn't she? In a car on the sands. Something about her scarf catching in the wheel. Yeah, I remember. Not long ago, was it? Terrible accident.'

'Yes,' I said, 'terrible.' I pointed back at the photograph. 'Either of them ever come in here? Or have you heard anything on the old grapevine about them? There's nothing that goes on in Torbay or the South Hams that you don't usually know about.'

He handed back the photograph. 'Don't know much really. I've never seen her around at all. Beautiful girl like that, I'd have known the instant she came in here. She'd have been the talk of the bar.'

'What about her husband?'

'Now he's different. I've seen him more than once. Not recently, mind.'

'When?'

'Oh, year or so ago, I suppose, was the last time.' He sniffed and his glasses started to slide once more. 'Wasn't he an actor at one time?'

'I gather so.'

'Well, could be about three years or more ago, he came in here quite a bit. With a crowd from the theatre. Must say I didn't take to him.'

'Why?' Tracy asked.

'Well, I don't think he was very popular even with his theatrical mates. You know, always last to buy a round, as I remember. And he didn't seem to be able to keep his hands off the girls. And good looking though he was, in a foppish kind of way, not all of them seemed to like it.'

'What about the last time he was in? A year ago.'

'Well, as I remember, he came in alone, which surprised me. But some time later a lady did join him.'

'Not the lady in the photograph?' Tracy queried.

'No, not her. I'd have known if it had been her. Not a bad looking woman, though, as I recall. I can't give you an exact description now.'

He turned to me. 'Why, what are you up to, Johnny boy? Can't you let old Ted into the secret?'

I shook my head. 'Sorry. Bit confidential and all that. Maybe one day. . .'

'Do you remember whether that lady was blond or brunette?' Tracy asked, half to cover my embarrassment.

Fingers went to the Brylcreem once more.

'Not really. All I remember is she was sort of classy looking. Not like those actresses with their painted faces I'd seen him with before. Oh, and she smoked like a chimney. I remember I had to send the boy over umpteen times to empty their ashtray.'

Tracy looked at me and smiled. 'Well, that narrows it down to a couple of million of us. If you start directly after lunch, Johnny, you should have tracked her down by the end of the century.'

I raised my glass. 'Thank you, Watson, for your encouragement.'

She raised hers. 'Think nothing of it, Holmes.' Then she laughed. 'Which probably sums up your feelings exactly.'

Four

It began raining. Devon rain. Falls sideways, not downwards, more easily to infiltrate your clothing. I cursed under my breath, put up my trench coat collar and braved it for almost half an hour before walking back to where I had parked the La Salle.

I started up and edged back up the narrow road, where I nudged into a gateway that was flanked by two large yews that would still hide the car from Mrs Briggs as long as she didn't decide to take a walk in the spring downpour. I deemed it a trifle unlikely, as I had only seen one sign of her that morning. She had white-washed the front step. Bobby Briggs certainly had a diligent wife, if not, in his opinion, a faithful one.

Through the small evergreen leaves, I could just about watch her house through my side window. At least I would spot her leaving or anyone calling, unless, of course, the visitor was under two foot tall. In which case, good luck to her.

Stake outs must be the most boring of all activities (or non-activities), and I'm afraid I spent my time not so much concentrating on Mrs Briggs as on the little problem landed in my lap by Diana Travers. I took out the notes I had written the previous evening, after I had at last managed to persuade Tracy to go home. (I should have thought of showing her the dilapidated state of my bedroom earlier, I suppose.)

Whilst I had actually got down to work on the case in the afternoon, after our noggins with Ted Shilling and a splendid Imperial lunch, I really needed time on my own to work out my real thoughts about Diana Travers and her dramatic suspicions. For whilst, from my office, I had rung a few theatrical friends in London to see if they could find out anything about Michael Seagrave through his previous acting career, and had visited the offices of the *Torbay Express* with Tracy to go through all their reports on the tragedy at Bigbury Sands, I could not fully explore my feelings about the lady who had commissioned the whole enquiry without risk of offending Tracy. After all, she was her friend. And I had only met Diana Travers a brief once.

So when the lights of Tracy's SS100 had finally faded into the darkness and I'd managed to switch my inclinations from the distinctly physical to the mental, I had put down on paper a few of my first thoughts about the Seagrave affair. I re-read it now in the car. They seemed far less significant in the damp light of day than they had in the gloaming of the cottage. Not so much thoughts, as questions really. Like why had Diana Travers waited until now to call someone in over her suspicions? The inquest, after all, had been some weeks before. What had suddenly made her so very sure her sister had been murdered and that the accident had been staged? She had provided Tracy and me with not a shred of evidence for her suspicions. She was relying on the existence of a motive as the sole *raison d'être* for her case against Michael Seagrave. Then again, why had she, seemingly, made no attempt to raise the whole tragedy with the Devon constabulary and air her suspicions with them rather than an unknown private eye like yours truly?

I also jotted down a note about Deborah's teddy bear, dolls and personal effects. For somehow, I just did not believe they were, in fact, the reason for Seagrave's visit to Diana Travers the previous morning – or at least not the sole reason. She had been too jittery. And the way Seagrave had been charging out of her drive in his Alvis indicated he was not exactly in a cool and balanced frame of mind either. But then maybe he never was.

So much for the question marks over my employer. The remainder of my jottings were about Seagrave himself and what courses of action I might follow. Number one on the list was to try and fabricate a natural reason for meeting the man, so that I could make some kind of judgment for myself about his character and capabilities. Tracy had never met him. Ted Shilling and Bobby Briggs were one step ahead of us in that regard. So the scrapyard king had an asterisk against his name. I could quiz him about Seagrave whilst ostensibly reporting back on his wife's seemingly dreary round. At this stage, I didn't want to come out in the open as to my motives, for South Devon is a tight little community and, like all such, tends to have big ears and mouths where you least expect them.

I took out the wedding photograph once more and propped it up against the steering wheel. Deborah had certainly been a very strik-ing-looking girl, like something out of *Vogue*, only with character. But it was not her I was interested in; it was her husband. I looked intensely at his face. A matinée idol looked back out at me. He had the dark, too-good-to-be-true looks of a Tyrone Power with features as regular as a Dick Tracy. He was, indeed, handsome to the point where character was replaced by anonymity. Stare as I might, I could not read anything but a smile in his face. I decided the sooner I met him, the better. That is, as long as he wasn't a murderer or, if he was, did not realize the real reason for my interest in him.

I put the photograph back in my pocket and opened my side window a little to prevent the La Salle steaming up totally. I could feel the horizontal rain starting to spray my hair and the cold wind to comb it, but I had to be able to see out, just in case Mrs Briggs decided to go on an expedition or admit an Errol Flynn by the side door. I wondered how experienced private eyes coped with two cases at once. I guessed they could afford a lowly-paid assistant to take care of the Mrs Briggses of this world whilst they reserved themselves for the *crème de la crème* of the criminal fraternity. I thought of Tracy. Trouble was, I could hardly ask such a silver-spoon sport to watch ironing, black-leading, white-washing, line hanging, tub thumping and shop tripping all day.

I sighed and went back to Michael Seagrave and how I could arrange a seemingly natural meeting. It took me at least quarter of an hour to hit upon a stratagem and even then I wasn't sure it was a good one: that I should pose as a Frazer-Nash fanatic, who just wondered whether, after the unfortunate tragedy, Mr Seagrave might just feel like disposing of the car involved to a worthy enthusiast. After all, how was anyone to know he had already sold it to Bobby Briggs? Except Briggs and his cronies, of course. And Seagrave wouldn't realize that I was, vaguely, a crony.

I was busy plotting my exact words of introduction after knocking at the Seagrave door, such as, 'I'm sorry to intrude at this time of grief, but I would like a word or two with Mr Seagrave about a rather personal matter. . . No, he doesn't know me, but if he is free I would appreciate just a moment or two of his time. Let me introduce myself. My name is White. Jack White. I am secretary of the British Sports Car Association and. . .', when I was abruptly woken out of my fantasy by a sharp, staccato rapping at my passenger window. It scared me to death.

I peered across and through the misting, to my horror, saw the unmistakably round and rubicund face of my quarry, Mrs Briggs. What could I do? I leaned across and wound down the window.

'Sorry to disturb you, sir,' she said in a Devonian accent as rich as could be, 'but I thought, seeing as how it's a mite damp and chill out here, you might like to pop inside and have a warm cup of tea. I've just put a kettle on the hob.'

It was lucky I was sitting down. Otherwise, the first passing feather would have felled me.

'Er . . . oh . . . er, thank you,' was my brilliant reaction to a cover blown. Dashiel Hammett would obviously never use me as a model for a hero. Splendid lady. She understood my embarrassment and went on, 'Don't feel you have to, like. But you've spent so many hours over the last few days in and around here, that I just felt I had to invite you in.' She held a workworn finger to her lips. 'S'all right. Won't breathe a word to my hubby. It's he who's employing you, isn't it?'

'I'm sorry –' I began, but she cut in.

'Don't you go being sorry, my love. I'm pleased as punch you've been watching me. Shows me old man bothers about me. What's more, proved my plan worked, didn't it?'

I couldn't reply because I hadn't the slightest idea to what she was referring. I'm afraid I just got out of the car like a lamb, locked it and followed her in to her spick and span home.

Two steaming cups of tea later, I had the whole story. And, what's more, the solution to my problem of keeping two balls in the air at the same time. It was all very simple, really, and my admiration for Mrs Briggs knew no bounds.

It transpired that while Bobby Briggs might well be the king of the south-western scrapyards and look after his business interests with a wily devotion, his attitude towards his personal and domestic affairs left a lot to be desired. (My choice of the last word is very deliberate.) As Mrs Briggs so neatly put it, 'I don't know why he bothered marrying. Instead of going to the altar, he should have gone to the ironmonger. Doormats are cheaper there.'

So after eleven years of grunts and neglect, Mrs Briggs had decided she had had enough. 'Not that I'd leave him, mind. Just give him a shock, like. See if that would do any good.' So she invented a lover. Persuaded her sister-in-law to write an affectionate letter, signed Bill, which she left around the house in the hope her husband would come across it. To hasten proceedings, she bribed the errand boy (Boy? He was at least twenty-eight, apparently) at the local shop to drop by around the times Bobby was expected home, so that a furtive figure could just be seen leaving the house or environs, as if to escape apprehension by an irate husband. I had always left the scene by the time I thought Briggs would be home, so I had missed this phantom Casanova entirely. But Bobby Briggs hadn't and indeed, from Mrs Briggs' gleeful account, had once almost caught the errand boy, but a Frazer-Nash proved no match for a push-bike over muddy fields.

On being challenged about having a lover, Mrs Briggs had parried the whole question by informing her husband, in no uncertain terms, that life with him was so downright boring and affectionless, that it was a wonder she didn't have three hundred and sixty-five lovers, one for every day of the year he ignored her. I asked if her decoy Don Juan campaign was bearing any fruit. She laughed and blushingly informed me that things were generally starting to look up, but all she would allow herself to admit to was being taken last Monday to the Gaumont to see Fred Astaire and Ginger Rogers in *Shall We Dance?*

'First time Bob's taken me to the pictures for donkey's years. Since *Red Dust*, I think it was. That Clark Gable. Now there's a *real* man. He wouldn't neglect no lady of his. . .'

I really took to Mrs Briggs. If I hadn't, I wouldn't have done the deal. It went as follows: I would pretend to continue my surveillance until her husband's ten pounds' credit was exhausted. She would corroborate my story, as far as she could, were it to become necessary. The problem of her husband not seeing my La Salle around would be covered by my stated decision to use ever differing cars borrowed from my friends for this particular assignment, as the big cream American number was, to put it mildly, a little conspicuous in any rural setting.

As I drove away, I told myself I really wasn't betraying old Bobby Briggs just to free myself up for the Seagrave case. I was – how could I put it without sounding too pompous? – helping mend a marriage? Giving a leg up to love? Bringing back domestic bliss? Spreading a little happiness as I go along life's highway?

By the time I reached home, I felt quite ill with all that sentiment. Relieved, but certainly a trifle dicky.

'What was that organization again?' the housekeeper queried, cupping her ear with a liver-spotted hand.

'British Sports Car Association.' I didn't know if such an organization existed, but if it did, it would embrace Frazer-Nash.

She thought for a moment, then looked me in the eye, as if to check if my old pupils were telling the truth. I forced myself not to blink, which obviously worked with her as a sure sign of sincerity. She was gone the next second to inform her employer.

I waited nervously until she returned, taking in the house and scenery. Deborah Seagrave's godfather's gold strike must have been akin to a 'mother load', for the house and estate were the far side of impressive, situated in a tightly rolling Devon landscape, all rises and dips that eventually flattened away to give a superb view of the distant sea from the front of the Elizabethan mansion. This was veritably a stone wonder of gargoyles and multi-mullions that spoke of minstrels' galleries, suits of armour and hot and cold running ghosts to go with them. I came to the instant conclusion that the house alone, let alone the remainder of the fortune that had bought it, could well have proved a powerful motive for murder.

A moment later and I was ushered into a vast drawing-room, where there was enough space to land a Tiger Moth. Standing by the windows, with his back to me, was a figure far taller than I had been expecting. He must have been at least four inches over grave depth. The housekeeper announced me, but still Seagrave did not turn round. It was not hard to detect the actor in him.

'Mr Seagrave?' I tried.

A 'Yes' filtered round the back of his head.

'I'm sorry to intrude, but I wondered if you could spare me a minute.'

'Go on.'

This was proving even more difficult than I had been expecting.

'Well, I'm from the British Sports Car Association – '

'Go on, go on,' his back rapped impatiently. 'I know that.'

I tried to spin it out. 'Well, Mr Seagrave, it's like this. Every member of our association is fanatical about the kind of sports car we in Britain make so well. In these days, when imported sports cars seem to be making some inroads into the British market – I refer, of course, to makes such as BMW from Germany, Salmson and Delahaye from France, Auburn and Cord from America, and so on. . .'

48

My rambling worked. He turned round impatiently and I glimpsed his face for the first time. It was somewhat of a disappointment. Not that he wasn't handsome. He was. His matinée idol looks were even more striking than the wedding photograph had managed to capture. And though he was tall, his head and figure were in perfect proportion to each other. My disappointment came from the mask-like anonymity of his handsomeness, at which the photograph had hinted. What lay behind the mask, I suspected I would only learn from Seagrave's actions, rather than expressions. I was none too keen on that way of picking up knowledge, just in case. . .

'Mr White, I am not a car fanatic, so I neither wish to hear an appraisal of the current sports car situation in the United Kingdom, nor have I any desire to join your association. I only agreed to see you because my housekeeper told me you wished to see me on a *personal* matter. Now, if you would be so kind, get down to the "personal" part of your patter right away and save me from all the rest.'

I cleared my throat.

'Well, you see, Mr Seagrave, it's like this. I am – personally – more a "one make" fanatic than most members of our association. That make is . . . er, Frazer-Nash.' I watched his eyes. They didn't blink but I, for one, did not necessarily take it as a sure sign of sincerity.

'So?' Seagrave queried and moved across me to fold himself into a tapestry-covered chair that looked as valuable as it looked uncomfortable.

'So I, er, wondered if, by any chance, you might have come to any conclusions about your own particular vehicle – the one that was involved in that most tragic of accidents. How can I put it?'

'Easily, Mr White,' he said icily. 'It is clear as daylight now why you have come. You read about my wife's death and instantly made a note in your mind that sooner or later I might get round to disposing of said Frazer-Nash, due to its calamitous connection, not really caring what price I got for it, as long as it went out of my sight. You waited until a decent interval had passed, then came knocking at my door in the avid hope that I would let you have an expensive British sports car at a knock-down price.' He wagged a manicured finger at me. 'That's it, isn't it? In black and white.' He laughed and added, 'Especially White.'

At least I was relieved he did not repeat 'Black.'

I shuffled my feet. I thought it would look good. Two can act, and I'd had a little experience.

49

'I'm sorry, Mr Seagrave, for coming round about such a matter – '

'You're not sorry, Mr White. But you will be now.'

I feigned incomprehension. 'What – what. . .?' I began and I could have written his next lines for him.

'Simple,' the matinée mask smiled. 'The car has gone.'

'Gone?'

'Sold. To a scrapyard dealer.'

I added 'horror' to my actor's repertoire.

'You mean you sold an almost new Frazer-Nash for scrap?'

'No. I didn't say that. I sold an almost new Frazer-Nash to a scrapyard dealer who, I dare say, is as much a Nash fanatic as you are, Mr White. He's using it as his personal transport, I believe.'

Seagrave reached across to a silver cigarette box, removed a 'Passing Cloud' and inserted it carefully into a silver and tortoiseshell cigarette holder. For a moment, he looked as if he were playing in *Private Lives*.

'I see what you mean about my feeling sorry,' I muttered, as he exhaled a Turkish aroma towards me.

'I'm so glad,' he smiled and rose from his chair. 'Now, if that's all you came about, Mr White. . .'

He moved towards me and the three-inch difference in our heights showed rather dramatically.

'Yes, well. That, I suppose, was all I really came about.'

'Good.' He moved past me and pulled a tasselled cord alongside the door. Somewhere in the house a distant bell clanged.

'Mrs Sayers will see you out. Goodbye, Mr White.'

I extended a hand but it wasn't grasped. A moment later, his housekeeper saw me briskly to the door. I crunched off down the drive to where I had left the La Salle, well out of sight of the house. After all, a British sports car fanatic could hardly be seen arriving in a flashy American vehicle. As I did so, a formation of Hawker Fury fighters flew overhead in a perfect V, their biplane wings glinting silver in the sun. For a second, the sight took my mind off my disappointing visit to Seagrave, but it was hardly a consolation. It simply reminded me of all the current war talk in the papers and the urgent expansion schemes announced for the RAF, which would soon replace these Furies with monoplane fighters such as the Hurricane and Mitchell's even more advanced Spitfire design. What was, in a way, worse, was that I knew if the dreaded happened and war came, the quacks would never allow me to get behind the controls of any machine, let alone an eight-gun fighter that could top an incredible three hundred and fifty miles an hour.

That evening I spent a therapeutic and reflective few hours at an old hobby of mine – making flying models of planes. After all, these I was still qualified to fly. At that time, I was putting the finishing touches to the balsa skeleton of a Hawker Hart, which is a bomber version of the Fury. That done, I started the tricky operation of covering the skeleton with gossamer-thin tissue paper, which later I would shrink with water, then dope silver for strength and final finish. It was while I was applying the tissue across the stringers of the rear fuselage that the telephone interrupted my thoughts. I answered it, my fingers still covered in balsa-wood cement.

It was Tracy. With the inevitable question and an unexpected invitation. I duly answered the first by recounting my more or less fruitless visit to Seagrave and reacted to the second with pleasure – an invitation to lunch at Burgh Island Hotel on the morrow, Saturday, where she anticipated we might be joined by Peter Courtenay and his enamorata, Priscilla (Prissy) Wagstaff. So by the time I threw a cloth over Groucho's cage and went up to bed, I was feeling much more A1; and looking forward to a few hours by the seaside like a kid with a new bucket and spade.

The showers of the morning had given way to unbroken sunshine and Bigbury Bay scintillated in its warmth. I drove down towards the beach and parked my car in the huge garage built opposite Burgh Island to house both the cars and the chauffeurs of the hotel's guests. The tide had only just started to ebb, so I had to wait a while for the hotel's unique form of ferry – a caterpillar tracked chassis upon which is built a passenger-carrying platform and driver's position held by stilts some fifteen feet or more off the ground or water. This contraption, however Heath Robinson, serves admirably as a means whereby, at high tide, hotel guests can be transported to and fro across the short distance to the mainland without the wetting of so much as a plus-four or a dancing pump, or the risk of a queasy tummy that water-borne transport might induce. At low tides, of course, the Island is readily reached across the sand bar that the receding waves reveal.

Full as the sea tractor had been when it eventually arrived, with a gay young crowd seemingly hell-bent on going up to play golf at the

Bigbury Golf Club, I was the sole passenger on the way back, though I could see plenty of other guests disporting themselves on the tiny island ahead, tennis seeming an obvious attraction on the courts to the right of the startlingly white and modern hotel. Its design, even now in 1937, some eight or nine years after its completion, is considered by many to be far too advanced in style to be either compatible with taste or the Devon countryside and coastline. But needless to say, its clean, curved and somewhat outrageous architecture is beloved of the smart set and the richer members of the theatrical fraternity, who never cease to remind the less sophisticated that Noël Coward – they pronounce his name in hushed tones, as if it were *he* who has just replaced Edward VIII on the throne – chooses to spend many of his vacations there.

As far as I was concerned, I love the place because it is always gay and alive. The architecture I can take or leave and it certainly doesn't offend me.

Once off the tractor, I climbed up the steps and made for the Ganges bar. But there was no sign of Tracy or Peter and Prissy, though I was rather thrilled to see the unmistakable figure of Agatha Christie seated in a corner reading a book. I had just finished one of her latest, *The ABC Murders*, and was half tempted to go over and tell her how much I had enjoyed it. But she looked too engrossed in her reading for me to interrupt. As I left the bar, I smiled to myself as I wondered what she would make of Seagrave and Diana Travers' suspicions. One thing was sure, it couldn't be less than I had so far.

I made my way across the lawns to the steep steps cut into the rock that lead down to the hotel's private playground – a wonderfully sheltered private beach that, through the clever use of artificial dams, is not subject to the tides. In the centre of the splendid sea-water pool thus created is, incredibly, a bandstand on which I had on quite a few occasions seen Harry Roy and his band perform. Naturally enough, it is to the beach that most guests gravitate when the sun shines, for there is waiter service for the odd gin fizz cocktail and even for exotic seafood snacks, complete with lobster tails, should they be desired.

Before I was down the long flight of steps, I spotted the slender form of Tracy supine to the sun's rays at one end of the somewhat crowded paved area that borders the cliffs. Next to her were arranged three deckchairs. On each was an object to pronounce possession – a towel, a bathing cap and a copy of what looked like *The Illustrated*

London News. Clever girl. She'd anticipated our arrival. I threaded my way through the bronzing guests towards her, tossing my car keys onto her rather damp Jantzen-clad tummy to announce my arrival.

She looked up, shading her eyes.

'Oh hello, Johnny. Are you alone?'

I laughed and pointed to the other gay young things around us.

'Hardly, old girl.'

'No, you idiot. I meant you haven't seen Peter or Prissy around, have you?'

I removed the towel and sat down beside her.

'No. Agatha Christie, yes. Peter and Prissy, no.'

'Yes, I saw her too. The barman tells me she may be planning to set one of her whodunnits here. Anyway, Johnny, did you bring your trunks?'

I nodded. 'I have them on underneath my flannels.'

I undid two more buttons of my shirt and relaxed back in the old deckchair.

'Ah, this is the life,' I grinned. 'Thanks for inviting me. It's just what I needed.'

Tracy sat up. I noticed quite a few male eyes swivel in her delectable direction.

'Seagrave case getting you down?'

'No, not really. I feel better this morning.' I lowered my voice. 'Anyway, the Seagrave affair isn't really a case yet. It's just a set of suspicions inside Diana Travers' head, isn't it?'

She squinted her eyes at me and whispered back, 'Sounds as if you've already made up your mind that Seagrave is innocent.'

I shook my head. 'Not at all. I was hoping my meeting with him would give me some kind of intuitive feeling. But it didn't, more's the pity. He could be innocent as the day is long or the nastiest bounder the world has ever seen.' I chuckled. 'Comes of all that acting experience, I would imagine.'

'You were an actor,' she reminded me.

'Only for a short while, filling in time after I was grounded. And if Denham Airfield hadn't been near Alexander Korda's Denham Studios. . .'

'. . .you wouldn't have been an actor at all, I know.' She smiled. 'I hardly believe you were. I've seen *Things to Come* three times just because you said you were in it and I haven't spotted you yet.'

'Not surprising. I was the 898th extra in the "Everytown" scenes and one of the rocket technician's assistants, who ended up on the cutting-room floor.'

I was starting to feel distinctly hot in my shirt and flannels.

'Like a swim?' I asked Tracy.

'No, thanks. I just had one before you came.' She lay back again on her towel. 'You go ahead.'

I did. I went back up to the hotel to strip off, in case I offended the more delicate sensibilities of the smart sunning set and soon was back and in the cooling water.

I swam out to the far rocks and clambered up onto them. Looking back, the hotel guests, reclining, tanning, sipping, parading, posturing and pontificating, seemed like actors and actresses in a play and hardly real at all. Above the cliffs, the dazzling white hotel appeared like some ethereal palace that would disappear again at the wave of a wand or the snap of a finger.

I soaked up the warm spring sun for a while and lazily watched a Tiger Moth doing its routine rounds of the Devon beaches, towing an advertising banner for the *Sunday Despatch* – one of the aeronautical experiences I did not envy, for towing anything robbed an aircraft of its freedom of manoeuvre and lightness of control, and to me, was akin to hitching a caravan to a racing car or a brewer's dray to a Derby winner.

After ten minutes or so, I decided it was a trifle unsporting to leave Tracy alone for too long, so I stood up preparatory to diving back into the water. As I angled my arms for the dive, a shriek of girlish laughter emanated from behind me. I looked around to see a bathing-capped girl of no more than seventeen clambering down towards me, having obviously climbed the rocks from the sea side. I moved sideways to let her pass and she smiled a big thank you, before shouting back over her shoulder.

'I told you, Michael, you'd never catch me.'

As she splashed me with her dive into the pool, I looked back and to my horror, saw who this Michael was. Instantly, I crouched down again and put my head in my hands. Hairy legs flashed past and it was not until I heard the splash that I dared peep out through my fingers.

Seagrave, by now, had almost reached the bandstand in the middle of the pool and the girl was alreading climbing up the ladder onto it. I cursed my luck, for bathing trunks are not exactly the greatest garment for hiding one's identity. All I could do was turn sideways, so my hand hid more of my face. I determined that from now on Johnny Black, like Sherlock Holmes, would assume theatrical disguises when assuming identities other than his own. Had I worn a deer-stalker, a false moustache and hair-piece and affected a stutter, I might not be imprisoned on a rock like an unthinking Rodin's 'The Thinker'.

The wind being off the shore, their voices carried clearly from the bandstand.

'Wow – the pool's much warmer than the sea.' A girlish giggle.

'Early in the year yet. Rather surprised you accepted my challenge to brave the open water.'

'You knew I'd accept.'

'Did I?' Those two simple words were said with a suggestion of intimacy that rather betrayed Seagrave's theatrical background.

Moving my hand and head slightly, I could see the two figures were now close to each other, reclining back on the bandstand boards.

The girl mumbled something I couldn't catch in reply, and then he asked, 'Do you think you can persuade your parents?'

'Gosh, I hope so.'

'Try and make it a further two weeks instead of one.'

'I'll try. I'm sure Father will have to go back to London, even if he allows Mother to stay on for a bit.'

'That's all right, isn't it?'

A pause. 'Mother on her own may be more of a problem.'

'Why?'

'She won't have anything to do but worry where I am all the time.'

'Doesn't she like me?'

Laughter. 'She thinks you're positively charming. But then she doesn't know. . .it all, does she?'

'You think she will disapprove if she finds out?'

Silence. Then, 'Oh, come on, Michael, let's enjoy now. Don't let's worry about what might happen.'

'All right, Susan. But will you promise to ask your parents tonight?'

'I promise.' Then, excitedly, 'Now, race you back to the hotel.'

Two splashes followed and I dared to look round. Both were athletic swimmers and were out of the water and starting up the cliff steps in no time at all. When they had disappeared from view at the top, I at last plunged back in the water and over-armed it back to an expectant Tracy.

'Did you see him?'

I laughed. 'Tracy, he almost trod on me.'

'He didn't recognize you?'

'I don't think so. Unless he's one of those people who can tell a person from their hands.' I dabbed myself with Tracy's towel and sat down. 'You don't know who the girl is, by any chance?' I asked.

'No, never seen her before.'

'Name is Susan, from what I could hear.' I recounted their bandstand conversation. Tracy grimaced.

'Hasn't taken him long, has it?'

'You mean, to recover from his grief and get on the trail again?'

She nodded. 'From what you overheard, it would appear she may know about his wife and the way she died.'

'Could be. If she does, she clearly isn't bothered by it. It seemed to me, she was leading him on, as much as he was leading her.'

Tracy thought for a moment. 'I assume he wants her to stay on here at the hotel for longer than her parents had planned.'

'Looks like it.'

'I wish I knew who the family is.'

'Well, they're not actually poor to stay in a place like this.'

'You implying that Seagrave might already be after another heiress?'

I shrugged and Tracy went on, 'He could be just after her because she's young and pretty. After all, he has Deborah's money now.'

'Could be.'

She looked at me.

'You don't like the feel of it, do you?'

I sighed. 'Maybe I'm old-fashioned or something. But I do think it's a little early for Seagrave to be girl chasing again. Mind you, I saw enough of that kind of thing in the four years I was with my uncle in Kenya. There, as Cole Porter so catchily puts it, "Anything goes".'

'Devon is hardly Happy Valley,' she laughed.

'Thank the Lord, old girl.' I lay back in the deckchair and closed my eyes.

After a while, Tracy commented, 'I'm surprised Peter and Prissy aren't here yet. It's nearly twelve.'

'They'll turn up. PC is not exactly renowned for his punctuality. At Brooklands, they're always surprised he remembers to turn up in time for the races.'

But we had to wait another twenty minutes before we saw the dashing couple descending the cliff steps.

'Sorry, darlings,' Prissy exclaimed in her familiarly loud and flamboyant manner, as she trod elegantly through the maze of tanning guests. 'All PC's fault. Met some old chums of his father's in the hotel lobby. Just had to hob-nob. Know what he's like. Worse than a woman.'

She collapsed in the deckchair next to me, crushing the *Illustrated London News* beneath her. I felt a hand on my bare shoulder. I looked up. Peter had arrived a little more discreetly.

'Apologies, old boy, old girl. Bit late setting off, then got waylaid in the lobby, like Prissy said. Couldn't ignore the Prendergasts – old friend of the family and all that.' He winked. 'Anyway, they've got a rather fetching daughter.'

I vaguely remembered Peter talking of the Prendergasts before. Something about their having made more than the odd million out of paper-making. The Prendergast Mills, that was it.

Peter hovered by the deckchair we'd reserved for him.

'Anyway, old sports, now we're here, how about us all quenching our thirsts?'

'Hang on a minute, PC.' I interrupted. 'How old is their daughter?'

He laughed. 'Bit on the young side for you, old boy, I'd have thought. Can't be more than seventeen or so.'

'Regular features, fair skin? Blondish hair from what little I could see peeping out from under her bathing cap? Oh and her name, I think, is Susan?'

Peter looked at Tracy in amazement. 'It's all right, PC,' she came to my aid. 'Johnny's not head over heels. We're both interested in her, as a matter of fact.'

He sat down at last. 'How's that, old girl?'

So we told him.

And that's how we came to find out that Michael Seagrave would be landing much more than a beauty if he succeeded in hooking this nubile Susan of the bandstand.

Five

I felt sorry for PC and Prissy. For Seagrave's unexpected appearance had really put paid to our having lunch at the hotel for fear he might spot Mr John White from the British Sports Car Association. So we packed up, took the sea tractor back to Bigbury, picked up the three cars and, at PC's suggestion, had a road race along the coast to Bantham. Luckily, we met neither police nor obstructive four-legged transport and arrived at our designated hostelry – an old haunt of Peter's – in double-quick time. Much to our racing driver's surprise and chagrin, Tracy won. More by guile than driving skill, however. For half-way there, she had honked her horn endlessly at PC's Bugatti ahead of her and when she had gained his attention, had pointed down at one of his rear wheels as if he had tyre trouble. When he had slowed to check, she zoomed past with a flourish and a 'fooled you' smile.

The rest of the day was spent on Bantham beach, Burgh Island mocking us in the distance across the river estuary. By the time I got home, Groucho didn't seem to recognize me at all. I failed to get a squawk, 'Drop 'em' or 'Hello, baby,' out of him. It wasn't until I saw my reflection in a mirror that I discovered the reason. My face was now the colour of the jolly old lobster we had devoured at lunch. I should have realized that spring sun, shimmering sea and brisk breezes can be real burners after a winter's gloom. A face as red as Seagrave's Alvis was hardly a compelling advertisement for a private eye. After all, if he's not bright enough to protect his own skin, how can he be any good at protecting that of others?

Sunday dawned showery and, luckily, my complexion by then had shed around a third of its fierceness, my time in Africa obviously having toughened my skin somewhat. I walked down into Dartington and bought myself the only paper the little local store had left, the *Sunday Dispatch* – so much for the power of aerial advertising – but found, on reaching home, that I could not settle down to reading. In fact, I found I could not settle to anything, my mind being more than preoccupied with the bandstand conversation and all it might imply.

I decided to forget a day of rest and take a trip to the Imperial in Torquay. But just as I was donning my trench coat, the telephone clanged. It was one of the old acting buddies whom I had asked to dig around to see if they could unearth anything about Seagrave's past. Ten minutes later, I left to go to see old Ted Shilling at the Imperial, with some very interesting information indeed.

'Got some special news for you, Johnny boy,' Ted beamed, as he splashed some soda into my Scotch.

'Not another certainty for tomorrow's two thirty,' I sighed. 'You know I've foresworn betting since my Grand National win. Quit while you're ahead. That's my motto.'

He leaned forward onto the bar. 'Not about horses, Johnny. Next best thing, though – women.'

He laughed and had to push his glasses back up his nose.

'Women?'

'Women. Or rather a woman. Or rather a girl.'

'Girl?'

'Don't act stupid, Johnny boy. You know what you asked me last time, about that fellow Seagrave, who he came in here with and all that?'

'Yes, tell me,' I said with growing interest.

He leaned right across the bar and said behind his hand, 'He's been in again.'

'Seagrave?'

He nodded. 'With a girl. Pretty little thing.'

'Blond, regular features, around seventeen and answers to the name of Susan?'

He frowned. 'No. Red head, snub nose, around twenty and from what I could overhear, was called Daphne.'

I took a draught of my Scotch. 'Gets around, this Seagrave.' I removed Ted's frown by telling him about the blond girl at Burgh Island, then asked, 'Don't know any more about this Daphne, do you?'

'Well, happens that I might. That evening I had a temporary barman to help me. Stan Timmins. Now he's seen too many Fred Astaire flicks for his own good, he has. He is dance mad. Even learning

59

ruddy tap now. That's how he claimed to have met the girl.'

'At a dance?'

'No, at that ballroom dancing school that opened a year or two back. You know, near Woolworths. He spends most of his wages there, from all accounts.'

'This Daphne is learning to dance too?'

'No, Johnny, she's one of the teachers there, isn't she? Or so he says. Hasn't taught Stan though, much to his disgust.' Ted sniggered. 'His teacher's got a face like the back of a train compared to her, I gather. I guess they reserve this Daphne for the better class of student – and not for the likes of young Stan.'

'Thanks Ted,' I raised my glass.

'What for?' he pretended. 'Didn't have to go out of my way now, did I? I just stand behind the bar and keep my eyes and ears open, that's all.'

'Anyway, thanks. You may have given me the first decent lead I've had so far.'

He leaned forward again and his glasses were now perilously near the precipice. I took the liberty of pushing them back for him. Wasn't the first time.

'Going to brush up your own technique then? Quicken your quickstep, tune up your tango, freshen your foxtrot?'

I smiled. 'Thought I might. Bit of a waste of time though, if I end up with the train.'

He laughed out loud. 'You won't, Johnny boy. One look at the likes of you and they'll pedal out their prettiest, don't you worry.'

I sipped at my Scotch thoughtfully. For right then, getting to see the right dancing teacher wasn't really my main worry. The telephone call from my friend in London had seen to that.

Next morning, before leaving for Torquay, I telephoned Mrs Briggs to check that our subterfuge seemed to be still working. She roared with laughter and reported that my last progress report to her husband, where I had invented seeing a male figure hovering around her house, had worked a treat. That very night he had taken her to see Ronald Colman in *The Prisoner of Zenda* and then had taken the whole of Saturday off and taken her to Dartmouth and Blackpool Sands in the Frazer-Nash. She said it was the first time he had taken her to a beach since their courting days.

Once in my pokey office, Babs fixed onto me like a leech and tried to suck me dry as to how I was getting on with my 'Big Case'. I replied, 'Fine' and 'It's a bit early yet to report any progress but I've put out a few feelers here and there.' My guarded replies patently disappointed her, so I changed the subject and stunned her by asking where she had learned to dance.

After a baffled silence, she stuttered, 'Nowhere, Johnny, nowhere.'

'Picked it up as you went along?'

She shook her curls. 'Haven't been along very much.'

'You can dance, though?'

'Sort of. All right on the waltz and the quickstep. But I sit out the rest usually. Why do you ask?'

'Well, I just wondered if you knew anything about that ballroom dancing school up by Woolworths.'

'The Adrian Feather Tap and Tango Academy,' she intoned with reverence.

'Is that what it's called?'

She nodded. 'I've got a friend who goes there. It's quite posh inside, she says. All palms and shiny panelling. And they've got *four* radiograms.'

'That's a lot,' I smiled. 'But I dare say they need them.'

She suddenly grasped the edge of my desk, her eyes more goo-goo than ever.

'Coo, Johnny, why do you want to know about the dancing school?' she asked breathlessly. 'Something going on there? Spies, are they? My friend says Adrian Feather's real name is Gottenberg. So they could be.'

I shook my head.

'White slavery. That's it, isn't it? Wow! To think we've got white slavers right by Woolworths!'

I reached across and patted her hand

'Hang on, Babs. It's nothing like that at all. I'm not investigating the dancing school. I want to use it. Learn the latest dances. All that. Perhaps even toy with tap.'

She slumped like a rag doll. 'Oh,' was all she could find to say.

'So,' I said, 'do I have to make an appointment with them or can I just walk straight in? What does your friend do?'

'She has a class once a week, I think. But she says sometimes one or two of the teachers are just sitting around listening to records. So

61

you could try just walking in.'

I got up from behind my desk. 'I think I'll do that, Babs.'

She looked horrified.

'You mean you're not going to work on your Big Case this morning?'

I danced around her question. 'Private eyes needs fancy footwork sometimes, Babs.'

She held the door open for me. 'If anyone rings, where shall I say you've gone?'

'To Gottenberg,' I grinned, cad that I am.

I went to my La Salle first. Took out the false Ronald Colman moustache I had put in the glove locker before leaving home – one of my theatrical left-overs – and a dab of glue later, left the La Salle as Mr Tom Conway, a dapper but slightly shy chap who wished to brush up his Terpsichorean technique.

The academy was just as Babs had described, and once inside there seemed to be more palms than people. Adrian Feather né Gottenberg, greeted me himself, his very English apparel of black coat and striped trousers contrasting heavily with his Conrad Veidt accent. I explained what I was after and he listened patiently.

After a few minutes' thought he said, 'If you're not quite sure of ze exact height of your fiancée, then it may be somewhat difficult for me to find a match for her.'

'Perhaps, if I could see some of your instructresses, then I would have a better idea.'

He struck a pose. 'Well, vone or two are busy with zeir students right now, but I vill see vat I can do.'

I nodded my thanks and he disappeared behind a large screen decorated with a sun-ray motif. A couple of minutes later, he was back, ushering in two girls; one a willowy blonde around twenty-six with a longish nose and powder an inch thick; the other, praise be, more or less matching Ted Shilling's description of red head, snub nose, around twenty et cetera. All I needed to discover now was whether she answered to the name of Daphne. But dear Adrian didn't help. He proffered the blonde.

'Zis is Miss Randan.' Then the red head. 'And zis is Miss Phipps.'

I pretended to appraise both. 'I think that, er, er – Miss, er . . .' I pointed to the red head, '. . . is nearer my fiancée's height.'

Adrian almost yawned as he explained. 'Mr Conway here is most insistent he takes lessons from someone who is as near his fiancée's height and figure as possible, girls.' He turned back to me. 'So you zink Miss Phipps is nearer your ideal, Mr Conway?'

I would have fingered my moustache at this point, but I was afraid it might come off. 'Yes, well, er – Miss. . .er. . .'

'Phipps,' Adrian repeated.

'Miss Phipps certainly has a figure very similar to my fiancée. The height I'm not quite. . .'

He led the red head up to me. 'Perhaps, if you tried a turn with Miss Phipps, it might help you decide.'

He went to a radiogram in the corner of the small dance floor and put on a record – 'I'm Young and Healthy' from the film *42nd Street.*

I looked as nervous as I could, then put my arm hesitantly around the red head's waist, as if she were made of porcelain. We did a couple of turns, then I stuttered, 'Miss Phipps, I've never danced with anyone before without. . .er. . .knowing them.'

'Don't be shy,' she smiled. 'Think of me as your fiancée. What's her name?' Her accent was two parts Cockney to one part Devon. I found out later she'd been born in Balham.

I thought quickly. 'Rebecca.'

'Nice name.' We swirled on and I winced as I deliberately trod on her toe. I was reckoned quite a hoofer at parties and it was difficult pretending to need lessons.

'Maybe I would feel better if I knew your name.'

'Oh. . .all right. Mine's Daphne. Daphne Phipps.'

I breathed a silent sight of relief and disengaged.

'Vell, vot do you think, Mr Conway?' Adrian Feather asked, rather impatiently.

'Yes' I said. 'Fine, Mr Feather. Er, I think Miss Phipps is just the girl I'm looking for.'

I had to attend the academy for three mornings in a row, before I felt I had wormed my way sufficiently into Daphne Phipps' confidence to suggest a little extra-mural activity. But after my tango lesson of the Wednesday, which ended at twelve thirty, I dared to suggest she might like to join me for a quick drink 'to celebrate my good progress in your hands', before she trotted off to lunch. She eyed me a little

63

suspiciously but soon accepted, when I explained my usual haunt was the Imperial bar.

'We're not really supposed to,' she had grinned, 'but seeing as how you've got a fiancée. . .' Then she added with a Cockney lilt, 'But not a word to Mr Adrian.'

I think she was disappointed when she found she had to walk, but I had deliberately left my old La Salle behind, for the same reason I was sporting a moustache. I just hoped none of my old cronies would be around at the hotel, but it was a risk I had to take. As we walked into the bar, I lifted a finger to my lips as Ted Shilling's jaw dropped when he spotted me. He winked his understanding and went on serving his customer, whilst I propelled Daphne to a secluded table in the corner where I hoped I could remain incognito.

'I like it here,' she said.

'Been here before then?' I asked.

'A few times. Someone brought me here only last week, 'smatter of fact.' She looked up. 'In case you're wondering, mine's a gin and orange.'

I went to the bar and waited for Ted to finish doing the rumba with his cocktail shaker.

'That the girl, Ted?' I whispered when I'd got his attention.

He nodded. 'She'll have a gin and orange too, I'll be bound.'

'You're bound,' I said.

He fingered his upper lip and started to pour out the gin.

'Look like Errol Flynn,' he muttered.

'Funny,' I said. 'They sold it to me as a Colman number.' I leaned forward. 'By the way, may name is Tom Conway.'

He chuckled. 'He's got a moustache like that as well.'

'Who has?'

'Tom Conway. The actor fella. Often in double features, You know, George Sanders' brother.'

Hell. I'd forgotten. My alias could certainly have been better chosen. I added a splash to my Scotch and picked up the drinks.

'Wish me luck, Ted,' I said out of the corner of my mouth.

He laughed and winked. 'Be a change for the likes of her, I expect.'

'What will?'

'Someone trying to get something out of her, rather than into her.'

I raised my eyebrows and returned to the table. Really, Ted can be a little too racy at times. And I don't just mean the two thirty at Newton Abbot.

It took me two more rounds to really get her going. The trouble was she wanted to talk about everything under the sun but what I was interested in – her men friends, with particular reference to Seagrave. After twenty minutes I knew her father was now a docker in Plymouth; her mother was a daily maid for a lady in Plympton but didn't like it; her sister had run off with a door-to-door brush salesman from Exeter and her brother was next door to being an alcoholic and was the reason she had left home and taken a tiny room above a shop in Torquay that 'sold the fanciest frocks this side of Bristol'. There, apparently, she spent most of her time playing Bing Crosby and Rudy Vallee records on a wind-up gramophone, if she wasn't reading romantic novels from Boots library or sitting in the one and threes at a Gaumont or Odeon.

This final piece of riveting information, at last, gave me an intro. As you may gather, she very rarely seemed to stop for breath – save to down some more mother's ruin.

'I don't much like going to the cinema alone,' I ventured. Thank goodness, it worked.

'Oh, I never go alone. No.' She looked across at me, eyelids a'flutter. 'Always get a young man to take me, don't I?'

'I bet you've got lots of boyfriends, Daphne – a girl with your looks.'

She tidied a non-existent stray hair from her perm. 'Oh. . .I have my share, certainly.'

'You must meet lots of young men in your work.'

She made a face. 'Don't go for many of them. Not my type. They're either too nervous or too bold. Besides, if they were any good, they'd know how to dance, wouldn't they?' She suddenly stopped and a blush fought a battle with her rouge. 'Whoops, sorry. I don't mean to include you in that lot, Mr Conway, honest I don't. You're different somehow. A real gentleman, you are. 'Sides, you've obviously got a lot of money behind you, if you don't mind me mentioning it. I mean, just look where you go for a drink. Most of my dancing partners look as if they can hardly afford the lessons, let alone take a girl out to a place like this.'

I smiled. 'So you like a man with a little bit of money, do you, Daphne?'

She looked a trifle taken aback. 'Well, why not? My old mum says money can't buy happiness, but as I always tell her, when she's off to clean somebody else's silver or polish their heirlooms, lack of it gets misery for free.'

I laughed. 'So you aim to marry a man with money, eh? Well, you're living in the right place, Daphne. Plenty of well off farmers round here. Then there are the holiday makers in the summer.'

She sipped her gin and orange, then smiled. 'Can you see me, Mr Conway, as a farmer's wife? All that mud, cows and horses and things. No, not for me. None of that. I will only settle for someone with a bit of sophistication.'

She glanced up at me, her eyelids slightly lowered, whether from the gins or an attempt to be alluring, I wasn't quite sure. 'More like yourself, really. Pity you've already found yourself a Miss Right.'

'Well, yes,' I stammered. 'And then again, no. But you sound as if you might have somebody in mind?'

She sighed. 'Having in mind and having in your pocket, so to speak, are a bit different, Mr Conway. But I can't deny. . .' Her voice trailed away, but I helped her back on this rather promising path.

'The man who brought you here last week, I would hazard a guess.'

She played with her glass with crimson-tipped fingers.

'Might be.'

'Is he nice?'

She pursed her equally crimson lips. 'Well, don't know about nice. But he's certainly exciting.'

'Been out with him long?'

'So, so,' she hedged. ''Nough times to know.'

'That you like him?'

She suddenly looked hard at me. 'Here, if you don't mind me asking, why are you so interested in my boyfriends?' You're not one of those – '

I cut her off. 'No, Daphne, I'm definitely not one of those.'

She looked down at her Ingersoll watch. 'Hang on, I'd better be going. Had no idea it was so late.' She rose from the table. 'I won't have time to grab a sandwich if I don't get a move one.' She smiled and, for a second, let a touch of innocence through her brittle defences. 'Anyway, thanks awfully for the drinks. Will I see you tomorrow?'

I realized it would take a few more lessons to glean what I wanted, so I nodded. At that very moment, I saw what I had been dreading the whole time – a crony bearing down on me.

'Hello, Johnny. Hey, love the new moustache, what?'

Daphne frowned at me, as I rapidly starting propelling her towards the exit.

'Hey, you said your name was Tom, not Johnny.'

I thought quickly, a bit too quickly as it turned out.

'It's my other name,' I muttered. 'Mother christened me John Thomas Conway. But I prefer Tom.'

'Oooh,' she cooed as we went through the door. 'John Thomas, eh?' With a dirty chuckle, she added, 'I hope your fiancée likes your John Thomas anyway. I'm sure I would, if I was asked. Bye.'

She blew a kiss as she sashayed down the hotel drive. 'By the way, love your new moustache too. Don't you go and shave it off.'

When she was out of sight, I instantly disobeyed her last injunction and a few minutes later, it was again bristling in the glove locker of my La Salle.

When I got back to my office, Babs was waiting impatiently at the door.

'I'm so glad you're back, Johnny,' she gasped. 'You've had a phone call.'

By her expression you would be tempted to think it was either the Irish Sweepstake committee or maybe even His Majesty himself.

I went in. 'Calm down, Babs. Who was it from?'

She consulted a scrap of paper in her hand.

'A Miss Diana Travers, she said her name was.'

'Any message?'

'Yes. She said would you contact her directly you're back from Gottenberg.'

I laughed. 'You didn't tell her I'd gone there, did you Babs?'

She blushed heavily. 'Did I do wrong, Johnny?'

I put my hand reassuringly on her shoulder. 'No, Babs, not to worry.'

'I must say, she did seem a bit surprised when I told her.'

'I bet she did. Anyway, thanks, Babs. You had better get back before Mr Ling starts ranting and raving.'

Diana Travers was in when I phoned and, seemingly, in a somewhat tetchy mood. I quickly explained about Babs' message but all she really wanted to hear was whether I could go up to Ashburton that afternoon and explain my progress. I decided I had better, so we made an appointment for three o'clock.

There was, thankfully, no red Alvis in the drive when I arrived and Diana Travers, with the minimum of greeting, ushered me into her drawing-room. As I sat down, she lit up a Balkan Sobranie in her long holder.

'So, Mr Black. I had been expecting you to call before.'

'I'm sorry, Miss Travers, I was going to ring directly I had any real leads, but it's still fairly early days and – '

She cut in. 'I would like a progress report from you at least twice a week, Mr Black, if that's not too much trouble.'

'Yes, fine. I'll remember that.'

She relaxed back in her chair and crossed her slim, elegant legs. In a curious way, her impatience with me heightened her physical attraction and had lent an excitement to her face that had been lacking at our first meeting.

'So, what have you discovered so far, Mr Black? I do hope you're making *some* progress.'

I had prepared what I was going to tell her on the drive over – which was, really, everything save for the information that my theatrical friends in London had provided. At this stage, it seemed to me premature to involve her with that. And, maybe, rather foolish.

By the time I'd finished, she was on her third Balkan Sobranie. As silence then ensued, I went on.

'So, Miss Travers, I intend seeing Miss Phipps a few more times, in the hope that I can discover exactly why a man like Michael Seagrave would be seeing a girl from a ballroom dancing school, when heiresses seem much more his cup of – glass of champagne.'

'Have you any other routes of enquiry? This Miss Phipps may prove a blind alley.'

'Before I left Bigbury on Saturday, I made an arrangement with the man who is in charge of the hotel garage and chauffeur's quarters. It cost a little, but I think it may be worth it. He is going to ring in whenever he sees Mr Seagrave's Alvis. I've given him a description of both car and driver so he shouldn't make any mistakes. Besides, Alvises aren't exactly Morris Eights. They're pretty thin on the ground down here. So I should be able to keep track of at least some of the times that Mr Seagrave is seeing Susan Prendergast.'

'Is she pretty?' Diana Travers asked, stubbing her cigarette into a Queen Mary Maiden Voyage ashtray.

I trod carefully. 'She's pleasant enough. Vivacity, I would say, was her main attraction.'

'Seventeen, you say?'

'I believe so.'

'Michael will be hanging about outside schools soon.'

I made no comment, but went on, 'Then I may have to pop up to London some time to acquaint myself a little with Seagrave's background. I gather he was in rep in Bromley and also, I believe, in Croydon – my old home town.'

She ignored my homely remark. 'I would have thought it was far more important for you to be spending your time in Devon, rather than running up big expenses going to London. It's not so much Mr Seagrave's background that needs looking into, as what he's been doing round here. After all, he didn't murder my sister in London, did he?'

'A private investigater needs all the information he can get on a case, Miss Travers. Ninety-nine per cent of it may well be irrelevant but that one per cent – '

'Don't give me a lecture on detection, Mr Black. After all, I gather you have not been practising your profession all that long, have you? Lectures should only follow considerable experience, I would have thought.'

I didn't rise to it. My sorely needed income from Miss Travers, once terminated, would also prevent my gaining any of that experience.

She rose from her chair and I took it as a signal that the audience was at an end. But, without warning, her mood totally changed. With a now alluring smile, she said, 'Thank you, Mr Black. You seem to have made quite a promising start.'

I dipped my head and made to leave, but she went on, 'I usually have some tea around this time. Would you care to stay and join me?'

As she was now standing between me and the door, and her invitation, whilst softly delivered, was accompanied by a look in her eyes that defied contradiction, I said, 'Some tea would be very pleasant.'

And so it turned out to be. Between sips, Diana gave me a slight glimpse into her private life for the first time, and gushed on about the kind of friends she liked, honest and fearless, it would seem, and thus, rather thin on the ground – and how she hated parties of any kind, particularly of the weekend variety, as they brought out the worst in people didn't I agree? I wasn't sure I did, so parried the question with a smile. Thereafter followed her favourite films (strong dramas), actors (Colman, Cooper, Leslie Howard), and relaxations (tennis and croquet).

When I did at last manage to leave, I was more than intrigued as to why she had suddenly felt the need to turn on the charm.

Six

At the Friday morning's hoofing lesson, the moustached John Thomas Conway at last made some headway. The ambitious Miss Phipps agreed to come to the cinema and have dinner with me that evening, 'seeing as how you're a gent and your fiancée is away for the weekend'. Whether, in her mind, she thought she might replace my fictitious fiancée, I did not know, but I certainly hoped the evening would end with some useful information, rather than endless embarrassment.

In the afternoon, I went over to see Bobby Briggs. He was armpit-deep in the bonnet of a crashed Avon Standard Ten, when I arrived.

'Hello, Johnny' he smiled. 'I can guess why you've turned up.' He wiped his greasy hands on an even greasier cloth.

'Not sure you can,' I replied, peering into the rather ritzy interior of the special bodied Standard.

He sniffed. 'You've come to tell me you've worked off what Black Eye owed me. That's it, isn't it?'

I had to admit I hadn't thought of that, my guilt towards him having obfuscated my mind about the duration of my sleuthing services – or, to be more currently accurate, non-services.

'You're right, Bobby,' I invented quickly. 'My observation on your wife's activities really terminated yesterday afternoon.'

'Well, thanks, Johnny, for what you've done. Must have been a boring old job keeping an eye on my old woman.'

I turned away, so he wouldn't see my face.

'Just sorry I didn't turn up too much. I must say, your wife is a most industrious lady. Seems to me she's always on the go. If it isn't washing, it's ironing, mangling, white-washing, black-leading, shopping. She hardly has time for anything else, I would have thought.'

'But you said you saw a figure lurking one day?'

I shrugged. 'Could have been anybody, couldn't it? Poacher, tramp, trespasser, even the village idiot, for all I know.' I grinned.

71

'Your village got an idiot?'

'Yes,' he grinned back. 'Me.'

'You, an idiot, Bobby? Not in a month of Sundays.'

He put an arm on my shoulder.

'Yes, I am. And you know I am, don't you, Johnny?'

I didn't like the tenor of the twinkle in his eye.

'No, I – '

'It's all right, I don't hold it against you.'

'Hold what?' I asked, but I was now rather afraid I knew.

He laughed. 'My wife has told me everything. All about her arrangement with the errand boy and her other little arrangement with you, old lad.'

I could feel myself blushing.

'I'm – er – sorry, Bobby, er. . .'

'No need to be sorry – except about your professional skills, of course. Fancy getting spotted by my wife so quickly. Just hope you're cleverer with your other clients, that's all. Otherwise, your Black Eye won't even last the ruddy month out.'

I took his hand. 'You've got a rare lady there, Bobby.'

'That's why I'm not annoyed with you, you idiot. You only met her once and I reckon you summed her up right on the button. She's quite a one, my Ada. Taken her for granted all these years and then she comes up with a ruddy clever scheme like an imaginary Casanova. You have to hand it to her.'

I sighed with relief that the subterfuge was now over.

'So she's happier now, is she? I'm glad.'

He nodded. 'The daft thing is, Johnny, so am I. I should have spared some time to go out with her right from the start, really. Think of all the ruddy years we've wasted, not going to the flicks or the beach or even out for a meal somewhere. No wonder we grew apart.' He nudged me in the ribs. 'Funny thing is, all our new outdoor activities haven't half improved our indoor ones. Get my meaning, Johnny?'

I'd got his meaning and was glad. For both of them.

'Bobby, I'm very pleased things are turning out so well. And when you want the money I owe you, just give the word, old chap.'

'You've done more than enough, don't worry.' He winked. 'What I'm getting now is worth more than a tenner.'

The time had now come to bring up the real reason for my visit. I pointed to the low cycle-winged sports car parked behind his office hut.

'How's the old Frazer-Nash going?'

'Like a bird. Noisy one, mind you. But the racket's half the fun of those things. Like to have a look at it?'

We walked over to the car, its British racing green coachwork shimmering its shine back at us.

'Simonized it yesterday, I did. Like ruddy new.'

I walked around it, taking particular note of the multi-spoked wire wheels with their projecting centre lock spinners.

'Get in,' Bobby urged. 'You feel really something behind the wheel. King of the Road.'

I climbed over the cut-away sill, there being no doors, and eased myself in behind the large steering wheel. The bonnet ahead was shorter and much lower than I was used to with the La Salle, but the fold-flat windscreen was a joy.

'Like it?' he enthused.

I nodded, then looked back and down to my right. The knock-off spinner was clearly visible proud of the skimpy rear wing and I had visions of a long scarf being easily gobbled up by the wheel's wire spokes.

I clambered out again and peered underneath the rear of the car on the passenger side. The chain-drive mechanism was quite evident but, as the inquest had reported, was much less likely to have caused the tragedy than the spinners in the wire wheels.

'Bit old-fashioned, isn't it?' Bobby commented.

'You'd think they'd have got round to prop-shafts and spiral-drive by now, wouldn't you?'

'Frazer-Nash are a bit like Morgan, I guess. Do things their own way.'

'Don't we all?' he smirked.

I toyed with the outside handbrake and gear lever that sprouted from where the driver's door would have been.

'Haven't found anything in the car, have you?'

The scrap dealer frowned. 'What do you mean?'

'You know, any bits and pieces Seagrave might have left in it by accident.'

He thought for a second. 'Not really. Just got the car, the instruction book, the log book and the original sales invoice from Torbay

Motors.' He grinned. 'What did you expect me to find? Bits of scarf?'

'No. Just wondered, that's all. People do leave things in cars sometimes, when they sell them.'

He came up to me. 'What's your interest, Johnny?'

His eyes narrowed and he looked more like a bulldog than ever.

'Oh, nothing,' I shrugged.

'Nothing, my eye,' Bobby persisted. 'I thought it was funny when you asked about the Frazer-Nash. Not your kind of car, this isn't. Too ruddy stark and old-fashioned. You go more for the ultra modern, don't you, Johnny? Like that La Salle I sold you. Not this kind of iron hard, haemorrhoid special.'

I wondered how much I should tell him. I had toyed with involving Bobby Briggs before, because he, like Ted Shilling, knows most of what is going on in Torbay and the South Hams, legal or illegal. And thus could be a damned useful set of extra eyes and ears. Especially to a single-handed sleuth.

'All right, Bobby. I'll come clean. You're right. I'm on a case. I want to find out as much about the previous owner of this car as I can.'

A slow smile softened his tough face.

'Seagrave? Might have known it. Didn't like the feel of him one bit. Though I got a good deal out of him, mind.' His voice went to a whisper. 'What's he been up to, then, Johnny? Or can I guess?'

I put my finger to my lips. 'I think for the rest of this little tale, we'd better go to your office, old chap.'

We started walking over.

'You mean my old scrapyard might have ears?'

'Why not?' I shrugged. 'It's got just about everything else.'

I kept my disclosures to the minimum and made him swear to keep his mouth shut. For it would be a disaster if word of my investigations got out. And probably not just for me.

All that Bobby Briggs really knew, by the time I took my leave, was that someone (unnamed) was employing me to double check on the facts of Deborah Seagrave's death; and I let him live with his own assumption as to who my employer might be – Mrs Seagrave's or someone else's lawyers. For Bobby had jumped to his usual conclusion that money lies behind everything in the whole wide world; and thus that Deborah Seagrave's will might have been a bone of conten-

74

tion amongst members of her family and if they could hang something around her husband's neck – like a noose – then they might be, as they say, quids in.

I myself left the scrapyard little wiser than when I had come. Not that I really expected much from examining the Frazer-Nash, for it had, no doubt, been gone over with a fine-tooth comb by the Devon constabulary many times and I had read their detailed evidence at the inquest from the files in the *Torbay Express* offices. That's why I had not placed much priority on bothering Bobby Briggs about the matter before. But all the same, there's nothing quite like seeing for yourself. And from the car's seat, it was clear as daylight that, thousand to one shot that it might be, Deborah Seagrave's death could have been caused by her scarf tangling in those spinning hubs.

When I got back to my office, there was, surprisingly, no sign of Babs around. I guessed Mr Ling was keeping her nose to the grindstone and her hands to packing and invoicing all his tin, bakelite and celluloid Hong Kong novelties. Babs had presented me with an example that reposed on my windowsill – a tiny tinplate clockwork aeroplane, with an evil-smelling celluloid pilot sitting in the cockpit. 'To remind you of your *real* lover,' she had cooed. I thanked her for the thought, but added that I hoped I didn't smell like that in my flying days; and that it wasn't the reason my student lost all his senses and dived us both into terra ultra firma.

Whilst I was still gathering my thoughts, the phone rang. It was Tracy. She was staying in London and wanted an update on how I was doing. I gave her one, more or less, and she wished me luck on my date with Miss Phipps. I thanked her and she then added that she had just met a man who might be of some use to us.

'A friend of mine wangled me an invitation to a reception Alexander Korda was giving at the Ritz for the cast of his new film, *Fire over England*. You should have been there, Johnny. Come to think of it, I take that back. If you had come, I might have missed out on meeting the most gorgeous hunk of man I've ever clapped eyes on.'

'I don't have an identical twin, old girl,' I teased.

'Shut up, darling. It was that Laurence Olivier. You know, the virile young actor who's all the rage right now. Trouble was, I think he really had his eyes on someone else. Pretty girl I've never come across before. A Vivien somebody or other. Plays a lady-in-waiting or something in the film, with whom he's supposed to have fallen in love.'

'Okay, okay. But get to the point. Who is this man you met who might be useful?'

'A Stanley Trenchard.'

'He's an actor?'

'No, an agent. That's the point. We got talking and, apparently, he took on Seagrave when he was only just nineteen. Thought he might have potential, with those looks and everything. When it soon proved his judgement was wrong, Trenchard dropped him.'

'Bit long ago, isn't it, all that?'

'Might be. Who knows? But an interesting fact he let drop might help to explain Seagrave's connection with Miss Phipps.'

'Oh?' I said, now genuinely interested. 'Tell me more.'

'When the agent discovered him, he wasn't an actor at all.'

'What was he?'

'A professional dancer. He was paid to sit around in *thés dansants* ready to partner idle ladies like yours truly.'

I was silent for a moment, savouring this new piece in the jigsaw of Michael Seagrave. Then I asked, 'When did Trenchard drop him from his books?'

'About five years ago, I think.'

'Just because he didn't show any promise? With Seagrave's Tyrone Power looks I would have thought a good agent, like Trenchard must be, could have made some money out of him – after all, Alex Korda doesn't invite riff-raff to his parties.'

'Well, I'm only passing on what he told me. Like me to try to make an appointment for us to see him?'

'Us?'

'Yes, you and me. Tell you what, darling, if you popped up sometime over the weekend, we could possibly see him on Monday.'

'Where are you staying?'

'Unfortunately, with a rather snooty and excessively puritan aunt of mine in Chelsea. A family cross I have to bear, but luckily, only about once a year.'

'If you can try to make it Monday, any time from two or so onwards, I'll get up to London in the morning.'

She seemed a trifle disappointed that I was obviously not going to help her out with her aunt. But there were things I wanted to do with my cottage that had to be started sometime and the coming Sunday seemed like a good day.

'All right, darling, see you then. Drive carefully.'

'I wasn't thinking of driving.'

There was silence for a second, then she said disbelievingly, 'Johnny, you're not thinking of doing anything as stuffy and old-fashioned as coming by train, are you?'

'No, old girl,' I replied jauntily. 'I'm going to try to cadge a lift on a plane.'

Daphne Phipps, given a choice of Barbara Stanwyck in King Vidor's *Stella Dallas* and Ronald Colman in *Lost Horizon* annoyingly chose the former. Still, I suppose it was just as well. My moustache would have featured in the latter.

After the show, I took her to a small restaurant where I knew I was unlikely to meet any of my friends. All through dinner, however, she insisted on reliving the film and enthusing over Barbara Stanwyck's performance – an actress Daphne obviously found much to her taste, being gutsy, ambitious and very certain of where she wished to go in life. So it was a long and rather tedious time before I could get her back to reality. In fact, we were at the coffee and brandy stage by then and she was starting to show some of the effects of the alcohol with which I had continually plied her. Her green eyes had exchanged excitement for a kind of tired sensuality and her thoughts were certainly not as marshalled and sequential as they normally were.

'I like a happy ending,' she sighed. 'Life should always have a happy ending, don't you think so?'

I nodded. 'Yours will, Daphne, don't worry.' I then smiled, 'Just be careful of us men, that's all. Don't want to risk ending up with a rotter, do you?'

'Rotter?' She swirled her brandy in her glass. 'You're not a rotter, are you?'

'Hope not. But there are quite a few about, you know.'

'You don't need to tell me about that, Tom. Meet all sorts in my job, I do. Nice ones, nasty ones, decent ones, dirty ones. . .'

'How did you meet that fellow you told me about? The one with a bit of money, who takes you to the Imperial sometimes.'

'Oh, him.' She shook her head. 'No, not through dancing. No, he's no need to come to a place like ours. Dances like a dream, he does. . .er. . .or so I'm told.'

77

I couldn't figure whether her last comment was to conceal she had in fact danced with him, or was, in fact, the truth.

'Your fiancée – what was her name again? Rebecca, that's it – is she a good dancer?'

I nodded. 'Very good. Loves it.' I looked hard into those green eyes. 'Always dragging me off in the afternoon to *thé dansant,* that kind of thing. That's why she said I should have lessons, so that I could keep up with her.'

'Funny that, my friend used to be a – ' She stopped suddenly. 'Oh, never mind.'

'No, go on.'

She shook her head. 'No. Not important.' This time she looked me in the eyes. 'Do you mind me asking you something?'

'Try me.'

'Well, you don't strike me as the kind of man who would come to a place like ours.' She grinned into her brandy. 'Or be dragged around by no girl, fiancée or not. It's been bothering me ever since I laid eyes on you. So what – '

I didn't like the way the conversation was going, so I cut in, 'That's what I meant earlier about the male species – appearances can be deceptive.'

'All the same – ' she sipped her drink reflectively.

'Anyway,' I said, 'I take it this fellow of yours isn't the type to be dragged around either. Or is he?'

'Not ruddy likely. He knows where he's going, he does. Nothing would stop him doing what he wants.'

'What does he do for a living? I mean, where does his money come from?'

She looked at me suspiciously. 'Oh, he – er – inherited most of it.'

'Lucky man. Must be very nice to have had rich parents.'

'No, it's nothing like that. He's had to work.' She stopped and found refuge in her brandy.

'But I thought you said he'd inherited money?'

She put down her glass. 'Now, Tom, don't let's keep talking about my friends, for goodness' sake.' Her eyelids fluttered. 'After all, I don't keep asking you about yours, do I? Fact, I don't wanna know. I like to think of you as, well, sort of unattached, like.'

She extended a hand towards my face. I drew back a little, in case her fingers found the secret of my moustache.

'You know something, Tom, you're quite a handsome chap. Do you know that?'

'Oh, I wouldn't say that.'

Scarlet tips brushed my cheek.

'I like handsome men. My friend is ever so good looking too. But in a different sort of way. But there I go again. Talking about him, when I've just ticked you off for the very same thing.'

'Oh, I don't mind.'

Her hand thankfully receded, as she looked appraisingly at me.

'You know something, Tom? Maybe you'd look even more dashing clean shaven, despite what I said the other day.'

'Oh, I don't think so. Most people tell me I look better.'

The hand returned and, calamity, closed over my upper lip. The green eyes scrutinized my face.

'There. Let me see. . .yes. . .definitely. You'd definitely look better without it. I know it. You're the open-air type. Moustaches like that are more for gigolos and fancy men, actors . . . that kind of person.'

I didn't dare tell her how very accurate her last named was, but gently took her hand down from my lip.

She frowned. 'Ever so stiff, that.'

'What?'

'Your moustache. I've felt other men's and they haven't been as stiff as that.'

'Virile hair,' I grinned sheepishly. 'Runs in the family. You could have brushed out a stable with my father's moustache.'

She laughed. 'Oh, you are a one, Tom. I like a man with a sense of humour. That's the only thing about my friend – ' She stopped once more, so I helped her.

'He hasn't got one?'

She shrugged, then looked at her watch. 'Cor, it's almost midnight. I'll have to go. My landlady locks up at twelve.'

She took hold of my hand across the table and squeezed it affectionately. 'I'd like to invite you back, but she would throw me out. She's ever so strict.'

'That's all right, Daphne,' I smiled, then added, 'Must annoy your friend that, doesn't it?'

'Not really. He takes me to a ho. . .' Her caution fought the drink and, unfortunately, won. She raised my hand to her lips and kissed it softly.

'Thanks a lot, Tom, for this evening. It's been lovely, it really has.'

'A pleasure. You filled in beautifully for Rebecca.'

She kissed my hand again and looked at me, her eyes now soft and sad.

'Did I really? You know, I don't think I'd mind doing that again, if you'd like. You're ever so nice, Tom.'

'But what about your friend?'

She seemed not far from tears, as she answered, 'I don't think Michael would really care. That's the awful shame.'

She did not seem aware she had let slip his name.

'Oh, he must – ' I began, but she continued, her voice now beginning to break.

'No, Tom, his trouble is he's too much in love with himself to bother too much about anybody else.'

I signalled to the waiter and quickly paid the bill. We walked slowly up the street, her head resting against my shoulder, to where she lived about Riviera Modes, 'the smartest dress shop this side of Bristol'. As she was about to put her key in the door, she suddenly turned and threw her arms around my neck.

'Tom, you will be my friend, won't you?' she asked, her voice strangely desperate, as if pleading for help.

I hugged her for a moment and then said quietly, 'Of course I will, Daphne. Promise.' I tilted up her chin. 'You're afraid of something, aren't you? Please tell me. I might be able to help.'

She looked up at me, then closed her eyes.

'No. . .no. . .I'm not. I'm sorry, I'm just a bit tired, that's all.'

She moved away from me and back to the door.

'Daphne. . .' I started.

She looked round and on her cheek a tear glistened in the light from the street lamp.

'. . . be careful.'

She took a deep breath and forced a jaunty smile.

'Always careful, aren't I? Us hoofers can't afford to be anything else. Never put a foot wrong, that's our motto.'

She blew a kiss and was gone.

As I walked back to my La Salle, I prayed fervently that Daphne Phipps would live up to her motto.

I looked out of the inverted triangle of my window. But the sharply tapering lower wing cut off most of the view of the ground. Even so, I thanked my lucky stars that a flying chum of mine at Plymouth aerodrome had been able to wangle me a free RAS (Railway Air Services) ticket to Croydon. For, at least, I was airborne again, even though, damn it, I wasn't in the green leather pilot's seat I could see ahead of me.

We hit a thermal as we banked out over the sea and the Dragon Rapide creaked and vibrated its reception. A middle-aged passenger alongside me gripped the side of the seat in front with white knuckles. How could I tell him that the motion of the air was as natural as the motion of the sea, only, for me, a thousand times more exhilarating, more poetic.

He smiled at me nervously. 'Noisy beast, isn't it?' he said to cover his embarrassment.

'A little,' I said and turned back to the window.

For again, to me, the pervading beat of the Gypsy Queens that filled the cabin was nearer Beethoven than a bugbear and I relished every crescendo, as the throttle settings were changed in the climb.

Very soon, however, at around eighteen hundred feet, we were in the cloud that had threatened since dawn, and even the very limited view I had enjoyed before disappeared, as if in wisps of silken wool. Though slightly disappointed that the world was no longer spread out below me, I at least found some solace in my cocooned state – I had a little time to think and in my very favourite environment. I hoped the latter, as it had on many previous occasions, might prove an inspiration. I certainly needed some bolt from the blue, or on that day, I guess, grey.

We landed at Croydon just before noon, neither late nor early, as the flight was unscheduled. Normally, the Rapide, after its stop at Bristol, would have flown north to Birmingham and then on to Liverpool. But on that day, as luck would have it, that particular plane was being exchanged at Croydon for an ex-Imperial Airways Rapide that was joining the RAS fleet. Hence the chance of a free ride for yours truly.

Tracy picked me up in her SS 100 and, bless her, had brought a spare flying helmet and goggles for our mad-cap dash, top and windscreen down, into central London. Being driven by Tracy was certainly the next best thing to open cockpit flying; and I had not a moment of fear with her capable hands at the wheel. For has she not, on more than one occasion, won the Women's Open Race at dear old Brooklands, I told myself.

We grabbed a speedy lunch in a favourite haunt of Tracy's in Knightsbridge, during which we mainly discussed my rather enigmatic employer. Tracy was as non-plussed as I was by her abrupt change of mood that afternoon. I added that Diana Travers was still oozing charm when I had telephoned in my promised twice weekly progress report on Saturday evening, despite the fact that I had discovered nothing very concrete or convicting.

'Maybe she's fallen for your own very distinct charms,' Tracy smiled. 'After all, she doesn't seem to have a suitor at the moment, as far as I can tell.'

'Heaven preserve me,' I laughed, crossing myself.

'You're being unkind, Johnny. She's quite a looker in my book. And she's not exactly on her uppers. You could do a lot worse.' She raised her wine glass and grinned. 'Mind you, you could do a lot better.'

We clinked glasses. 'Let's drink to that,' I laughed. 'There's something about Diana Travers that's not quite...right, somehow, and I get a feeling she knows a good bit more about this whole affair than she's letting on.'

'Because you saw Seagrave's Alvis leaving that morning?'

'Not just that.'

She leaned forward at the table. 'Come on, Johnny, I know that look. What do you know that I don't?'

I recounted the telephone call I'd had from my actor friend in London, and his revelation that Seagrave had often been seen with Diana Travers a few years ago, and that many people were surprised when they learnt he was to marry her sister and not her.

She sat stock still, more than a little stunned.

'Good Lord,' she gasped, then added, 'Have you told Diana you know?'

I shook my head. 'No. I think it better that she tells me first.'

'Maybe she never will.'

'Maybe.'

She thought for a moment.

'Maybe she hasn't told you because it's totally irrelevant to the question of whether Seagrave murdered her sister or not.'

'Maybe. And maybe because it is *wholly* relevant to the case. After all, it could provide a motive for her to kill her sister, couldn't it?'

'You're joking, Johnny,' Tracy exploded. 'I know Diana at least well enough to know she's no murderess. Anyway, the whole thought is preposterous.'

'Is it? Think of it this way: Diana might not have intended to kill her sister. They could have had a hell of a quarrel and, in some kind of jealous brainstorm – '

She shook her head. 'And you mean to say that Michael Seagrave concocted the car accident to protect Diana? I can't believe it. From all accounts, he doesn't come over as the kind of guy who would help anybody but himself. Anyway, if it were true and he is protecting her, why the blazes is she employing a private eye to prove that *he* did the murder? Wouldn't she just let the whole affair end with the inquest findings?'

I looked hard at her. 'Come on, Tracy, you know exactly why. She may never have forgiven him for what he did to her.'

'Johnny, thousands of women have actually been jilted at the altar and not resorted to murder or mayhem, for goodness' sake. Besides, from what you say, she wasn't even engaged to him. They were just friends.'

'All the same,' I started, but then stopped.

Tracy smiled seductively. 'You're letting your imagination run away with you, my darling. Now, if only you'd do that a little more often with me, then. . .'

I glanced at my watch, then got up to pay the bill. '. . . then Johnny wouldn't be a dull boy?'

She joined me and linked arms. 'We ought to go and see that agent. There'll be time afterwards to test your imagination.'

'I thought you said you were staying with a strict and bible-thumping aunt?'

She kissed me on the cheek. 'I am. But she announced this morning that she would be out this afternoon and evening attending a Temperance rally in Aldershot. We'll have her place to ourselves, my darling, so start buffing up your – whatever you need to buff up.'

'My last train back leaves at seven thirty.'

'A sleeper?'

'Don't think so.'

She narrowed her beautiful eyes. 'What a pity, darling. I have a feeling you may find it a rather tiring afternoon.'

Stanley Trenchard's offices in Wardour Street were somewhat of a disappointment, for I guess I had been expecting something akin to a set out of a Hollywood musical, all glass,white paint, chrome trimming and ultra-modern curved furniture. But the curves were restricted to a secretary who looked like Bebe Daniels, the rest being distinctly nineteenth century and about as dramatic and exciting as an accountant's mind.

However, the man himself made up for it more than somewhat, being larger than life-size in almost every way. He must have weighed eighteen stone without his beard, and reminded me strongly of Charles Laughton in *The Private Life of Henry VIII*. Maybe, as a friend of Korda, he took pains to accentuate the resemblance.

We got through the introductory pleasantries in next to no time, Tracy seeming to want to propel the meeting along at a rate of knots for reasons I could guess only too well.

'So, Mr Black, what can I do for you?' He placed his hands together in front of him, like a Buddha idol.

'Tell me about Michael Seagrave.'

'Oh, I hope you won't find your visit to London too disappointing, Mr Black, for I don't know that much about him. And what I do know is pretty old hat by now. I *know* next to nothing of his recent life, beyond what Miss Spencer-King has told me.'

'No, it's his background that I'm more interested in, Mr Trenchard.'

'Well, where would you like to begin?'

'At the beginning, when you first met him.'

He glanced at Tracy. 'I've told Miss Spencer-King some of this already. I apologize for any repetition.'

She smiled her forgiveness and he began.

'I first met Michael Seagrave some years ago in a hotel in Brighton, where I was staying . . .' He stopped awkwardly, then added, '. . . with my wife and, er, there was this very handsome young man obviously employed by the hotel as a professional dancing partner for unescorted ladies at the *thé dansant* and in the ballroom of an evening.

'His dark good looks certainly seemed to command interest from the female guests, so, at the end of the weekend, I approached him and asked if he had ever thought of becoming an actor. Well, he expressed some interest in the idea, so I left him my card. When the summer season was over, he turned up at these offices to see me and, to cut a long story short, I took him on my books.

'He was, as I remember, almost twenty then and I managed to get him a few non-speaking roles in various second features and the odd part in provincial rep. But somehow, he did not seem to attract the attention of those who matter in this business, nor quite have the impact that his looks really promised.'

Trenchard shrugged. 'Maybe he didn't work at it enough. Or people were put off a little by his manner. I found he tended to lord it a little and he really did not have the experience to justify such an attitude. And he was very impatient too. Always berating me for not landing him star parts from day one. Michael Seagrave was a young man in a hurry and he thought I was being dozy.'

'Did he make any particular friends at that time?'

His moon face broke into a sly smile. 'Lady friends, do you mean?'

'Yes. Or any others that spring to mind.'

'Young Michael, I'm afraid, was more successful with the ladies than with us men. Men just didn't seem to go for him. Maybe they saw him as too much of a rival, I don't know. Anyway, he more than made up for it with the ladies, from all accounts. I've had more than one actress sobbing over him in this very office, I can tell you.'

'He loved them and left them?'

He nodded. 'Occasionally, they left him, I suppose, when they discovered his true nature.'

'Remember any in particular?'

'Not that would interest you, I would have thought.' He fingered his beard. 'There was one, though.'

'What happened? Do you remember her name?'

'Yes,' he said reflectively. 'She was one of Cochrane's young ladies, in the chorus. Cute little thing. Nifty at tap.'

'Was? Do you mean she is no longer on the stage, or what?'

'No longer doing anything, I'm afraid. She took her own life. Electric heater in the bath. Soon after Michael and she split up, apparently.'

'Because of that?'

'Maybe. Who knows? Who knows?'

'Have you any idea why they parted?'

'There was talk at the time that she was jealous of another woman. But, as I remember, Seagrave didn't seem to go straight from her to anyone else.' He smiled. 'So, to be honest, Mr Black, I don't really know.'

'Have you ever heard of a Diana Travers?'

He thought for a second. 'Yes, I think I have. Isn't she the sister of that poor lady Seagrave married – the one who was killed in the Bugatti?'

I nodded. 'Frazer-Nash, not Bugatti. You're thinking of Isadora Duncan.'

'Ah yes, but I am right?'

'Yes. But I really meant, did you hear of her years ago, around the period, say, that this dancer died?'

He shook his head. 'Can't say I did. Or maybe I've just forgotten. I have so many people on my books at any one time that I can't keep track of everyone's dalliances – even if I wanted to.'

Disappointed, I turned to my next question.

'Tell me, Mr Trenchard, why did you eventually part company with Michael Seagrave? Was it only because his career was not progressing as well as you thought it might?'

He took a deep breath and looked from me to Tracy and back again.

'Well, er, not quite, Mr Black. But I'm not sure I should say anything more really.'

Tracy came to my aid and said in her most wickedly persuasive manner, 'Oh, Mr Trenchard, after I've persuaded my friend to come all the way from Devon just to see you.'

The little girl look of disappointment hand in hand with big girl glamour was a combination that even a hard headed agent could not resist.

With a rather wheezy sigh, he relented and went on, 'Let me just leave it that Michael Seagrave sometimes seemed to carry his acting on into his private life. Or so two of the girls on my books complained at the time.'

I frowned at Tracy. She frowned back.

'I don't quite understand.'

He looked reluctant to enlighten me.

'Let's put it this way, an incident occurred which could have proved ugly, but luckily did not. But nevertheless, I felt it better to ask Mr Seagrave to find new representation. One has to be careful of one's reputation in this business. I represent many very famous names, who would quickly become alarmed and, perhaps, fly the fold, if any unpleasant scandal. . . You understand.'

Tracy smiled seductively. 'But I thought, Mr Trenchard, scandals were what show business was all about.'

He chuckled. 'Wild gossip, infidelities, who's chasing whom, that frivolous level of scandal, maybe, Miss Spencer-King. But perhaps the word "scandal" is not quite the right description for my problem with Michael Seagrave.'

'But the word "unpleasant" is,' I chipped in.

He did not respond, but his expression told all.

'You are really talking about Mr Seagrave's sexual proclivities, aren't you, Mr Trenchard? He liked acting out fantasies?'

He suddenly rose from behind his desk, grunting with the effort. 'I fear I have said too much already, Mr Black. You must not ask me – '

Tracy and I rose as one.

'All right, we won't embarrass you further, Mr Trenchard,' I said, rather reluctantly. 'Many thanks, however, for seeing us at all and at such short notice.'

He saw us to the door.

'I hope, Mr Black, that whatever this case is on which you are working, my name will never be quoted.'

'I give you my word on that.'

He extended a large and puffy hand.

'Well, goodbye. And as Miss Spencer-King told me over lunch that you were a brilliant pilot, happy landings.'

His grip was theatrical in its intensity.

'Thanks,' I muttered, as Tracy kissed him on the cheek.

Once Bebe Daniels had seen us off the premises and we were back on Wardour Street, Tracy turned to me.

'I don't suppose even the Spanish Inquisition would be able to get from him the names of those girls who complained about Seagrave, do you?'

'No,' I rejoined. 'But we may not need them.'

'How so?'

'I don't suppose Seagrave suddenly stopped acting out his private fantasies when he left show business.'

'You mean – ?'

I nodded and climbed into her SS. 'That's right. I think it's high time I took another dancing lesson.'

Seven

As luck would have it, I didn't actually need a sleeper back to Devon, as Tracy had prophesied. For when we had got back to her aunt's place in Chelsea, we discovered, to our surprise, the owner still in situ, lace handkerchief to nose, complaining that she'd had to cancel her attendance at the Temperance Rally, due to a sudden attack of what she claimed was influenza – 'Timed and sent by the Devil, Mr Black, you can be sure of that.'

Tracy was not quite as certain, as she said as she drove me to Paddington Station.

'I should never have told Aunt Agatha you had come up to London. I think she timed and sent her own influenza to stop her niece going to the Devil in her absence.'

Be that as it may, the next morning duly found me round at Adrian Feather's dancing school and asking for my usual Miss Phipps.

'She is, unfortunately, not vith us today, Mr Conway,' Feather said in his Conrad Veidt accent. 'Perhaps this morning, you might like to try Miss Randan. You met her the first day you came, I believe.' He clapped his hands.

I remembered her, a willowy blonde with flour-bag make-up.

'Oh,' I said, 'she's rather tall, isn't she? I mean, not the same height as my fiancée.'

As I spoke, in answer to his clap, the blonde appeared by the radiogram, and somehow she seemed a good deal older than I remembered her. Feather beckoned her forward.

'Vell, you're no longer a novice now, Mr Conway. Perhaps it's time to spend an hour or so with a different partner. After all, in life –'

I felt embarrassed for Miss Randan, as I went on. 'But maybe I should leave it until Miss Phipps is back. When do you expect her in?'

He hesitated. 'Vell, ve are not quite sure at this moment. You see. . .'

As he floundered, the blonde cut in.

'She's disappeared. I'm ever so worried.'

Feather tried to stop her, but she went on, 'Daphne has told me about you. She thought you were ever so nice. Her friend, like. Otherwise I wouldn't bother you.'

Feather put his arm around her shoulder to try to propel her away.

'Now, now, Miss Randan, don't bother our students with our little vorries. Especially as there may be no reason to vorry at all.'

But Miss Randan shrugged him off.

'You don't know where Daphne might have gone, do you, Mr Conway?'

'That's more zan enough, Miss Randan,' Feather barked and reminded me of the times I'd watched Herr Hitler on Gaumont-British Newsreels.

'No, let her speak,' I said firmly. 'She's right. I am enough of a friend of Miss Phipps to be concerned if she has disappeared.'

Exasperated, Feather snorted and quickly left the room. I took Miss Randan's hand and led her to the gilt chairs that lined the dance floor. We sat down.

'Now tell me all about it, Miss Randan. When exactly did Miss Phipps disappear?'

'I suppose, on Sunday,' she replied, now in a voice so quiet I could hardly her it. Suddenly I realized why she looked older than I had remembered her. It wasn't age in her face. It was worry with a capital W.

'Neither of us had anything to do that day, so we were going to take the steamer to Dartmouth together. You know, a nice day out.'

'What happened?' I asked anxiously, getting more and more concerned by the second.

'Well, I turned up at her place. You know, over the dress shop, Couldn't get any reply. That is, until her landlady came to the door. She was very cross and said she hadn't seen Daphne since the previous afternoon. And she said, if Daphne stayed out just one more night, she would throw her out, lock, stock and barrel.'

'And as far as you know, she hasn't been seen there since?'

She shook her head sadly. 'No, Mr Conway. And she didn't turn up here for work yesterday, either. Not all day. Nor this morning. Oh, I'm ever so worried, Mr Conway. What on earth do you think can have happened?'

I couldn't tell her. 'Don't get too upset yet, Miss Randan – '

'Dolly,' she interrupted. 'Call me Dolly.'

'All right, Dolly. Miss Phipps may yet appear, hale and hearty and wondering what all the fuss is about.'

She did not look convinced. 'It's not like Daphne to just vanish without a word, it isn't. I know she's a bit madcap at times, but she's got her head screwed on all right. Besides, she wouldn't risk losing her job here. Not yet, anyway.'

She averted her eyes, as if she felt she had said something she shouldn't.

'What do you mean, "not yet"? Had Daphne got expectations of some kind, then?'

She looked nervously around the room.

'I don't know anything about that, really. No, it's just that. . .' Her voice tailed away.

I took her hand. 'What, Dolly?'

'Well, maybe I'm wrong to tell you this, because Daphne told me in the strictest confidence. Made me swear to die.'

'Told you what?'

'That she'd be coming into a bit of money soon. Didn't say from whom, or how, or anything. Just that she'd be more than all right pretty soon. Fact, she said she'd already got a hundred quid of it.' She leaned nearer to me. 'Showed it to me, she did, in her handbag. Big white notes, lots of them, almost like folded newspapers.'

'When was this?'

'Last week. Can't remember the day exactly. Tuesday, Wednesday, something like that.'

'Are you sure she didn't give you some hint where the money was coming from?'

'No. Not a dicky bird. Just winked and said there was more where that came from.'

I looked her in the eyes.

'Where do you think it was all coming from?'

She turned away. 'I don't know. Really I don't.' Then she added quietly, 'Unless it was from that man she was going out with.'

'Who was that?'

'Wouldn't tell me his name. Just said he was well off and that she rather fancied him.'

'Did you ever see him?'

'No. I saw his motor-car though once. Long, low, red thing, looked

90

ever so expensive.'

'Was it an Alvis?'

She shrugged. 'I couldn't say, really. I don't know one motor-car from another. Except a Ford Eight, that is. My dad's got a Ford Eight, otherwise I wouldn't even know that.'

Suddenly, footsteps resounded across the sprung dance floor and Adrian was back. Dolly instantly got up and moved down the line of chairs.

'I'm zorry to interrupt, Mr Conway, but, as you may imagine, I cannot let Miss Phipps' disgraceful dereliction of duty totally interrupt our day. Perhaps you vould like to carry on your conversation over a lesson with Miss Randan, ozerwize I must ask you – '

I got up myself, noticing Dolly's shake of the head out of the corner of my eye.

'No, I think I'll leave it for today, Mr Feather. I'm sorry to take up yours and Miss Randan's time.'

I looked across at her. 'If you would let me know if you hear from Miss Phipps, I'd be very grateful. And I will do likewise, of course.'

'Have we got your telephone number, Mr Conway?'

Hell's bells, I shouldn't have said that.

'Er, no, you haven't. Tell you what, I'll call in again later. And maybe, again tomorrow.'

I went over to Dolly and pressed her hand. 'Now, please don't worry too much. I'll make a few enquiries around and see if I can turn up anything.'

'But why should you worry, Mr Conway...' she began, but I cut her off.

'Didn't you say Miss Phipps regarded me as a friend? So what are friends for?' I smiled encouragement and then left, escorted all the way to the door by a now even more severe-looking Mr Feather. I suddenly felt like asking him whether he taught the goose-step at his academy, but resisted the temptation. After all, amongst the thousand things for which Herr Hitler claims fame, I don't think you'll find a sense of humour.

Daphne Phipps' landlady proved to be almost as humourless as Feather, né Gottenberg.

'Only give you five minutes, Mr Black. No more,' she had said, after I had introduced myself. 'I'm washing my hands of that Miss Phipps.

91

Tomorrow I'll be letting her rooms out to someone who won't alley-cat around to all hours like she did.'

She took me up to what was obviously her sitting-room. Neat and tidy, clean as a pin and smelling of the obviously new Rexine-covered three-piece suite. We both sat down and squeaked on the smooth, cold surface.

'Well, what d'yer want, Mr Black? Out with it,' she snapped, wiping her thick fingers in the folds of her apron.

'I'm worried about Miss Phipps, Mrs. . .?'

'Lovelock, Mrs Lovelock.' She sniffed self-righteously and patted her tight perm. 'And I wouldn't worry about girls like her. They never come to no harm, they don't, more's the pity. Just cause trouble for other people, that's all.'

'I think you may be wrong, Mrs Lovelock. You see, I have reason to believe that Miss Phipps hasn't disappeared of her own accord.'

She frowned. 'What d'yer mean? She's been kidnapped or something?'

Cackling, she added, 'Cor blimey, why would anybody want to kidnap *her*?'

I did not elaborate and not just because I was only allowed five minutes.

'Well, I'm not sure what's happened to her, but I am certainly concerned.'

'Hurry up, then, what do you want to know? I haven't got all day.'

'You don't happen to know where Miss Phipps went on Saturday evening, do you?'

She shook her head. 'No, I gave up asking her long ago, where she was off to. Only got surly answers and "Just out, nowhere in particular."'

'Did you see anyone call for her – in a car, perhaps?'

'No, can't say I did. I don't spy on my tenants, Mr Black.'

I forced a smile. 'No, of course not. So you have no idea where she might have gone?'

'No, I told you that. I heard the door go around eight, I suppose it was. I haven't seen hide nor hair of her since.'

I tried another tack. 'Ever seen a red Alvis come to pick her up?'

'Red what?' she scowled.

'Alvis. It's a long, low, sports car.'

She laughed. 'Not on your life. The only car I've ever seen come round for her is a battered old Trojan. And I only know its name because I read it on its radiator.'

'Did it come often?'

'Often enough.' She pursed her thin cracked lips. 'But come to think of it, I haven't seen it around quite so much lately. P'raps she was starting to give him the brush off.'

'Him? Who's that?'

'A shiftless-looking chap. Probably hasn't got a bean to bless himself with. Surprised he's got a car at all, I am.'

'Do you know anything about him?'

She screwed up her eyes at me. 'Why do you want to know, Mr Black? Think he might have something to do with our Miss Phipps' disappearance? I'll tell you now, she isn't the type to go off with the likes of him. She's not so attracted by the sound of wedding bells as the tinkle of cash registers. Get my meaning?' She chuckled the dirtiest chuckle I've heard outside a pilots' mess.

'All the same, do you happen to know his name?'

'Henry somebody, it is. Heard her call him Henry one day, when they were about to go out.'

'That's all you know, his Christian name?'

She patted her perm once more, as if it stimulated what passed for her brain.

'Let me think now. Yes... She told me once, in a nose-in-the-air way, that he's some kind of actor.'

'With a local company? It would have to be, really, wouldn't it?'

'It is. I remember now, she said he was at the Drake Theatre. Said the name like it was some posh place like the Theatre Royal in Plymouth, instead of the flea-pit it really is.'

I refrained from informing her that the Drake was owned and run by an old mate of mine from my acting days, Tubby Trouncer. And whilst the theatre was certainly on the small side, it boasted one of the better repertory companies around in the South-West.

'I think I'll pop round there,' I smiled. 'There can't be that many Henrys in any one company.'

'Well,' she laughed, 'you're not going to find no Henry Irvings there, that's for sure.' She consulted the bakelite clock on the mantle shelf, then got up. I took the hint and joined her.

'I'll be going then, Mrs Lovelock. Now if you hear from Miss Phipps at all, could you do me a great favour and contact me?'

I tore a sheet from my Lett's diary and wrote down both my Black Eye and home telephone numbers and handed it to her.

She sniffed. 'All right. Since you ask – '

'I'll pay for the calls, don't worry. Oh, and there's one other thing.'

Stifling a yawn, she asked, 'And what can that be, Mr Black?'

'You don't happen to know Miss Phipps' parents' address, do you? I know they live in the Plymouth area somewhere.'

She went across to an oak sideboard, picked up an address book and started flipping through the indented pages.

'Now, that I can help you with. I always insist all my tenants give me the address of their next of kin. You never know in this life, you see, Mr Black, do you?'

I had to agree with her. You never know in this life, it would seem. Never. Just as well, maybe.

I left it until eight before I turned up outside the well kept, but modest, terraced house near the Plymouth Devonport docks. I wanted to be sure at least one of her parents was back from work to greet the moustached Mr Conway.

Daphne's mother answered the door – smaller and frailer than I was expecting, but with her daughter's gritty look of determination in her eyes. I explained that I was a student at the dancing academy and was just enquiring when Daphne would be back at work.

She looked puzzled, then after looking me up and down, invited me in, apologizing for the smell of fish that permeated the place.

'I'm cooking my husband's supper. He loves a bit of steamed fish, he does, when he comes home.'

We went into the parlour. The black-leaded grate shone like a guardsman's boots. She took a huge black bundle of fur, that turned out to be a cat, off a chair. His green eyes flashed their anger at his displacement for a stranger. Mrs Phipps perched on the arm of the chair opposite.

'Now what's this about my Daphne? You say she's been away from work?'

I nodded. 'Yes. I just wondered if you knew when she might be returning.'

She rubbed her work-worn hands together.

'I didn't know she had been away. You see, we haven't got a phone and our Daphne isn't much of a one for putting pen to paper.'

94

Frowning, she went on, 'Anyway, Mr Conway, why did you come to us? I mean Mr Feather or that Mrs Lovelock, her landlady, would know better when she'll be back, wouldn't they? And how did you get our address? Did Daphne give it to you?'

The last statement was spoken with a high degree of disbelief.

I was about to give a hesitant and hedging reply, having no wish to worry the mother prematurely, when I suddenly had the urge to come clean as to who I was. I put my hand to my lip and winced, as I tore off my moustache.

'Look, I'm very sorry,' I said quickly, as Mrs Phipps put her hand to her neck in amazement. 'I have misled you. My name isn't Conway. It's Black, Johnny Black. No don't be alarmed, please.' I handed her my card. 'I run a detective agency in Torquay called Black Eye and I urgently need to get in touch with your daughter.'

Her mouth fell open. 'What's she done wrong? What's my Daphne – ?'

'Nothing,' I cut in. 'Absolutely nothing. It's not anything your daughter's done. The case I'm working on is about someone I think your daughter has been meeting recently.'

'A man?' her mother asked, her intonation hardly praising the male as a species.

'Yes, I'm sorry about that. A man.' I leaned forward towards her. 'Now, has Daphne recently told you anything about going out with a man with a considerable amount of money?'

I followed her nervous glance across the tiny room. On a table in the corner lay a handbag.

'Well, er, I don't know whether I should say. Oh, I do wish Mr Phipps was home. He'd know how to – '

'Look, Mrs Phipps, this is very important. You must tell me. What do you know about this man? It may be vital to my case.'

She started to bite at a nail. 'Oh dear, I don't know what to say. Really I don't.'

I pointed to her handbag. 'Has Daphne sent you some money recently?'

I could see my guess had been spot on.

'Oh dear, oh dear. . .'

'She has, hasn't she? A lot of money?'

'Please, Mr Black, are you sure our Daphne hasn't done anything wrong?'

'Sure,' I had to lie.

She took a deep breath. 'Well then, I got a letter from her about ten days ago, I suppose it was. I wasn't half surprised. She doesn't write normally more than once in a blue moon, as I told you.'

She got up from the chair arm, walked slowly over to her handbag and picked it up.

'But that wasn't the big surprise, Mr Black. When I opened it, you could have knocked me down with a feather.'

She opened the handbag and took out a bundle of notes. They were white and neatly folded.

'These were inside, see. Well, one more than I've got here, to tell the honest truth. Mr Phipps and I spent most of one of them the other day on a gramophone. For Daphne really, when she comes to visit. She does so like to listen to records and we thought it might save her being bored, you see.'

She unfolded the notes. There were four left. So Daphne had sent her parents the princely sum of twenty-five pounds. No wonder her mother's first assumption had been that it was her daughter who had done something wrong.

She looked up at me. 'I felt guilty the moment they arrived, I did. But Mr Phipps, he laughed at me. "Take 'em, old girl," he said. "Don't look a gift horse in the mouth," he said. "Depends what the horse has done to get 'em," I told him. But he laughed again and said that what our Daphne had written in the letter was probably God's own truth.'

'What had she said, Mrs Lovelock?'

'That she was going out with some fellow who had taken a real fancy to her. And that he was "loaded with money" – those were her exact words – and that twenty-five pounds to him was just a drop in the sea and there'd be more where that came from.'

'And that was all I she said?'

'Yes, as far as I can remember. I haven't got the letter any more. I threw it on the fire a day or two back.'

She suddenly came right up to my chair. "'Ere, Mr Black, I've just remembered. You didn't answer my question a little while back, did you? About why you've come all the way out here rather than making enquiries round Torquay. Mr Feather would probably have given you the name and address of Daph's landlady. I mean, she might be ill in bed or anything, mightn't she?'

I could see from her eyes she knew she was wishful thinking. So I had, reluctantly, to tell her that it wasn't just work to which Daphne had not returned.

She subsided into a chair.

'Oh, my Lord,' she gasped, biting the knuckle of her finger. 'I know what she must have done. What Mr Phipps will say, I just dread to think.'

'H'mmm?' was all I could think to say.

'She's run off with him without a word to no one. That's it, right enough. She's gone and run off.' She looked across at me. 'She was always headstrong, Mr Black. Always knew better than her old mum and dad. Wouldn't take no advice, never. And I know why she's not getting in touch. Because she's ashamed of what she's done, that's why. She's too ruddy afraid of what we might say.'

She stopped to bite a nail, then concluded, 'And he won't respect her for it, he won't. No man does. He'll love her and leave her, he will, once he's had his way with her. Oh, silly, silly, silly girl. The way to get any man to the altar is to make 'em wait for it.'

She blushed, as she realized the strength of her feelings had made her forget she was talking to a stranger.

'I'm sorry, Mr Black, for talking this way. But I know the truth of it, you see. I've seen enough of life. Daphne hasn't, whatever she may think. Maybe, one day, she'll learn after she's left high and dry by some man or other. . .'

Soon afterwards, I left the house, with her illusions still intact. I did not dare share my more terrible fears – that Daphne Phipps' learning days might well be over, at least in the world we mortals know.

Eight

'Things going wrong, Johnny?'

I looked up at Babs, who was making her third little visit that morning.

'What makes you think they are?'

'Each time I've popped by today, you've looked so – well, down in the dumps.'

I put on a smile.

'No, things are fine, Babs. I've just got my thinking cap on, that's all. It's a tight fit. Always makes me frown.'

She giggled and it was nice to hear. I needed a lorry load of giggles right then. For Daphne's disappearance and what I had learned from her mother the previous evening had certainly put a giant-sized dampener on my spirits. On the drive back from Plymouth, I had been tempted to involve the police right away, but the cold light of morning had exposed the frailty of my case only too well. For, after all, what could I prove? Nothing, as yet. I couldn't even demonstrate that Seagrave was actually the man that Daphne had told me about, let alone the man off-loading the fivers, in return for. . .? There, I don't even know that. It could just as well have been for her favours as for her silence. And if it was the latter, what was she being paid for being silent about? I had no evidence that she knew anything about Seagrave's wife's death. What's more, if my suspicions were totally wrong and Daphne eventually turned up safe and well, having gone off with some other fellow, as her mother had suggested, then there would be not only egg on my face, but big black blotches all over Daphne's personal reputation. The latter I certainly did not want and the former would hardly be the greatest launch in the world for Black Eye of Torquay.

'Still, anything I can do for you?' Babs went on, hopefully.

'What about Mr Ling?'

'He's always getting colic.'

'Must be the chink in his armour,' I grinned.

She didn't even blink. 'What must be?'

'His stomach.'

'Oh, yes, I suppose it must. Not surprising though, the rubbish I've seen him eat. Sweet and sour this, chow mein that and little wriggly things' She stopped as she saw me get up from my desk.

'You off now, Johnny?' she asked, her big eyes fluttering her disappointment.

'Yes, Babs, it's high time for me to take the stage once more,' I replied in a dramatically actor-manager manner.

She frowned.

'Don't worry, Babs,' I laughed. 'I'm only popping round to the Drake Theatre.'

'Coo, what are you going to see?'

'A dancer's friend,' I said.

She thought for a second. 'Haven't heard of that one. Anyway, best of luck in getting tickets for it.'

'Thanks,' I smiled. 'Right now, I need every ounce of luck I can get.'

To my relief, just one ounce did come my way. The theatre was open and the company was in rehearsal on stage. Directly I dropped the magic name of Tubby Trouncer, the stage doorman let me in and I walked around the back of the stage and down the side stairs into the modest auditorium.

The scene took me back to my brief days treading the boards, but it was only memory working, not the pull of nostalgia. For I had never been drawn to acting for acting's sake, but only as a fairly simple means of filling in time between my crash and my eventual resurrection. I understand the appeal of grease-paint and the roar of the crowd (in my case the latter was usually only a desultory handclap) but I suppose I'm nowhere near narcissistic enough myself either to need them or revel in them. So I was glad enough to pack it all in, once I had worked out what my resurrection was finally going to be.

I sat down quietly in a back seat. In front of me I could see the unmistakable dumpy silhouette of Tubby Trouncer bouncing away trying to get some sense into the still hesitant movements of the actors on stage. It was obviously only day one or two of rehearsal of a new farce of the Ben Travers variety – notoriously difficult to mount without the comic genius of a Robertson Hare or Jack Hulbert. By the end of quarter of an hour, I felt distinctly sorry for my old friend.

At the first real break, as the actors and actresses shuffled off stage, I moved forward and tapped on Tubby's rounded shoulder. It took a second for him to recognize me in the dim light.

'My God, it's you, Johnny.' He clasped me by the arm. 'Don't tell me, you're fancying the old footlights again.'

I shook my head. 'No, I'm letting others have a bit of a chance. Wouldn't be fair on people like Laurence Olivier, John Gielgud and Robert Donat, for me to return, would it?'

He laughed uproariously, then led me to the end of the row of seats to stand in the aisle.

'So, to what do I owe the pleasure of your company, Johnny, old lad?'

I kept my explanation to the minimum. He already knew about Black Eye, of course. He had even seen my advertisement in the paper.

'So you wonder if I've got a Henry in my company?'

I nodded.

'So that you can ask him some questions about a young lady who is involved in the case you're working on?'

'Right again.'

His normally jocular expression turned serious for a moment.

'This Henry of yours is not up to his little ears in something naughty, naughty, is he? Because I'll tell you, Johnny, I can't afford to lose any member of my company right now, friend or no friend.'

I didn't rise to his question. 'So you've got a Henry,' I smiled.

'Two, in fact, old love. But only one a young lady would deign to go out with. The other is seventy-two and would love to oblige, but time has rather robbed him of what little magic he might once have possessed.'

'I think it's the first,' I said.

He gripped my arm. 'Scout's honour, you're not going to get him into trouble?'

I gave the salute. He returned it the wrong way round, then pointed back stage.

'You will find him in the big dressing-room with the boys. He's wearing a tweed jacket and corduroys. Name of Henry Swindon. You can't miss him. Brushes his hair forward to hide his bald patch.'

He bustled down the aisle and up the stage steps ahead of me. 'But you've only got ten minutes, mind, old love. I need him in the next scene. Oh, and you can use my office, if you like. Swindon will show you.'

And with that, he exited stage left, every jaunty step of his reminding me of James Cagney. I exited via the door at the back of the set – a manor-house style library – and instantly regretted it. How was I to know I would trip over the maid necking with the butler?

'Yes, I've been out with her, so what?'

His eyes flitted nervously around the office, its walls lined with framed and signed photographs of minor stage stars.

'The "so what" is where has she gone, Mr Swindon?'

He re-crossed his legs, rasping the corduroy of his trousers.

'How should I know? I'm not Daphne Phipps' keeper, am I?'

I tried to soften his defensive tone.

'But you're her friend, aren't you?'

'Yes, well,' he cleared his throat, 'she's got other friends, you know?'

I leaned forward in my chair.

'Look, Mr Swindon, I haven't come here to accuse you of anything– '

'I should ruddy well hope not.'

'I just want to ask you a few questions about Miss Phipps, that's all.'

'Who asked you to?'

I thought quickly. 'Her friend at the dancing school, Dolly Randan. She's worried about what might have happened to her. That's all.'

'Oh. Her,' he said, with a certain amount of disdain and I could see he was trying to work out what the likes of me was doing with the likes of her, as they say.

'Well, fire away. I'm back on in a minute.'

'Okay, I'll make it brief,' I said firmly. 'Question one. Do you have any idea of where Daphne Phipps could have gone?'

He shook his head, then checked his bald patch cover had not been shifted by the movement.

'No. I mean Daphne is a pretty impulsive girl. She could be anywhere. Doing anything. With anybody, for that matter.'

'So you're not worried?'

'Not really. It's too early yet – a couple of days or so. Maybe I will be after a week.'

'Question two. Has she told you anything about a supposedly rich man she's been seeing recently?'

I noticed his hesitation.

'Daphne has lots of friends, I'm sure, that she keeps from me.'

I looked him directly in the eyes, which he averted instantly.

'Are you saying she has told you or hasn't told you anything?'

'Use your imagination, Mr Black. Would a girl be likely to tell one boyfriend about another boyfriend – especially if the first just scrapes a living as an actor and the other is loaded to the skies? Daphne wasn't that cruel, you know. Ambitious, but not a bitch.'

I passed on.

'Question number three. Have you noticed any signs recently that Daphne has, shall we say, come into a little money?'

For a second, annoyance flicked across his clean-cut but rather weak features. But he was the master of instant recovery.

'Hardly,' he smiled. 'Daphne has about as much chance of coming into money, as I have of being chosen by Lilian Bayliss to play Hamlet at her Old Vic.'

'Maybe,' I persevered. 'But that doesn't mean to say that a little bit of someone else's money might not have. . .' I was going to say rubbed off on her, but hesitated and changed to '. . .come her way.'

'You're back to this rich fellow you harped on earlier?'

I nodded. He shrugged.

'As I told you, who am I to know?'

'I thought you and Daphne are pretty close friends.'

'She doesn't tell me everything, any more than I do her. We're not married, you know.' He looked at his watch. I was amused to see it was marked 'Aeroplane'. I had seen them advertised in flying magazines – five shillings down or twenty-five shillings cash. 'I must be going. Mr Trouncer despises lateness.'

He rose from his chair.

'One last question, Mr Swindon.'

'Better be short.'

'It is.' I too got up. 'How can you afford to run a car on what Mr Trouncer must pay you?'

Now anger did flood his face and stay there.

'What the hell's that got to do with you?' He strode to the office door, then turned. 'If you want to know, Mr Nosey Parker, the car you are no doubt talking about was bought by three of us in the company, pooling every ruddy penny we've got. Twenty-seven pounds, ten shillings. And we take our turns in using it for our dates. That satisfy you?'

The slamming of the door would have precluded a reply, even if I'd had one ready.

I just did not believe the scene when I arrived back at my office. I well nigh walked out again, thinking it must be some nightmare or I must have come to the wrong address. But Babs ran up to me and confirmed that it was all only too real.

'It's all my fault, Johnny,' she gasped.

I tried again to open my office door fully, but it would not budge past the nearest of what seemed like a mountain of packing cases stacked inside.

'What *is* all this, Babs?' I exploded.

'Our latest consignment from Hong Kong,' she stammered. 'Jokes, puzzles, magic gardens, drumming teddy bears, celluloid George Formbys playing the ukulele – '

I stopped her there.

'Look, Babs, I don't care if they're bakelite Baldwins playing the bugle or tinplate Mussolinis doing the tango, what the hell are they doing in my office?'

Her eyelids would have fluttered, but they were now too wet.

'I told the delivery boy to stack them all in the last office on the left on this floor.'

'But my office is on the right. As you come in, anyway.'

'I know, Johnny, I know. I should have supervised him, but just then the phone rang and I had to answer it. It was Mr Ling, saying he was coming in after all and he expected all the invoices typed and I hadn't nearly finished them and so I panicked and sat down at my desk and forgot all about the. . .'

She couldn't go on for the sobs. I put my arm around her shoulder.

'All right, Babs. Not your fault delivery boys don't always know their lefts from their rights.'

She looked blearily up at me.

'You're not cross, Johnny?'

'No, not if you can help me clear my office in ten minutes flat.'

She almost collapsed with relief. 'Oh, you're an angel, Johnny.'

'Not yet,' I smiled, giving my door an extra shove, so that I could get in without tearing all the buttons off my sports jacket.

'Now, let's get down to shifting all these across the corridor.'

All went well, until Mr Ling turned up around half-way through the exercise. I think, had I known Chinese, in the next few minutes I would have heard every swear word in their ancient language. And the noise was not so much deafening as piercing. For Mr Ling's voice seemed to go up an octave with every extra decibel of sound and it speaks volumes for my, and Babs', eardrums that they're still intact today.

It was in the middle of this oriental cacophony, as luck would have it, that a packing case split, depositing celluloid George Formbys all over my floor. At this very point in time, Black Eye was privileged to have a visitor. Not any old visitor, either. But my one and only claim to an income. Miss Diana Travers.

'I must apologize, Mr Black,' she smiled.

It was quarter of an hour later, when my office had returned to its barren normality and my client was perched on the one and only guest chair.

'What on earth have *you* got to apologize for, Miss Travers?'

She took out her usual black Sobranie and inserted it in her holder. I offered her a light with a still shaking hand.

'Two things really. The unfortunate business of the toy and not giving you some warning of my visit. But I happened to be in Torquay, so. . .'

She was referring to her accidental step onto one of the George Formbys. Her heel had broken off his ukulele.

'Forget the toy, Miss Travers. I've already given Mr Ling one and threepence, which will more than cover the cost – and that's retail.'

'Add it to your expenses, Mr Black,' she exhaled towards me.

'No, I wouldn't dream of it. As to your second point, do always feel free to visit me at any time,' I smirked. 'But normally, I entertain clients away from this place for reasons that, I think, you may realize.'

She waved an elegant hand. 'Don't make apologies for your office, Mr Black. I'm well aware that your Black Eye agency is still in its infancy. One day, I'm sure, you will be so successful that you'll have plush offices in every city in the land. You'll be the British Pinkerton.'

I'll swear I blushed. 'I feel like the prize British idiot right now, Miss Travers.'

She leaned forward and I detected a waft of some exotic perfume through the cigarette smoke.

'Now, bring me right up to date. A little bird tells me you might have gone. . .quite far afield in your enquiries this week.'

I wondered who had said what to whom and why.

'Yes,' I confessed. 'I did go up to London on Monday.' I quickly added, 'But I managed to get a free ride up there and I'll pay for the return journey myself.'

'Why should you?' she cut in. 'The visit was made for me, wasn't it?'

I hedged. 'Only partly. I went to see Tracy too. We had lunch.'

She sat back and crossed her silk-clad legs.

'Oh, you and Tracy, are you. . .?'

'Just good friends,' I grinned. 'We've known each other quite a while.'

'Very beautiful, Tracy,' she mused. 'Like my sister. . .' She recovered and went on. 'Anyway, Mr Black, bring me up to date and tell me what you discovered on your five-hundred-mile trip. I'm all agog.'

So I told her.

'And that's all?' she queried as I finished. 'Just that Michael Seagrave seems to have carried a little of his acting over into his. . .' she cleared her throat, '. . .personal life?'

'Well, it was a bit more than that, Miss Travers. Mr Trenchard did state that, through his fantasies, an incident had occurred that could have raised quite a scandal.'

'So you said, Mr Black, so you said.'

She ran her tongue over her lower lip and the red lipstick glistened like blood. 'I'm sure Mr Trenchard was wise in giving Michael up.'

I noticed her very natural use of just his Christian name. In fact, it fitted my next question perfectly. I got up from behind my desk, went over to the window and turned around. Back-lit as I now was, I knew she would have more difficulty in reading my expression.

'Miss Travers, may I ask you a personal question?'

She recrossed her legs. 'Aren't you going to tell me what else you have done since we last spoke? I'm sure there's more than just London.'

'There is. But first, I would like to clear up a little matter that's been worrying me.'

She took the cigarette from her holder and stubbed it out in the ashtray I had personally whittled from the top of an old Gypsy six-cylinder.

'If it's money, Mr Black – ' she began, but I cut in.

'No, it's not money.'

'Then what's your problem?'

'Maybe there's not a problem, Miss Travers. I just want you to assure me there isn't.'

She fiddled for another Sobranie, as I went on. 'I would like to know why you haven't told me you knew Michael Seagrave a good bit before your sister met him?'

I saw her hand tremble slightly, as it tried to insert the cigarette into the end of the holder.

'Oh, *that*,' she sighed, and I was pretty certain her relief was feigned. 'I didn't tell you because it might be misleading – distract you from your main task.'

'And what's that, Miss Travers? Discovering whether your sister was actually murdered or that Michael Seagrave is the murderer?'

This time she lit her own cigarette. I didn't want to leave the window to do it for her. Unfortunately, it gave her more time to consider her response.

'I resent your tone, Mr Black. I'm employing you to discover the truth and nothing but the truth. If, at the end of your enquiries, you consider that Michael Seagrave did not kill my sister, then so be it. But that won't stop me from continuing to hold my own opinions or entertain my own suspicions.'

'Of course not.'

'Now, would you be so kind as to tell me how you found out about my previous. . .dealings with our suspect?' She smiled coldly. 'I take it you haven't exonerated our dear Michael yet and he is still a suspect in your book?'

'Oh, no. The more I dig, the more I feel Mr Seagrave may well be guilty of causing your sister's death, as you will hear in a moment. But in answer to your first question, I learned about your previous dealings with him from an old acting chum of mine in London.'

I moved a little further into the room, the better to note her reaction.

'He told me that his friends were very surprised that Michael Seagrave married your sister rather than you.'

Unfortunately, she rose from her chair and turned away from me.

'That's rubbish, Mr Black. Michael and I were never much more than acquaintances. These friends of a friend of yours can't have known either me or Michael very well.' She spun around. 'What are their names, by the way?'

'Turner. Jack and Jessie Turner.'

She laughed. 'Ah, the Turners. I remember them. He used to ape Jack Buchanan and she, Jessie Matthews. Pity neither of them had any talent, though.'

She came towards me. 'Or good memories, for that matter. I assure you, Michael and I never ever entertained any notion of marriage. The whole idea is ludicrous. That's why I didn't think it of any importance to tell you. We were acquainted, yes, but anything else – '

She dismissed the concept with a sweeping gesture.

I came back to my desk.

'So you do not believe it could have any bearing on this case at all?'

She returned to her own chair and elegantly arranged herself in it.

'I assure you, it doesn't. Now hadn't you better get back to the point of my coming here? After all, it saves you coming all the way up to Ashburton for your mid-week report.'

I smiled. 'All right, Miss Travers. Now you may think I'm being a little alarmist from what I'm about to tell you, but. . .'

I mused about Diana Travers all the way home in the La Salle. For my latest revelations about Daphne Phipps and her disappearance had effected a considerable change in my client's whole demeanour. From being a rather brittle, distinctly cool and apparently revengeful young woman, she had assumed a far softer image, her smiles becoming more of sympathy than scorn and her words losing their cold and sometimes cutting edge. Indeed, her very appearance seemed to change with her mood and I saw her as an attractive human being, rather than a beautiful weekly retainer. I liked to think it wasn't all an act to fool me.

Just before she left, she had turned to me and said, 'Are you sure, Mr Black, that you want to continue with this case?'

'Why on earth would I not?'

She put a hand on my arm. 'Because if your suspicions about poor Miss Phipps' disappearance are correct, we are up against a very dangerous man.'

107

'He is still Michael Seagrave,' I countered, hoping she would take my meaning without further elaboration.

She did and smiled. 'But the man I knew a few years back hadn't got his eye on a fortune. Money can change people, you know, change them drastically, dramatically . . . tragically.'

'Don't worry, Miss Travers. I can look after myself. If I couldn't, I would hardly have chosen my line of business.'

'It's not like flying.'

'No, I've learned that already. It would seem there is more turbulence on the ground than you will ever find in the sky. Anyway, it's not me you should be concerned about. If Seagrave did murder your sister and now, maybe, Daphne Phipps, then *you* might be in more danger. So, please, leave all the risks to me and keep out of his company. If he calls round, get your maid to say you are out. Just don't mix with him at all. Promise me?'

She took my hand. 'I promise, Mr Black. Now you promise to be careful yourself.'

'It's my second name,' I grinned. 'And by the way, my first name is John, but everyone calls me Johnny.'

'I know, Johnny. And don't forget, I have a first name too.'

'All right, Diana. I'll report again the instant I have any more news.'

And that's how we left it. Her change of attitude helped enormously, somehow. I guess because I now felt I wasn't just working for pounds, shillings and pence, but for a real live lady who had a giant-size problem to solve.

I was looking forward to a quiet evening in the cottage, where I could work out my next moves in peace, or as much peace as Groucho permitted me. So, as I neared journey's end, I was a little put out to see the unmistakable shape of a Frazer-Nash parked up my drive. I just prayed Bobby Briggs had not discovered that his wife really was having an affair with some errand-boy or other.

I pulled off the road and parked behind the Nash. As I did so, the bulldog figure of the scrapyard dealer legged it awkwardly out of his motor. If ever a man needed a car with a door, it was Briggs.

'I was just about to go,' he grunted. 'Thought you were out gallivanting for the evening.'

I shook his hand. 'My current case has curtailed my gallivanting, as you call it, by around ninety-nine per cent, damn it.'

'Won't do you no harm, Johnny. Keep you out of trouble.'

I laughed, 'I think, right now, carousing and cavorting might be infinitely safer options, old chap. However, to what do I owe . . .?'

He pointed to the sports car.

'To that, Johnny, to that. Thought I ought to pop over and tell you right away.'

I perked up my rather tired ears.

'Tell me what? Have you discovered something in the car?'

He shook his head. 'No, nothing like that. Don't suppose I will, neither.'

'So?

'So a man called round at the yard this afternoon. Never seen him before. He wandered around a few of the cars on the dump, but I can always tell when a caller is not really going to put his hand in his pocket.'

'So what was he really after? Buying the Frazer-Nash?'

He chuckled. 'No, not on your life. He was an ordinary sort of fellow. Plain as all get out that he didn't have Nash kind of money. No, after ten minutes or so, he sauntered up to me, nonchalant like and asked me about my car.'

'What was he after?'

'He pretended at first that he was just impressed with it, like. Then ended up with saying I must get people asking lots of questions about it. I said, not really. But he kept on and wanted to know whether I'd had any people interested in it recently, enquiring about it and all that. It was then I twigged what he was after. And remembering what you'd told me about Seagrave, I played it very close to my chest and said there hadn't been no one. I don't know whether he really believed me or not, but he left soon after that. So I decided then and there, I'd better drop by and let you know about it this evening. So here I am.'

I took him indoors and poured him the last of my Scotch. Amidst Groucho's 'Drop 'em's and 'Hello, baby's, I elicited more information about his intriguing scrapyard visitor.

'About medium height, he was. Sort of sandy hair, I think.' He gulped his drink as if it were Dawes lemonade.

'What do you mean, I *think*? It was either sandy or it wasn't, surely.'

'I couldn't see it all. He was wearing a leather helmet thing. Came on a motorcycle, see. An Indian, I think it was.'

'So other than his motorcycle helmet – ?'

'Didn't look like no motorcycle helmet I've seen,' Briggs interrupted. 'And his goggles looked a bit funny too. Still, you'll be wanting to know if he had any distinguishing features, won't you?'

'Guess so.'

'Well, he had a gingerish moustache, for a start. Then, let me see . . . yes, he talked a bit lop-sided like that actor fellow.'

I did one of my 'famous actor' imitations.

'Like him?' I grinned.

'Yes. Just like him. Now what's his name again?'

'Massey. Raymond Massey. Was in *Shape of Things to Come.*'

Briggs frowned, then went on, 'Yer, well . . . and then he had – I noticed it as he was putting on his gauntlets before he rode away – one finger that was a bit funny. Little finger, right hand, as I remember. Looked like most of the tip was missing, as if he'd had an accident.'

'That's really good, Bobby. Thanks. Sherlock Holmes couldn't have described him better.'

You could have knocked me down with a feather when Briggs actually blushed.

'Oh, well, it was nothing, Johnny. Just thought the information might come in useful, that's all.' His eyes brightened. 'Do you think it will?'

I sipped some more of my gin, which I had only poured to keep Briggs company. For gin is certainly not my tipple and thus will never be my ruin.

'Could well be. Then again, I suppose it might just be a genuine enquiry from a sports car nut. After all, Frazer-Nashes are a pretty rare breed, to say the least.'

'Didn't strike me that way, Johnny. I don't think he was no nut. He didn't want to know about the car. Just about who might have been asking questions about it.' He downed the last of his Scotch. 'Anyway, it's obvious you don't seem to recognize my description of him.'

'No, I don't, more's the pity. I haven't met anyone on this case yet who is sandy haired, with a ginger moustache and who talks lop-sided astride an Indian's saddle.'

Briggs guffawed. 'Now, come on, Johnny, take me seriously. I really reckon this guy has got something to do with this case of yours, don't you?'

I nodded. 'Sounds a bit like it.'

'You don't sound cock-a-hoop.'

Smiling, I proffered him the gin bottle, as the Scotch was, alas, no more.

'Been a funny day,' I said. 'Sorry and all that. I reckon I'm just hoping there won't be any more damned peopled involved in this case than I've got already.' I winked. 'Can't keep track of what I've got, d'you see?'

He laughed. 'Sorry already you took up sleuthing, Johnny?'

It was just then that Groucho took it into his head to shout suddenly, 'Stick 'em up'. I never thought I'd see the day when the scrapyard dealer got near to fainting with fright. But it just shows how wrong you can be.

Nine

By next morning, I had decided to drop in once more on the rehearsals at the Drake Theatre in the hope of catching Henry Swindon. I had no real plan in my mind, save to check whether he had come across anybody with a ginger moustache and a lop-sided way of talking – or long shot, had seen such a character with Daphne Phipps. For Briggs' introduction of the motor-cyclist with a head full of questions about Seagrave's old Frazer-Nash worried me. Somehow, I knew I wouldn't rest easy until I had, as the constabulary would say, eliminated him from my enquiries.

But just as I was about to leave the cottage, the phone rang. It was Tracy, all agog to hear the latest on the Seagrave case and to tell me she was about to flee her maiden aunt in her SS100 and belt it down Devonwards. Her ETA, six o'clock sharp at my cottage and I had better have a cool martini mixed in my hand.

I rattled off, at newsreel speed, a general outline of my most recent activities, then asked her if *she* had ever come across the said ginger moustache atop a Massey mouth. She retorted that, from the description, she was glad she hadn't and added a cautionary word about someone I had almost completely dismissed from my mind – the blonde of Burgh Island. Miss Susan Prendergast.

'Hadn't you better warn her off, or something?' Tracy urged. 'After all, if Seagrave did murder his wife and has now done away with the Phipps girl. . .'

'Point taken,' I said. 'But I don't think Seagrave has been back to see her over the last few days. The guy in charge of the hotel garage would have phoned me either at home or at the office. I gave him both numbers when I greased his palm.'

'That's a relief. Anyway, I think we should warn her off, all the same. You never know when he'll be back a-courting and don't forget, the Prendergasts are old friends of PC's family.'

'What do you mean, *we*?'

'Well, I thought you and I might have some lunch over at the island tomorrow. We can chew the cud and hopefully, whisper the odd disparaging word into young Susan's ear along the way.'

I laughed. 'We can hardly air our real suspicions, my love. We would be sued for slander in five seconds flat.'

'So we'll just drop the hint that Seagrave is a notorious womanizer and can be trusted about as much as Don Juan, Casanova. . .'

'. . . Crippen,' I added.

And that just about ended that, and with a 'See you at six', she was gone. A minute later, I was behind the wheel of the La Salle and heading for Totnes and Torquay.

I had noticed the police Wolseley tourer outside the theatre, its top down and the driver enjoying the sun. But I'd assumed, in my innocence, it was just parked there for some reason unconnected with Tubby Trouncer's enterprise.

Inside the auditorium, I saw how wrong I was. For there on stage were two uniformed policemen and a fellow in the kind of raincoat that shouts 'plain clothes'. They were gathered around old Tubby, and lo and behold, my quarry of the morning, Henry Swindon. Of the rest of the company, there was no sign.

I climbed up onto the stage, hardly believing the scene in front of me was real. For in the stage setting of the library, the group came over as distinctly theatrical, actors in some fictitious murder mystery rather than – who knew what?

The Inspector, for that's who the raincoat turned out to be, stopped talking to Swindon as he noticed my arrival. Tubby Trouncer immediately turned around.

'Good Lord, it's you, Johnny. I'm afraid I'm a bit busy at the moment.'

I was about to move away, when Swindon suddenly said, 'That's the man, Inspector. The fellow I told you about. The one who was asking a lot of questions about Daphne.'

The Inspector's eyes flicked from indifference to interest.

'Ah. Well then, you sir, may be just the man I should have a few words with.'

With a bony hand, he indicated one of the chairs on the set. What could I do but sit down?

113

'Could you tell me what this is all about first?' I asked.

'Just routine enquiries, Mr – er?'

'Black. Johnny Black.'

'I'm Inspector Wyngarde from the Plymouth division. We're just making some enquiries about a Miss Daphne Phipps.'

'Did her parents notify you of her disappearance?'

He nodded. 'That's why we're here, yes.'

I felt sort of relieved that now I would be having some official help and what's more, at the instigation of others and not myself.

'I'll give you all the help I can, Inspector.'

'I'm sure you will, Mr Black.' He turned to the rather frightened-looking actor. 'Mr Swindon here has been very co-operative, even though – '

'I know nothing,' the actor interrupted. 'Nothing about what has happened to Daphne.'

A thin smile flickered across Inspector Wyngarde's somewhat skeletal features.

'We are not saying *anything* has happened to Miss Phipps, Mr Swindon.'

'Oh yes you are, otherwise you wouldn't be here,' he went on rather breathlessly, then turned to me as if for help. 'That right, isn't it, Mr Black? You think something awful has happened to Daphne, the Inspector obviously does too, and you all come running to harass me with your questions. Well, I don't like it. I tell you straight. I was just one of many that Daphne went out with. So why don't you get off my back? I haven't done anything. I don't know anything.'

Tubby Trouncer put his arm around Swindon's shoulder.

'Now, calm down, Henry, no one is accusing you of anything. Johnny and the Inspector only came to you for your help in tracing Daphne. That right, Inspector?'

'Precisely, Mr Trouncer, thank you.' He turned back to me. 'Now, Mr Black, if you would like to tell me what your interest in this whole matter might be.'

So I told him briefly about Black Eye and that I had come into slight contact with Miss Phipps, while acting for a client who was checking up on a philandering boyfriend. Not exactly the truth and nothing but the truth, but there we are. I felt it decidedly premature to raise the whole question of Seagrave and the Frazer-Nash incident at this stage. For had not the gentlemen of the law and an inquest already

114

proclaimed Deborah Seagrave's death as an accident?

'I don't suppose you will divulge your client's name?'

I shook my head. 'Professional oath.'

He pursed what little lips he possessed. 'And did you trace your client's boyfriend to Miss Phipps?'

'Nothing I can prove. No.'

'But you are still interested in her, it would seem.'

'On the few occasions I've seen her, I grew to quite like her. She was quite a girl.'

'Was, Mr Black? Was?' he frowned.

'Is,' I quickly corrected myself.

He thought for a moment, his bony fingers rubbing an equally bony chin. I almost expected to hear a few clinks. 'In what way is she quite a girl?'

'Oh, quite a strong character. Knows what she wants. That kind of thing.'

'And what does she want, Mr Black?'

I smiled. 'I guess, more out of life than her poor parents.'

He looked surprised. 'You've met her parents?'

I instantly regretted mentioning them.

'Yes, I was over Plymouth way and decided to drop by, in case Daphne had gone home for some reason.'

'So you were the man the Phippses mentioned.' He turned to the still nervous-looking actor. 'And the man Mr Swindon mentioned. My, my, you do get talked about, Mr Black. Your ears must be perpetually warm.'

I didn't rise to it. Just went off Inspector Wyngarde in a rather big way.

He went on, 'You must have known Miss Phipps quite well to have her parents' address.'

'No, I got that from her landlady.'

'Ah yes. A Mrs Lovelock. We saw her earlier this morning. That's how we got hold of Mr Swindon's first name. Henry.'

'Did the same as you, old boy.' Tubby Trouncer interrupted with a shrug.

The Inspector took a deep breath, but his cadaverous chest did not seem to expand with it.

'So, Mr Black, you are only concerned with Miss Phipps' disappearance because you "quite like the girl". Nothing more?'

I didn't like shaking my head, but I had to.

'Well, I expect she'll turn up like a. . .well, she'll turn up, hale and hearty and wondering what all the fuss is about. If you hear from her or about her at all, do, please, contact us, Mr Black.'

He turned to the actor. 'That goes for you too, Mr Swindon. And do, please, try to relax. We don't get too worried about people who go off without explanation at this early stage. Now, after a week or two, that's another story. But I'm pretty certain you will hear from Miss Phipps soon. After all, from what both you and Mr Black have said, Miss Phipps is quite a character and more than able to look after herself. That right?'

We both smiled nervously. The Inspector looked at the watch that hung loosely on his wrist. 'Well, we should be going now. We wish to interview Miss Phipps' employer, Mr Adrian Feather, before we return to Plymouth. So, thank you all for your time and sorry, Mr Trouncer, for interrupting your, no doubt, valuable rehearsal time.'

With that, he strode off the set, trailed by his two doughty but silent constables.

Directly they had gone, Tubby turned to me.

'Hell, Johnny, I'm already regretting your having opened your Black Eye in the same town. First you, then the police. Where's it going to end?'

'I wish I knew,' I smiled. 'But sorry, Tubby, all the same.'

He grinned. 'That's all right, old boy.'

I took his arm. 'But I'm going to have to ask you one more favour.' I pointed to the actor who was just about to disappear into the wings.

'What on earth's that?'

'I want to ask Mr Swindon just one more question.'

'One?'

'One.'

'Okay.' He shouted across to the actor, who turned and reluctantly came back.

'What is it now, Mr Black?'

'Only one more question, I promise you.'

'Which is?' he sighed.

'Have you ever seen a youngish man with a ginger moustache and a lop-sided way of talking like Raymond Massey, hanging around Miss Phipps? Oh and he rides an Indian motor-cycle.'

He didn't take long in replying. 'No. But then I told you I don't know everyone she goes out with.'

'So my description doesn't ring a bell at all? I mean, in any direction at all?'

'None. As far as I know, I've never ever come across a man like that.'

'All right,' I smiled. 'End of Third Degree.'

The actor hesitated, then went off stage.

I turn to Tubby. 'Last gasp – I don't suppose you've seen him either?'

'Never,' Tubby laughed and affected a limp hand. 'I'm trying to give up men on motor-cycles.'

And on that frustrating note, I left. The Wolseley was still outside, with just the driver, staring up at the sun with his eyes closed, snatching a tan at the rate payers' expense.

When I got to the office, Babs was waiting with excitement written all over her, polka-dot frock and all.

'You've had a call,' she beamed and followed me into the office.

'Anyone important?'

'Ted Shilling. Up at the Imperial.'

'I know where he works, Babs,' I laughed. 'What did he have to say?'

She looked very serious. 'It's all right, Johnny, he is not after money this time.'

'I know, I know. Relax. Just say why he was ringing.'

She took a tiny notebook out of the pocket of her dress and held it up.

'I bought this specially for your calls, Johnny. So I'll always remember what they have to say.'

'You shouldn't have done that, Babs. Here, how much do I owe you?'

She looked horrified.

'Owe me? *You* owe *me*? After what you did for me yesterday, I owe you, Johnny. You saved my job.'

'Oh, that.' I waved my hand. 'After all, it cost me nothing to tell Mr Ling it was me who directed the errand boy. So how about the notebook?'

She hid it behind her back. 'Nothing doing, Johnny. My way of saying a little thank you.'

'Thank *you*,' I smiled.

She consulted the notebook again and started to read. 'Ted Shilling said to tell you that the man has been in again, but this time with a different lady. He said she was a good bit younger and a blonde.'

She looked up. 'Do you understand that?'

'Yes,' I said, with a deepening frown. 'Unfortunately, I do – only too well.'

She came towards me. 'Johnny, you look so upset. I don't like to see you like this.'

I put my hand on her shoulder. 'Don't worry, Babs, I'm all right. I'll tell you all about it one day.'

'Can't you – ?' she pleaded, but I cut in.

'I wish I could, but I can't. Look, Babs, leave me for a bit, would you? I need to make a call.'

She hesitated, then went to the door. 'Let me know if you need me.'

I saluted.

'Aye, aye, miss.' She perked up and actually missed the door knob, as she went out. I immediately rang the Imperial.

As I thought it could not have been anyone else but the young Susan Prendergast. Ted Shilling's description fitted her to a tee.

'She looked up at him like he was a god,' Ted observed critically. 'Hung on his every word, by the looks of things. And drank far too much for her own good at her tender age. I tell you, if she'd been my daughter, I'd have – '

'Look, Ted,' I interrupted, 'you didn't happen to see how they arrived, did you? I mean, did they come in a car or taxi or what?'

He guffawed. 'Johnny, I'm a barman. I mix drinks, right. That's my living. The spying I'm doing for you doesn't extend beyond my bar. It can't. So, no, I'm sorry. I only notice guests *after* they've arrived. I'm too busy for anything else.'

'Okay, Ted, I'm not criticizing. I'm grateful, for goodness' sake.'

'That's all right, Johnny boy, pleasure. Anyway, why is it so important to know how they arrived?'

I told him about my arrangement with the head of the Burgh Island Hotel garage.

The line went silent for a moment, then he said, 'So you can't understand why you didn't get a call that this Susan girl had been picked up?'

'More or less, yes.'

'Perhaps her parents dropped her off here. He wouldn't have rung you if they had taken their car out.'

'No, he wouldn't.'

'So that's what must have happened.'

'Maybe,' I conceded reluctantly, but somehow, I couldn't see a printing magnate just dropping off his seventeen-year-old daughter at a hotel, without first checking that the person she was claiming to be going to meet was indeed there.

'You didn't see anyone who might look like her father, or indeed, her mother, hovering around the bar door when she came in?'

'Can't say I did, Johnny boy. All I remember is that they were already chatting when they entered.'

'What time did they leave last night?'

'Around eleven. I made a note of the time.'

I did a quick calculation. She would not have been back at Burgh Island Hotel until close on midnight – that is, if she went straight back. I wondered what time my man at the garage retired to bed. I bet he would have been long gone by then.

'Okay, well thanks, Ted. I owe you one.'

'"Snothing. I'm sort of enjoying watching out for him now. Makes my job a bit more ruddy interesting. The Dick Tracy barman and all that.' He guffawed again and rang off.

I was indebted for his call. For it meant that I had put far too much trust in my check-point at Burgh Island, as a yardstick of how often Seagrave was seeing the vulnerable Miss Prendergast.

'I still don't see why all this is necessary,' Tracy grumbled, as she began draping my biggest bath towels over the washing line I'd hung down the centre of my bedroom, wall beam to wall beam.

I grinned. 'If it was good enough for Clark Gable and Claudette Colbert, it's good enough for me.'

She stopped and put her hands on her slim and delectable hips. 'Yes, my darling, but in *It Happened One Night*, it was Claudette who was objecting, not Gable.'

I put on my Gable voice, number seven in my limited repertoire of famous voices. 'Well, baby, it's like I told you, see. My old flesh is weaker than yours.'

She came over and put her arms around my neck.

119

'Why can't we just be weak *together*?' she cooed. 'Like the old days.'

'Because these are new days, my love. Remember what we promised ourselves? A few years of finding out about ourselves before – '

Her lips cut me off. After a rather pleasurable interlude, she whispered, 'Imagine this is just a break for half-time.'

I gently disentangled myself, for my flesh by now was feeling remarkably frail.

'Tracy, darling, if we do take a break, I very much doubt if I'll ever have the will-power to get back on the pitch. And I doubt you will either.'

'Let's try it and see.'

I took her face in my hands. 'Look, Tracy, the idea of us not having this cursed washing line between us tonight is the most seductive in the whole wide world, so try not to make the whole thing impossible. But if I don't have the washing line, the sight of you in your skimpies or whatever you call them, will be the last straw. . .'

'. . . that broke poor Tracy's back,' she enticed. Hell, she has more come-backs than Carole Lombard.

I took a deep breath. 'Tracy, will you just listen to me. I find you the most desirable girl I've ever met in my short career and probably, you'll still be heading the list when I'm in a bathchair, but, right now, we should stick to the arrangement we made. For goodness' sake, I've only just started in the profession that I hope will earn me the odd crust over the years and I'm still as penniless as a church mouse.'

Her lips interceded once more with a breathed, 'Infest me. . .infest me. . .'

Once I had surfaced, I went on, 'So if we spliced the main-brace, we'd have nothing to live on.'

'But my money – '

'That's it. Your money. I'm sorry, old girl, but I was brought up in the old Protestant ethic of the male being the bread-winner. And again, you still adore going to London and mixing with all those bright young things who have little to do but enjoy themselves. And why the hell shouldn't you? Then there's all those house party weekends.'

'I'll give them all up for you,' she said, but without a mountain of conviction.

'Maybe you will one day, my darling. But the life of a wife of a penniless private eye in Torquay would be coming down with a hell of a bump. I think, if you were honest, you're not really ready for that yet. Now come on, darling, admit it.'

She bit her lip. 'I guess we need two more towels.'

'I'll get them,' I said and went out to the linen chest on the landing. Never in the history of mankind have towels and blankets seemed so necessary, yet so damnably hateful.

'What are you thinking?'

Her voice startled me. I thought she had succumbed to the sandman at least half an hour before. I rearranged my frame on the spindly camp-bed, Tracy being at least a foot higher on my own bed behind the towel and blanket curtain.

'Guess,' I said.

'Seagrave?'

'Who else?'

'Think he did it?'

'It or its?'

'Either. Both.'

'First "it" being his wife, maybe. Second "it" being Daphne Phipps. I don't know. I just don't know. I thought I sort of did until. . .'

'Until what? Don't leave me in the air.'

'Well, until I saw Henry Swindon with the police yesterday. He was distinctly jumpy and defensive. Not quite like someone who is as innocent as a new-born babe would be.'

'No actors can be as innocent as new-born babes,' Tracy laughed, then added, 'Sorry, go on. Are you going to say you think Swindon might be behind that girl's disappearance?'

'I really can't say. I just have a feeling he might know a little more than he's ready to admit at the moment.'

'So you'll keep an eye on him?'

'As far as I can. Single-handed. I can't keep an eye on everyone who might have some bearing on this case.'

'You need a trusty girl assistant, my darling.'

Drat, I should have seen it coming. I changed the subject. I had no desire for Tracy to end up missing as well.

'And then again, there's this ginger-moustached guy with the Massey mouth.'

'And the Indian motor-cycle.'

'Spot on. He's the kind of complication I don't need at the moment.

I don't even know how to go about tracing him, let alone eliminating him. No one I've asked so far has ever clapped eyes on him.'

There was silence for a moment, only broken by the hoot of a barn owl outside on a forage from Dartington Woods.

'Maybe ginger moustache and Swindon are one and the same,' she offered.

I had already thought of that one. 'But Briggs said his hair was sandy coloured. Swindon's is brown.'

'So actors have access to wigs.'

'There's another problem. Swindon has a part share in an old Trojan. He's most unlikely even to have a part share in an Indian motor-cycle as well. Besides, he does not look the motor-cycling type. The wind would expose his bald patch too much.'

'Didn't you say Briggs reported that ginger moustache was wearing some kind of helmet?'

'Yes, that's true,' I replied reflectively. 'A funny kind of helmet, he said. Same went for his goggles. I had forgotten that.'

'What was funny about them?'

'I didn't go into it. I just took it that they were probably old-fashioned or somewhat eccentric.'

'Supposing they were new-fashioned?'

'What do you mean?'

'I mean, what else do you wear helmets and goggles for?'

I sat up so suddenly in my camp-bed that the frame collapsed.

'Hell, Tracy, you're right. I should have thought of that myself.'

She pulled aside a towel and peered down at me sprawled on the floor.

'And you call yourself a flying fanatic, darling.'

She sat up and leaned towards me, thus giving me a glimpse of rewards I definitely did not need at that moment.

'Whoops, what's happened to your bed?'

'It's grounded,' I grinned. 'A bit like me.'

She extended an arm. 'Here, let me help you up.'

I must now draw a discreet veil over what happened next and resume the Seagrave saga as from the next morning.

Ten

Before we left for Burgh Island, I leafed through the telephone book to find the numbers of all the aerodromes and flying clubs I knew of in the vicinity. One by one, I rang them, but, unfortunately, could not raise a reply from over half of them, efficient administration not really being the forte of the flying fraternity. Those that did have the old phone manned, pleaded complete ignorance of anyone with a ginger moustache and lop-sided way of speaking. So having drawn a blank, I resolved to phone the non-repliers again on my return from the Island.

However, our luck was in, as far as our proposed visit was concerned. For the sun was bright and hot enough to crack the hedges when we left – and that meant that our little heiress might well be enticed down to the beach where Tracy and I would have more chance of meeting her accidentally than in the hotel. But all this, of course, assumed that Seagrave would not have got to her first. To find out more about the chance of the latter, I ended my phone calls with one to the hotel garage at Bigbury. To my relief, no red Alvises were reported as having checked in so far that morning, and my spy confirmed that he had not actually spotted an Alvis since our little palm-greasing arrangement. I just hoped Seagrave had not got to his palm first.

As always in good weather, the journey to Burgh Island was a delight, as the road via Kingsbridge, Churstow and Aveton Gifford passes through some of the most charming and serene scenery Devon has to offer; breath-taking glimpses of estuaries and the sea to the left, the dramatic rolling outline of Dartmoor to the right. And us in the middle, windscreen and hood lowered, eating up the miles at a fair rate of knots in Tracy's SS.

The journey went only too quickly and in seemingly no time, we were parking between a stately Daimler Straight Eight and a real cad's

123

car, the low and racy Railton Fairmile. I re-greased my contact's palm, then Tracy and I set out hand in hand across the thin strip of sand that the tide had left exposed between Bigbury and the island.

Quarter way across, Tracy kicked off her shoes and started to pull me towards the gently lapping water. I had no alternative but to follow suit and doff my socks and brogues. For I have a feeling that even the Thin Man would lose a little of his magic if he tried to warn off näive heiresses with his shoes squelching and brimful of the old briny.

Tracy started to trail her hand in the water, then flick some in my direction.

'Oh Johnny, if only we could forget all about the horrors going on in the world and just be kids again.'

I stopped and looked across at her. She looked stunningly beautiful against the sea's shimmer, more like some magical seductive water sprite than a child. Though her grin was always that of a mischievous kid. It reminded me of the day she had climbed down from the cockpit after her first solo, smiling the smile, not of mature achievement, but of immature delight.

We splashed lazily over to the Island and the reason for our slow pace was not hard to define. As we put our shoes back on, sitting on the slope that winds up round to the hotel, Tracy sighed.

'Well, here goes, darling. I just hope our Susan likes the sun as much as we do.'

I stood up and helped her to her feet.

'I just hope she's around at all. And that our friend hasn't spirited her away somehow. But Lord knows how.'

'Maybe he's got a boat. That could be it, couldn't it? He picks her up and sails or motors her round the coast to Torquay. It's not very far, after all, and would not take long in one of those new speed boats. That would explain no Alvises.'

I had to admit it was a possibility, but now we were nearing the hotel, the grounds seemed to be alive with guests in sporting apparel, either off to tennis or swimming, golfing or sunbathing. From then on, we kept mum and joined a frisky group of young men and women in boaters and big floppy hats, making their way to the steps that led down to the private beach.

Once down, our frisky friends appropriated all but one of the last vacant deckchairs. I offered it with a gallant flourish to Tracy, who accepted with a 'We'll take turns'. She relaxed back in the chair, the split in her skirt revealing her long brown legs.

'She's not here, yet,' she breathed.

'I know,' I whispered back. 'Just our luck.'

'Maybe the whole family has upped and left.'

'Doubt it. She was still around the night before last. More likely they'd leave at the weekend than mid week.'

I sat down on the platform beside her.

'However, I'll go and check at the desk if she doesn't turn up in the next quarter of an hour or so.'

And that's how we left it. I took off my blazer and cravat and loosened my shirt and very soon regretted not having brought swimming gear. For the private beach was a veritable sun trap, the rock walls bouncing their heat back into the pool area. Tracy seemed to thrive on it, but of course, the few garments she was wearing were gossamer light compared to my flannels, shirt and socks.

I watched her anoint her arms and shoulders with sun-tan oil. It smelt of warm coconut. She smiled down at me.

'Ten more minutes and you can have the chair.' Winking, she added, 'I don't want you getting haemorrhoids.'

I laughed. 'Have you felt this platform, Tracy? It's like a grill. It'll be burns yours truly will be getting, not what-you-m'call-its.'

Just then, I thought I heard a very familiar sound. Coming from across the rocks and out to sea. A moment later and my suspicion was confirmed. It was, without doubt, the distant hum of a Gypsy Major. My adrenalin rose instantly.

Tracy, as always, sensed my reaction.

'Down, boy,' she smiled.

I was down. Down for ever, damn it. Every beat of the Gypsy Major reminded me.

We both looked out across the rocks for a first glimpse of the aircraft.

'Probably towing a banner to exhort us to drink Ovaltine,' she smiled, 'or Guinness.'

'Well, it can't be for the *Sunday Dispatch* this time. It isn't Saturday.'

We waited, scanning the sky. It was not long in coming. But this was no weary work horse towing a drag-producing banner, but a bright red and yellow biplane, with long, sleek floats projecting beneath it that only just missed the flag pole atop the hotel tower, as it flew across.

'Whew!' Tracy sat up. 'That pilot's got some nerve.'

'Just showing off, I expect,' I smiled. 'We've all done it at some point in our careers. Pilots are rarely introverts, you know.'

From the sound of the aircraft, it was clear it was circling to land on the water, somewhere over to our left, where the bay stretches across to Bantham.

I got up.

'Not time yet,' Tracy grinned.

'No, I'm not after your chair. I'm interested in that seaplane. I think I'll go up and get over to the beach. Watch it taxi in and anchor.'

She looked at me strangely. 'But what if Susan P suddenly appears?'

'Get into conversation. Begin the therapy. At least, keep her here until I'm back. I won't be long.'

I was pretty hot by the time I had climbed up all the steps to the hotel, but the breeze at the top refreshed me, as I descended again to the sand causeway between the island and Bigbury-on-Sea. By the time I reached the beach, there were quite a few people gathered to watch the Fox Moth seaplane taxiing into its anchoring point. I joined them by the edge of the water and was surprised to see how far in the Moth could get without grounding, demonstrating the effective buoyancy of its floats.

Two small boys started to wade in towards the Fox Moth the moment its propeller ceased to turn, their gleeful shouts betraying the excitement they felt at its arrival. I waited and watched, as a slim figure in flying helmet and goggles climbed out of the rear cockpit, down onto the port side float and threw out a small anchor. He then reached over to the door of the forward cabin to help his passenger alight. As he did so, the passenger emerged and I immediately recognized the bland but handsome features of Michael Seagrave.

Just as I was recovering from the shock, the pilot, before stepping down into the water, removed his own flying gear and for the first time, I could see him clearly. Sandy hair, ginger moustache and a lop-sided mouth – Briggs' brief description could not have been more spot on.

I guess I stood mesmerized for a few seconds too long, for as Seagrave let himself down from the float into the water, our eyes met. I instantly turned and moved back through the onlookers, hoping against hope that Seagrave's memory of the man from the British Sports Car Association was as fleeting as our present eye-to-eye. I did not dare look back as I made my way up onto the island and down again to the private beach. But as I descended the cliff steps, I saw right away that Tracy had company and the company we had been seeking – the blond Miss Prendergast.

'Ah, Johnny,' Tracy beamed, but her eyes belied her smile. 'Meet Susan Prendergast. Susan, Johnny Black.'

We shook hands. She was certainly a pretty girl, more outdoor Scandinavian than an indoor English rose and with a freshness that only youth and inexperience can provide.

'We've been talking about the seaplane, Johnny. Apparently, it's been dropping by quite often recently.' She turned to Susan. 'Bringing a friend of yours to visit, you tell me.'

'That's right,' the young girl blushed. 'He always flies low over the hotel as a signal that he's arrived. When I hear it, I order drinks from the bar, then come down here.'

'Your friend a pilot?' I tried.

'No. A friend of his flies him over.'

'I used to fly,' I went on. 'Maybe I know this friend.'

'Well, his name is Tom Dawlish.'

I pretended to think. 'Name doesn't quite ring a bell yet. Tell me, what flying club does he belong to?'

She laughed. 'I'm not sure he belongs to any. You see, he works for an aerial advertising company. Normally, he's towing those banner things all over the sky.'

'Is that who the seaplane belongs to – the advertising company?'

'I believe so. My friend hires it from them when he wants to.'

I looked back towards the cliff steps. Still no sign of Seagrave or the pilot, but I knew I had to move fast.

'Your friend wouldn't by any chance be a Michael Seagrave, would he?'

Her eyes sparkled in the sun. 'Yes. Why, do you know him?'

'Not really. But I know a bit about him.'

She looked at me with a desperately sincere and serious expression.

'He's a wonderful man and, as you know something about him, you will remember what a terrible tragedy he's trying to recover from.'

'Yes. His wife was killed, wasn't she?'

'Killed?' she repeated in horror. 'You make it sound so. . .brutal.'

'Death can be brutal, Miss Prendergast.'

'But it was an accident. Her scarf got caught in the car's wheels. Accidents aren't brutal, Mr Black, just very, very tragic.'

I was about to comment, when I saw I no longer had her attention. She was staring up at the cliffs and waving. I did not need to look at whom.

Tracy came across and took my hand.

'Well, Susan, maybe we'll see you later when your friend has gone.'

'Oh – that would be nice but, er, Michael is taking me up on Dartmoor after lunch.'

'By seaplane?' I asked incredulously.

She giggled. 'No, Mr Black, by car, of course. He's having a new one he's bought delivered here at noon. It's smashing too. I've seen the sales catalogue. It's a Lammas–Graham Coupe.'

She said the name with considerable reverence. I knew the make. Brand new on the market. Supercharged American engine, British bodywork à la Bentley. A cool seven hundred pounds. Seagrave wasn't wasting time spending his wife's fortune.

Tracy squeezed my hand. 'We had better not keep you from your friend, had we, Johnny?'

'Thanks. Bye.' The young girl waved and ran off towards the steps.

'We'd better keep facing towards the water,' Tracy remarked between gritted teeth. 'Otherwise, he'll spot you.'

'I have a feeling it may be a bit late for that. Our eyes met as he was getting out of the plane.'

'Think he recognized you?'

'I have no idea. All I wish is that we'd brought our swimming gear. Then we could have swum away from here and onto the rocks and out to the beach, without having to test his powers of recognition.'

'Perhaps we will be able to sneak up the steps whilst he's still in the throes of greeting his new beloved, poor girl.' She looked behind for a split second, then squeezed my hand until it hurt.

'Watch out, Johnny. Forget what I just said. He seems to be making straight for us.'

I'm afraid I forgot myself at this point and came out with a combination of words that even Bernard Shaw hasn't used yet. Then I took a deep breath and turned around – to find Michael Seagrave only a couple of feet away, his Tyrone Power features now anything but bland, in the distortion of his anger.

'All right, Mr White of the British Sports Car Association,' he railed, 'or is it really Mr Black, as I gather you've just told Susan?'

'I have to confess, Mr Seagrave, that it is Black.'

'You don't need to confess, Mr Black. I knew your real name some time ago.' He laughed. 'You don't think I swallowed all that twaddle you told me the day you called, do you?'

By now, he was uncomfortably near and I could smell whisky on his breath. He must have a different yardarm from me. I let him rail on.

'First of all, I'm not such a complete ignoramus that I don't know the main motoring clubs. And there's no such organization as the British Sports Car Association. Secondly, my gardener told me you arrived in a big plush American La Salle – he read the name on the bonnet. Now, no British sports car buff would go around in a La Salle, would they, Mr Black?'

'They might. It's pretty fast, you know.'

He grabbed me by the front of my shirt.

'Don't get funny with me, Mr Black. I know your little game. You're trying to stir up dirt about me, aren't you? And I can guess who is employing you to do so.' He started to push me with his fist.

It was then that Tracy, bless her, tapped him on the shoulder.

He looked around sharply, but she adroitly side-stepped. I'm afraid I couldn't resist it. I cut down on his grasping hand with my right, then prodded forward with my left. His feet slipped on a patch of wet on the platform, and one more prod and he fell backwards into the water with an almighty splash, much to the intrigued onlookers' amusement.

Tracy, ever gallant, extended a hand to help him back onto the platform, but he shunned her generosity and made rather a meal of clambering out on his own.

'You'll pay for this, Black. You'll pay for everything.'

I couldn't help but smile.

'What have I done, Mr Seagrave?'

He looked down at his sodden and dripping clothes, then shook himself like a dog. Susan Prendergast ran to his side.

'You know what you've done, only too well. And I suppose today you were going to try to tip a little of your poison into Susan's ear.'

'He didn't say anything really, Michael. Please don't quarrel. Especially in front of all these people. He mainly talked about. . .'

I suddenly recoiled as I felt a hand on my shoulder. I looked round and into a ginger moustache. With all the brouhaha, I had completely forgotten about him.

'Want me to take care of Mr Black for you, Michael? You know, whilst you get yourself dried off and all that.'

Seagrave glowered. 'No, thank you, Tom.' The glower turned to an empty smile. 'As Susan says, we don't really want to upset the guests any further with our, er, differences of opinion.'

He turned back to me. 'However, I will say this, Mr Black. If I get any more evidence of your meddling in my affairs, I shall inform the police and my lawyer of your activities. Meanwhile, I will have a word with the owners of this hotel to see that you are never allowed to visit here again.'

He frowned at Tracy's laugh.

'I'm sorry, Mr Seagrave, but you forget I've been a witness to this whole affair.' She extended her arm towards the other still avidly interested guests. 'As have these ladies and gentlemen here. We all saw who was the initial aggressor and it was not Mr Black.'

He was about to retort, when Tracy added, 'Hang on, Mr Seagrave, let me ask you a question. How well do you know the owners of this hotel?'

His rapid blinking stood in for an answer.

'I thought so,' Tracy grinned. 'Well, I should warn you that I know them very well and my family have known their family for many years now. So I would advise you to proceed cautiously. For who knows? It might be you who ends up being blackballed, so to speak, and not Johnny here. You wouldn't want that, would you?'

With an almost imperceptible bow of the head, Tracy took my hand and we moved off through the still gawping onlookers.

'Do you really know the owners that well?' I whispered.

'No. But we make a great team, don't we?' she whispered out of the corner of her mouth, then added in a gangster's-moll style accent, 'Me, I maka with de mouth. You, you maka with de fists.'

I laughed out loud. For, drat it, there was no doubt she'd hit the old nail on the head.

For the second time running, we missed out on eating at the hotel. For neither of us much felt like sitting at a table with Seagrave, either in earshot or eyeline. So we apologetically cancelled and took our custom to the diminutive Pilchard Inn, an old smugglers' retreat that lies at the end of the hotel's drive and the only other building on the tiny island. There we bought a bottle of wine and some bread and cheese, which we then took outside to enjoy whilst we sat on the sea wall.

Tracy pointed out across the bay below us.

'Ginger moustache didn't stay long, did he? Can't have had time for more than one drink before he left.'

'Worried about the aircraft and tides, I expect. Either that or he's not such a chum of Seagrave's to be asked to stay to lunch.'

'Hired hand only?'

I shrugged. 'Maybe. But would he send just a hired hand to enquire at scrapyards about the Frazer-Nash? I would doubt it, somehow.'

I poured us both a glass of wine and rested the bottle against the wall, out of the sun.

'It's a pity Seagrave came on the scene so soon. I was just starting to get on well with our Susan.'

I tore off a hunk of my bread. 'Yes, the whole morning has hardly gone to plan, has it? But I suppose we do have some sort of silver lining – we've now put a name to our scrapyard visitor, Mr Tom Dawlish. So when I get back, I'll make a few calls and find out which of the two aerial advertising companies around here employs him. I would like to know, for instance, how long he has worked for them and a little bit about his background.'

'Think he may have had something to do with the death of Seagrave's wife?'

I shook my head. 'Probably not. But he may well have had something to do with Daphne Phipps' disappearance.'

'How so?'

'Well, if our worst suspicions prove right and the girl was black-mailing Seagrave for some reason and has been killed to keep her silent, then why has no body turned up yet?'

Tracy put down her glass.

'Because no one, as yet, is looking for a body. She hasn't been missing long enough yet.'

'Maybe. And perhaps she's been buried in some remote place somewhere. Devon is hardly over-populated and a body might not be discovered for years, even centuries.' I looked across at her, squinting in the midday sun. 'But the sight of that seaplane has opened up another possibility in my mind.'

'Oh, hell's bells, Johnny, you don't mean – ?'

'I do. A weighted body dumped in mid-English Channel from the Fox Moth would probably never be found – except by fishes.'

She put down her hunk of cheese and grimaced.

'Thank you so much for spoiling what little lunch we're grabbing.'

'Sorry.'

'You shouldn't be,' she sighed. 'Because you may be dead right.' Smiling, she added, 'Sorry, that wasn't meant to be a funny line.'

'Nothing is funny in this case, Tracy – except funny peculiar, that is. Sometimes, I feel the more we discover, the less we really know. My nightmare is that the whole affair may end with no one being able to prove anything specific about anybody.'

'What you might call, a dead-end,' Tracy laughed. Her impish grin lifted me right out of my self-pity, which was, no doubt, just her intention, bless her cotton socks.

Eleven

He smiled and put his hands to his ears, as a General Aircraft Monospar roared overhead, its Popjoy engines at full chat.

'Sorry, Mr Black, my office is hardly soundproof.'

'That all right, Mr Withers, the sound of aircraft is the stuff of life to me,' I smiled across at the manager of Skytrail Advertising, to which company, based at Haldon near Teignmouth, I had traced Tom Dawlish.

'Before I answer how long Tom has worked with us,' the manager resumed, 'could I ask why you would be interested?'

I glanced quickly at Tracy, whose tanned legs I could see were clearly indicating Mr Withers had other interests than aviation.

'I'm an ex-flier myself and I'm preparing a register of pilots in the West Country, with their backgrounds and qualifications and so on, which could be of some use to people like yourself – responsible men in aircraft and aerodrome management.'

'Ah, I see. Well, in that case, couldn't you approach Mr Dawlish direct?'

Tracy, good girl, recrossed her legs and smiled enticingly.

'Mr Black likes to talk to employers first, to get their evaluation of their pilots. You see, the proposed register will only contain the names of those with a proven track record of safe, sound airmanship.'

I couldn't have put it better myself.

'A splendid aim, Miss Spencer-King. Not every pilot is a good one, I'm afraid. However, Mr Dawlish is not amongst their number. He has, so far, given me no cause for complaint at all.'

He smiled. 'He perhaps has an over-fondness for that seaplane of ours. He did once use it without prior permission but that's the only slight blot on a pretty perfect copybook.'

'I'm glad to hear he's a good pilot. But back to his experience. How long has he been with you?'

'About a year, I suppose. He joined us at the beginning of last summer, when one of our pilots, poor lad, came in too low over those trees at the end of the drome. Wrote off a Miles Hawk and almost himself. Tom towed sky signs most of the summer and did charter work and tuition during the winter. Now of course, he's mainly back on sky signs, when the seaplane is not being chartered by someone or other. He's proved our best pilot on water by far. So the Moth is almost his private preserve.'

I waited for a Percival Gull, I could see through the window, to land, then asked, 'Do you know where Mr Dawlish worked before?'

'As I recall, he came from a charter firm based in Croydon. Before that, he worked in France. Out of Nice or Marseilles, I forget which one. Is that enough for your register, Mr Black?'

'For the time being, I guess so,' I smiled.

'Would you like me to ask Mr Dawlish to get in touch with you? Or perhaps, some of my other pilots? I have three I could name who – '

Tracy and I rose from our chairs, as if tied together.

'That's very kind, Mr Withers,' Tracy beamed. 'But we'll have to make that some other time.' She tapped her platinum watch. 'Mr Black and I have another appointment before our day is done.'

He rose from behind his cluttered desk and almost knocked over a pile of old *Flight* magazines stacked in a corner.

'Well, you know where to find me, Miss King,' a ready blush spreading across his podgy features.

Tracy glanced wryly at me. 'We know where to find you, Mr Withers,' and the emphasis was heavily on the plural 'we'.

Tracy had to leave soon after we got back to my cottage.

'There's a Birthday Ball over at Dartmouth. Mother and father are going, so little daughter has to trot along in attendance,' she had told me. 'Can be back some time Sunday, if you want me.'

What could I say, as her delicious lips met mine, but a scarcely audible 'Yes'?

So there I was an hour later, listening to the news on the wireless and trying to silence Groucho long enough to hear about a new convict escape from Dartmoor Prison, when the phone rang. It was Tubby Trouncer with a distinctly disturbing request. Would I contemplate treading the boards again that evening – like in an hour and a

134

quarter – because one of his actors had not turned up all day and another had 'flu?

'Only small part, old chap. About six lines in Act Three. I'd do it myself, but I'm already standing in for the chap with 'flu.'

I suddenly had an awful presentiment.

'The actor who hasn't turned up wouldn't be Henry Swindon, would it?'

'How did you know, me darling? Have you put a jinx on the fellow?'

I didn't explain. 'I can learn the lines all right, maybe, but what about the movements?'

'Show you when you arrive, old bean. Simple as all get out. You follow a girl in Act One, just stand by the library door in Act Two and follow another girl in Act Three. Thanks a bundle, old chap. Don't be late, will you? Curtain up at seven thirty.'

With that he was gone.

Five minutes later, so was I, breaking the odd speed restriction in the La Salle. No actor worth his salt misses a curtain. And no private eye worth his Cerebos misses an opportunity to make some instant enquiries into the disappearance of a major 'dramatis persona'.

By the time I came off stage, bewildered and perspiring like the proverbial pig, I had experienced the clearest of reminders of why I had so willingly given up being a Thespian. One, I was too petrified ever to be truly relaxed in front of a live audience and two, I didn't have enough talent to act my way out of a paper bag.

Tubby Trouncer praised my stand-in performance to the skies, but for purely selfish reasons. He wanted me to repeat the terrifying role the next afternoon and evening, if Henry Swindon still had not turned up and the 'flu hadn't flown. I was totally non-committal, not because I didn't want to help my old friend out, but because Henry Swindon's disappearance had added a whole new dramatic dimension to the Seagrave case – a dimension that might call for more urgent action than parading about on a Torquay stage. What poor Tubby couldn't know was that my acceptance in the first place, for the one night, was more selfish than selfless and as accommodating for yours truly as for him.

But my first probings amongst the case proved fruitless. No one could even hazard a guess as to where Henry Swindon might have gone, nor why on earth he should risk his job with the company to miss both rehearsals that day and the evening performance. Everyone seemed to agree that whatever his other shortcomings might be, Swindon was a true trouper and not one to go AWOL without warning.

All I really discovered from them was where he lived – in a tiny boarding house in Babbacombe – and that he hadn't taken the Trojan because one of the other actors had the car for a couple of days. I asked Tubby Trouncer while he was praising me to the skies whether he had been in touch with the boarding house. He replied that he had and all they knew was that Swindon had gone out the previous evening fairly late and they had not seen hide nor hair of him since. On further probing, I gathered that fairly late meant around ten, a fairly late hour for an evening stroll, not that Henry Swindon looked the evening stroll type.

I hid my worst worries from Tubby, for he had enough of his own without my adding mine. But he twigged that something was up, nevertheless.

'Don't think anything – anything nasty – has happened to Henry, do you, old love? I mean, like falling off a cliff in the dark or. . .something to do with the case you're working on, perhaps. Do tell me, if there's something I should know. I mean, that Daphne what's-her-name girlfriend of his hasn't been found yet, has she?'

I shook my head. 'No, but don't get all het up yet. It may all just be a curious coincidence, the two of them vanishing without a word. Who knows, they may have gone off somewhere together, mightn't they?'

Tubby's beady eyes brightened. 'They might just have, at that.' He slapped me on the shoulder. 'Must love and leave you now, old bean. got things to do. Scene shifting wasn't up to scratch tonight, did you notice?'

After he had gone, I wandered wearily back to the 'boys' communal dressing-room. By now, only one of the cast was left and he had already removed his make-up and was donning his normal clothes.

'Wasn't so bad after all, was it?' he smiled.

I sat down in front of the big bulb framed mirror that had to serve four of the cast and opened my cleansing cream.

'Bet it was from where the audience was sitting,' I chuckled.

He finished putting on his sports jacket and sat down on a stool just up from me.

'Don't run yourself down so. You were all right, you were. Tubby was quaking in his shoes until you said you would stand in. Funny of old Henry to let him down.'

I started to remove my pretty standard five and nine make-up.

'Tell me something, Terry,' I said. 'Have you noticed anything –
well, strange about Henry recently? Anything that might help explain
his absence today?'

He furrowed his young brow and though the gesture was sincere,
somehow looked the very essence of a juvenile lead acting worried.

'Well, he's been het up about the police coming round and all that.'

'And all that, including my visits, no doubt,' I grinned.

'Yes, I suppose so. Henry sort of felt he was being got at. You know,
suspected of somehow causing that girl's vanishing trick.'

I continued smearing away at my face with cotton wool.

'Yes, I gathered that. But you haven't notice anything else? I mean
like any changes in him or in his habits?' Then I added quickly, 'Or a
sudden flush of money?'

The actor almost fell off his stool with laughter.

'Henry, come into money? You must be joking. He's one of those
chaps who will always be next to broke, the way he lavishes what little
he's got on booze and lady friends.'

'So no changes?'

He thought for a moment. 'Can't say there have been. Unless you
call getting interested in cars, a change.'

I finished wiping my face with a towel. 'Interested in cars? What do
you mean?'

'It's like this. Henry has never shown any real enthusiasm for
motor-cars, at all. He only bought shares in that old Trojan so that he
had something to cart his girlfriends around in. What he knows about
what makes them go can be written on the back of a Penny Black.'

I turned to him. 'So what's the change?'

'Recently, he's taken to talking about them a good bit. Not just
ordinary motors, mind you.' He took a packet of Players out of his
pocket and offered me one. I turned it down. He lit up himself, then
slipped the cigarette card out of the packet. It showed an ultra-modern
Cord Sportsman convertible.

'See this card? Well, Players are running a second series of motor-
cars right along now and the other day I had a British sports car card
that he took a fancy to, so I gave it to him. The next thing I knew, he
brought in a sales catalogue for the car that he had specially sent off
for. I laughed like a drain, for the price was out of this world. Around
six hundred and fifty pounds, as I remember.' He pointed to the Cord

137

car. 'And the car wasn't even modern like this one looks. It appeared distinctly old-fashioned to me. Even had the gear and brake levers outside, would you believe?'

I believed. 'The car's name wouldn't have been Frazer-Nash, would it?'

His eyes brightened. 'Yes, that's it. Frazer-Nash. I remember I made a joke about the double-barrelled name. That you must be paying three hundred odd for the Frazer and three hundred odd for the Nash.'

I sighed. For now I was even more worried about what might have happened to Henry Swindon. 'You don't know why he wanted the catalogue, do you?'

The actor shrugged.

'Search me. I even asked him that myself, considering he can't even afford to buy a single wheel for that kind of car, let alone the whole shebang.'

'And what did he say?'

'Something about, "there's no harm in dreaming, is there?" And. . . er, oh yes, "you never know when your ship's going to come in".'

I got up from my stool and wearily reached for my jacket. For now I had a distinct feeling that Henry's ship might well have belonged to Daphne Phipps – and could have sunk with all hands.

Saturday morning saw me in Ashburton good and early. When I rang her, Diana Travers didn't seem to mind the hour and immediately saw the need for some urgency.

She looked considerably less composed than usual, when I arrived. Though immaculately dressed in cream slacks and a polka-dot blouse, her face betrayed her worry and her fingers trembled slightly as she fitted the inevitable Sobranie into her holder.

I quickly brought her up to date with my enquiries, amplifying on the sketchy outline I had given her over the phone. She remained silent for a moment after I had finished, then said quietly, 'Johnny, I think we should call the whole thing off. It was a mistake my involving you at all in this – '

'Nonsense,' I cut in. 'Why are you saying that now, just as we are starting to learn something?'

'Learn what, Johnny? We've learnt nothing. All we really know is

138

that two people you have been interviewing have gone missing for some reason. We can't even connect them with Seagrave or the pilot or anything.'

I stood up.

'Look, Diana, you're not proposing to drop the whole thing because we're not making progress, but because we are. You're just afraid of what we might be uncovering right now and afraid – '

'All right, so I am,' she snapped. 'So what? Do you think I want to see you or anybody put at risk by continuing this investigation. Don't you see, Johnny, that if our worst suspicions are correct, we're not just up against a man who may have covered up killing his wife – who knows, he may have strangled my sister in a fit of rage on the spur of the moment – but a man who is capable of planning and carrying out wholesale murders of anyone who gets in his way. What's more, it looks almost certain he's not acting alone. That fellow Dawlish seems to be involved in far more ways than just being his pilot.'

She too rose from her chair and went over to the French windows.

'Where will it end, Johnny? If I had known even half of what I know now, I would never have started it.' She turned around to face me. 'Don't you see, it's all far too hot for us to handle. Just two people. What we need is – '

'The police,' I chipped in. 'If you are afraid of us continuing alone, why don't we just go to the police and lay our cards on the table. Air our suspicions. Let them take the whole thing over.'

She came quickly across to me and grasped my arm.

'Please, Johnny, not yet. I don't want the police involved.'

'Why not, Diana?' I looked her straight in the eyes. 'Are you holding something back from me?'

She let go my arm and stubbed her cigarette out in an ashtray.

'No, Johnny, it's not that. It's just that they won't take any notice of us. We have no proof of anything, anything at all. They might even blow the whole thing by going prematurely to Michael directly and putting our suspicions to him. It wouldn't be any help to us. Just put us more in his firing line. And him on his guard.'

'But Diana, he knows who I am and it's pretty obvious what a private eye would be doing. So he's on his guard already.'

She took out another Sobranie. 'Look, Johnny, the time to go to the police is when we have even the tiniest shred of evidence or proof of any of our suspicions, not before. Please believe me.'

'But we won't get that, if we call the whole thing off. Seagrave will stand a good chance of getting away with – '

'Murder,' she whispered. 'But he's bound to slip up sometime, surely. I mean you can't hide bodies for ever.'

I sighed. 'You can, Diana, if you know where to put them. Like I told you, anchored to the bottom of the English Channel, for instance.'

'You think that's what has happened to Henry Swindon too?'

I shrugged. 'Why not? If it's worked well for one, it will work for another. Why should Seagrave give up a tried and tested method?'

She thought for a moment. 'Because it would mean trusting that pilot fellow twice, wouldn't it? Michael's not exactly the trusting type. Also, why should that pilot be sticking his neck out for Seagrave?'

I rubbed my fingers together. 'A little thing called money. Seagrave's got plenty of that now.'

'So you don't think any bodies will turn up?'

'I doubt it somehow.' This time I grasped her arm. 'That's why we've got to go on, Diana, don't you see? At least until we can go to the police with something concrete. Otherwise, Seagrave, if he's as guilty as we think he must be, stands a good chance of escaping totally scot-free. And you can hardly want that, Diana, surely? Remember you owe it to your sister to discover the truth.'

She was silent for a moment, then, to my surprise, threw her arms around my neck. 'Oh, Johnny, I'm so afraid. For us both. I never guessed it might turn out this way.' She looked up at me. 'Michael must be mad, mustn't he?'

'Not more than mad for money, perhaps. The glint of gold can twist the sanest mind.'

She rested her head against my shoulder. 'He might actually like. . . killing people,' she whispered, almost as if to herself.

'What made you say that?' I asked softly.

She suddenly moved a little away from me, back to the cigarette box, where she began fumbling for another Sobranie.

'Oh, nothing. Just a thought,' she smiled weakly. 'People have been known to enjoy such things, I believe.'

I sensed further probing would be counterproductive.

I said, 'So you agree for me to continue on the case? At least until we turn up something really positive.'

140

She lit her cigarette with a trembling hand. 'I suppose we had better. Otherwise, my sister. . .' She didn't finish the sentence, but came over and took my hand.

'You will be careful, won't you, Johnny. If Michael has done away with the girl and the actor, then he won't be likely to balk at a fourth.'

This time, I put my arms around her neck.

'Or a fifth, Diana. Now, for goodness' sake, take extra precautions yourself. Keep your doors locked, whether you are in or out and don't take unnecessary risks outdoors. Keep your eyes peeled for anything unusual and watch out in case you're being followed. If you are worried about the slightest thing, come round to me either at the cottage or Black Eye. Or give me a ring.' Then I added, 'And don't forget, living so near the Moor, you've more than just Seagrave to worry about now. There's that escaped convict.'

She smiled weakly, then stood on tiptoe and kissed me softly on the mouth. She tasted of sugar and spice and all things nice.

'I should have met someone like you long ago,' she breathed.

'I would have been an impecunious pilot or a penniless actor then,' I countered, somewhat embarrassed at my pleasant but rather profit less predicament.

She relaxed against me.

'It was just my luck to meet the *wrong* penniless actor,' she said and her sigh had the depth of the deep blue sea.

From Ashburton, I drove straight into Torquay. For there was one other person I had promised to keep updated about Daphne Phipps: her friend at the dancing school, Dolly Randan. To save another embarrassing meeting with her German boss, I decided to catch her as she left at lunchtime for her afternoon off.

To fill in time until twelve thirty, I went into the office. There was no sign of Babs, as she wasn't really expecting me in, but I could hear the merry clacking of her typewriter up the corridor. But on my desk was a note neatly penned in her roundest of round handwriting.

'10.30 a.m. A Mr Briggs rang. Says would you ring him back sometime? Cheers, Babs.'

I was quite glad to have someone to talk to, so I rang him right away. At first, I thought he must be out, for he took ages in answering.

'Sorry, Johnny, had a customer. Took a ruddy hour an' a half of my time before settling on a Hillman Minx wing for half a crown.' He laughed. 'And people think scrapdealers make a load of money. I ask you.'

'You rang me, Bobby,' I reminded him.

'Oh, yer, I did, didn't I? Now don't get excited, old son. I haven't come across anything startling. I just thought I might let you know that I've found a little bit of evidence that might bear out old Seagrave's story.'

My ears perked up. 'And what's that?'

'It's like this, Johnny. The Frazer-Nash is going well enough, but I thought I'd take down the transmission to have a dekko at the wear and tear on the chain, and check on its tension and all that. So I don't get no problems later. Well, as I was dismantling it, I found a little shred of cloth caught in a couple of the links. Seems like a woollen material of some kind, but it's so covered in oil that it's difficult to tell. And I found another few shreds wrapped around the back of the nearside wheel hub. So you can see why I rang, Johnny. Looks like Seagrave's story of the scarf killing his wife could be the honest truth, couldn't it?'

I tried to hide my disappointment. 'Could be, Bobby. But we know from the police reports at the time that they had found bits of scarf caught in the car's wheel.'

I heard Briggs sniff. 'Yer, well, suppose so. Just thought you'd like to hear some confirmation, that's all. You asked me to –'

'I know and thanks, Bobby. You did just right.'

'Can I throw the bits of cloth away now then?'

'I guess so.' I stopped, as I suddenly had a thought. 'No, don't. Not yet. Tell you what. I'll pop by on my way home this afternoon and pick them up from you.'

'Only a few shreds, Johnny. Hardly worth the petrol your swank La Salle will guzzle.'

'Well, you never know,' I said. 'See you later.'

And that was that.

For the next ten minutes or so I sat back in my chair with my feet on the window-sill, watching the seagulls catch the thermals from the harbour and soar lazily over the tips of the many masts, enjoying the heady freedom of the air. But my mind wasn't really with them that morning. Henry Swindon's disappearance had seen to that. I soon turned back to my desk and made a call to the theatre, where I was put through immediately to Tubby Trouncer.

'No, old bean, no sign of him. And it's the dress rehearsal for next week's show too. As far as I'm concerned, if he doesn't surface by lunchtime, he's out of this company for ever. Now, Johnny, as to this afternoon's matinée and this evening's performance' – I held my breath for his next utterance – 'you'll be relieved to hear I don't need you really. Percy has recovered from the 'flu, so I'll play your part. But anyway, thanks a bundle for last night.'

Wearily, I put the receiver back on the hook. Then I spent the next quarter of an hour wracking my brains for some plan of action that could somehow trigger Seagrave into betraying his hand. For a short while I even toyed with a direct confrontation with the man, but doubted that he would be sufficiently disturbed by the suspicions of a fledgling private eye working from a tiny office rented from a Hong Kong novelty import company, to really get rattled. After all, even well established private eyes with a fine track record are hardly the police. Now if they went to him with the same accusations, then he might just be panicked into some move that might betray him.

It was that last thought that gave me the idea. I immediately dialled a London number and soon was explaining my stratagem. Thanks be, it was received with the same degree of enthusiasm as it was delivered.

As intended, I caught Dolly Randan just as she was leaving work, looking rather different in her modest spring coat and hat from how I remembered her on the dance floor.

Taken by surprise, she refused my offer of a drink at the Imperial or even a coffee at the Kardomah, pleading that she had a date in the afternoon and she had to eat, wash and dry her hair at home first. But after a promise that I would drop her home afterwards, she did agree to walk back with me to where I had parked the La Salle and have a brief chat in the car.

The sight of the big cream American car certainly seemed to impress, for before she would get in, she insisted on walking round it twice.

Once inside, she said, 'Coo, it's like something out of the films, isn't it? Just the kind of car that Daphne is always on about. Suit her down to the ground, it would.'

She looked across at me. 'You've shaved off your moustache, Mr Conway. I think you look nice like that. I prefer clean shaven men.

They're less sort of' – she blushed – 'tickly.'

I took a deep breath, then came clean as to who I really was. She sat open-mouthed at my revelation that I ran a detective agency.

'Oh, Mr Black, I never would have guessed. Did you ever tell Daphne who you really are?'

I shook my head. 'No. I felt mean not doing so, but I couldn't right then. You see, in my business, secrecy and subterfuge are very often the name of the game. Clients expect you to be discreet and not reveal any details of your assignment and, especially, who you are working for.'

I laid it on thick because the last thing I wanted was to give her any clue as to my real interest in her vanished colleague.

She sat with her hands discreetly folded in her lap, as I informed her that no one seemed to have seen or heard from Daphne Phipps since that Saturday afternoon. But when I went on to tell her that her actor boyfriend had also now gone missing, her hands and eyes gave away her agitation.

'Well, I never,' she said quietly. 'He's gone too.' She turned to me. 'You don't think they could have run off together, do you?'

'What do you think?' I replied with a smile that said 'no'.

'H'mm. P'raps not. Daphne liked someone with a little bit of money, she did.'

She sat silent for a moment. Then twisting her fingers together, said, 'Someone's not employing you, are they, because they think Daphne's done something wrong?'

'What makes you say that?'

She suddenly reached for the door handle. 'I'd better be going. . .'

I grasped her arm. 'No, Dolly, not yet. I'm Daphne's friend, not her enemy. I'm trying to find her in case she's in some sort of trouble.'

She looked hard at me. 'Are you telling me the truth?'

'Yes, I am, I promise.'

'You told us all a lie about who you were.'

'But that was different. It's sometimes my job to adopt a different personality. But I promise you I am speaking the truth now.'

At last, she looked away, 'I hope you are.'

I squeezed her arm reassuringly, and she went on, 'Well, you see, I'm just a bit worried about where Daphne got all that money I told you about the other day. Never seen so many five-pound notes, I haven't.'

144

'You think she might have come by them dishonestly?'

She shook her head. 'No . . . well . . . I don't know . . . not really. Daphne was ambitious all right, but not a thief or anything like that. No, not Daphne.'

'So how do you think she came by them?'

Her eyelids fluttered. 'Well . . . er . . . from some man or other, I expect, like I said. That rich fellow she said she was going out with. He might have given it to her.'

'He might have. But it was a lot of money. And I know for a fact that Daphne had given her parents quite a bit as well. Now why should a man dole out that amount to a girl he could not have known all that long?'

'Maybe he really loves her,' she tried, but I could tell she didn't believe it.

'Look, Dolly, this is very important. I don't want to worry you unduly, but I think Daphne may be in very serious trouble.'

She looked at me in horror. 'You mean she's gone into hiding so that. . .'

'So that what, Dolly?'

She hesitated, so I helped her. 'So that the police don't catch up with her?'

She looked terribly flustered. 'Oh, Mr Conway, I mean, Mr Black, I don't know what I'm saying, I really don't. Daphne's my friend and I mustn't speak ill of her.'

'But I think you've a shrewd idea of what she was up to, Dolly. To save you the embarrassment, I'll say it. You think she was blackmailing somebody, don't you?'

She shook her head, this time more out of bewilderment. 'I really don't know, Mr Black. I suppose she might have been. She was ambitious all right, but – '

She turned to me and her eyes were wet with incipient tears. 'Oh God, you don't think something terrible's happened to her, do you? I mean, like. . .if she was doing what you say, then – '

'Someone might want to silence her?'

She closed her eyes tight shut at the thought.

'No, Mr Black, that can't be true.' Her voice became almost a shout. 'It mustn't. It *mustn't.*'

Her hand reached for the door handle once more. 'I must go. I've stayed far too long already.'

I reached across her and relatched the door. 'I'm dropping you home, remember?'

She wiped her eyes with her fingers. 'Oh yes, of course. Well, could we go now, please? I've got to get my hair done and dried before I go out again.'

'Okay,' I smiled. 'I'm sorry to have upset you.'

She sniffed. 'S'alright, Mr Black.' Smiling through her tears, she added, 'Sorry for getting like this, only, you know, Daphne is my friend and friends sort of feel responsible for each other don't they?'

I put my hand on her shoulder. 'Daphne is lucky to have you, Dolly.'

But my attempt at bucking up her spirits seemed to have exactly the opposite effect. She burst into floods of tears that even my handkerchief, considerably larger than her own, could hardly stem.

Bobby Briggs was lolling about in the hut he called an office, when I arrived, reading one of those thriller magazines with the most lurid and blood-drenched cover.

'You should read these,' he winked as he saw me. 'Might give you some ideas.'

'I need a few,' I laughed, 'but I don't think they'll give them to me, somehow.'

He put down his penny dreadful, rummaged in a drawer of his desk and handed me a well thumbed envelope.

'They're inside,' he sniffed, 'for what they're worth. Don't know why you want 'em, meself.'

I peered under the flap. A few limp and oil-blackened strands stared back at me.

'Nor do I, really,' I smiled.

'How's it all going, Johnny? Think you'll ever crack your first case?'

I shrugged. 'I'll only know that when I have . . . or haven't.'

He reached down and from a bottom drawer of his battered old desk, brought out a bottle of Johnny Walker.

'Like a snifter, old son? Might cheer you up.'

I didn't turn it down. He poured a tot into an already dirty glass that stood on his desk then looked around for something for me. At last his fingers curled around what, to my amazement, looked like a small cut-glass vase.

'This do, Johnny?' his bulldog face beamed. 'It should, you know. Got this out of an old Isotta-Fraschini, big as a hearse it was.' He

146

affected what he thought was a posh accent. 'Fitted in the back of the division for a nosegay from his lordship's ruddy gardens, don't you know, old boy?'

The vase duly filled up with golden liquid and was pushed my way.

'Bottoms up and death to the Kaiser,' he toasted.

'You're a bit out of date, Bobby, aren't you? It's Herr Hitler we're supposed to be wary of now.'

'*Him*,' he sniffed. 'He's just a jumped up housepainter, isn't he? Why, with his dainty little moustache, he couldn't frighten a mouse. Now the Kaiser – he was more of a man. I mean, you had to take a bit of note of what he did. . .'

I sat down opposite him and for a moment, let the burn of the Johnny Walker take over. For I didn't want to come on to my request too soon. Luckily, Briggs was in a bullish and talkative mood.

'When I heard the crunch of your car coming in, Johnny, I thought for a minute you were the police coming back.'

'Coming back?' I queried.

'Yer. Been once today. Thought at first they may have come to give the old Frazer-Nash the once over again. But no, they wanted to sniff around the yard.'

'What for? I smiled. 'You been dealing in cars with a dodgy pedigree again?'

'No,' he sneered. 'Gave that up ages ago. No, you must have heard about this con on the loose? The triple murderer who sawed through his cell bars.' He guffawed. 'Some bloody cake his missus must have baked him to hide the hacksaw. Anyway, they were sniffing around for him. Here about twenty minutes. Thought they'd never go. Bad for business, you know, having a ruddy police car hanging about so long outside the yard.'

Good old Bobby. He had given me just the intro I needed.

'That reminds me, old chap. Got a little favour to ask of you.'

He downed some more Scotch, whilst he tried to divine from my expression how big this favour might turn out to be.

'Yer, well, you'd better try me, hadn't you?' he smiled.

'You haven't got a half-presentable Wolseley in the yard, have you?'

He thought for a moment. 'What d'you mean by "half-presentable"?'

'Well, not over two or three years old. Must be black and not under fourteen h.p. Oh, and it's got to be a runner.'

147

'What a pity. Got a snappy little Wolseley Ten out there. Only needs a tweak to the chassis and a couple of front wings – '

'No. Must be fourteen or eighteen h.p. Don't want to buy it. Just borrow one for a morning, that's all.'

He put his glass down and leaned forward, his canny eyes almost glowing with interest.

'What are you up to, Johnny? Why do you want a car for a morning? And not just any old car, but a big black Wolseley?'

I could see by his expression he was over half-way to guessing, so I came clean.

'Don't just want any big black Wolseley, either.' I grinned. 'I want you to fit it up with a few temporary little extras as well.'

He chewed on his lip. 'Now, let me guess what one or two of them might be, shall I? First on, I reckon you need a chrome bell. Then how about a sign front and back and a nice long radio aerial, whipping in the wind.' He laughed. 'Should have taken more notice of the one that called this morning, shouldn't I?'

I drained my delicate vase. The substitute for flowers buoyed my spirits beautifully.

'You have the picture, Bobby. Now where can I find a Wolseley like that?'

He sat back in his chair. It creaked ominously.

'Let me see. I can mock up all the fittings, I think. May have to make do with a brass bell instead of chrome though. As for the car. . ., well, leave that with me for an hour or two. My wife's uncle has got a '36 Fourteen. He might be persuaded to lend me it for a few bob. Then, if he won't, there's a farmer over Newton Abbot way I know who's got a '35 Eighteen. Only trouble is he sometimes puts sheep in the back. Still, I could always clean it up for the day. When is the day, by the way?'

'Monday,' I said. 'Have it back by lunchtime.'

He prodded his thick finger at me. 'You've got to promise me first this 'ere car won't come to no harm. Don't want any wild chases or anything.'

I crossed my heart. 'All it's going to do is drop someone at a house, then wait outside until he comes out again.'

He chuckled to himself. 'You're a right one, Johnny boy, I'll say that. You realize you're risking the nick, impersonating a policeman.'

'I'm not impersonating anybody,' I said self-righteously.

148

'Oh, aren't you?' he mumbled in disbelief, then pointed down to his penny dreadful magazine.

'Well, you just be careful, old lad. In last month's issue, a guy called Barry Blood got machine-gunned down in a street just for pretending to be a cop.'

'Serves him right,' I smiled, 'for having such a silly bloody name.'

Twelve

Once I had left the scrapyard, I felt there was very little I could achieve on the Seagrave case until Monday came round. So, for once, I had a quiet evening, give or take Groucho, and then went to bed early with Dashiel Hammett's *The Glass Key*, which I had bought a couple of years earlier and never got around to reading.

Sunday morning dawned bright though breezy, which enticed me out into what passed for my garden. By lunchtime, I was quite pleased with the clearances I'd made and the ground I'd dug. Indeed, the plot was now assuming some form of order and set off the cottage to a little more advantage. It was about time.

After lunch, I marshalled my thoughts for the morrow and wrote down a check list of questions I wanted asked. I had hardly put down my Conway-Stewart, when I heard a screech of brakes outside. It could only be one person and so it proved to be.

Once I had got him inside and propped a Scotch in his hand, I asked him about the uniform.

'Don't worry, old boy,' he laughed, slapping my back. 'You didn't think old PC would forget a PC's uniform did you? It's outside in the Bug.'

'Are you sure it will fit?'

'Course. Prissy thinks I've missed my vocation. I tried it on at Nathans to make sure you could get into it and I thought her eyes would pop.' He laughed. 'I reckon she's got a hankering for fellows in uniform. If a war comes, Heaven forbid, I'll have a job holding her, I wouldn't be surprised. Think of the choice she'll have then, with hundreds of thousands in khaki and two shades of blue.'

'Well, thanks for coming down, PC. I appreciate it.'

'Nothing to it. My ERA is all stripped down at the moment, so there was nothing to keep me in London. And Prissy has gone off this weekend with Mater and Pater to Monte Carlo for a couple of weeks.'

He looked around the room. 'Tracy not here?'

'She will be,' I replied. 'She, too, has been with her folks. She'll turn up any minute, I expect.'

He sat down and spread his long legs out in front of him. 'Now, old boy, bring me bang up to date on this old case of yours. After all, if I'm to be an inspector tomorrow, I should be pretty clued up, what! By the way, I've thought of a damned good name for myself, if you don't object.'

'Which is?'

'Eric Roger Ambleforth, Inspector from Plymouth Division. Get it, old boy? The initials – ERA help me remember who I am.'

'Fine,' I agreed, for Peter Courtenay's memory was certainly not as sharp as his driving skills. Then I started 'clueing him up', as he would have it and by the time Tracy arrived, he was totally in the picture and pretty word perfect.

'Have you heard the news?' Tracy asked, as she bounced in, all bright eyed and bushy tailed. 'They have caught that convict. Thank the Lord for that.'

'How do you know?' I asked.

'Friend of Daddy's knows the governor of Princeton. News came through just before lunch. But they think he may have killed again before they caught him.'

'Why don't they know for certain, old girl?' PC queried with a frown.

'No body, apparently.'

'Then what makes them suspect he's done it again?'

'I don't know all the facts. But it seems he was wearing a jacket with a few blood stains on it when they picked him up just outside Widdecombe. The jacket had a wallet in it and the reasoning goes he may have killed someone for the money. He's apparently a totally hardened and ruthless individual for whom murder is all in a day's work.'

'Hell, poor fellow,' I remarked. 'I mean the victim, not the convict. That is, if there is a victim. Maybe he only beat him up to get his jacket. Let's hope so.'

And that's how we left it and gave the news no further thought. For the deed of the morrow seemed of far greater moment.

PC left around eleven and I persuaded Tracy to go about quarter of an hour later under the pretext that I needed all the sleep that I could get that night, so that I would be fresh for the morning. I hated seeing her leave, but I couldn't go through another night with a towel and blanket curtain. It wasn't fair on either of us.

Precisely at eight thirty the next day, as arranged, I arrived at Briggs' yard. There, gleaming black in the intermittent sun, stood a '36 Wolseley Fourteen saloon, with a 'POLICE' plate front and back and a chromium bell mounted on the front bumper.

Bobby Briggs caught me inspecting the last mentioned.

'Cost you extra, that will, Johnny. Took me two hours last night that did, because I couldn't get a chromium bell.'

'What have you done, then?'

'Silver cigarette paper, old love. And not just from packets of ten or twenty. Big sheets from twenty fives and fifties. Stuck on by yours truly. Me better half thought I'd gone mad.'

'What's the damage?' I asked.

'Well then, let's see. Fifteen bob to my wife's uncle for the car, ten bob each police plate, four and six for the brass bell, pound for the aerial, ten bob for all the fitting and thirty bob for all those cigarettes.'

'Which you'll smoke in no time,' I smiled and proffered him a fiver and a ten shilling note. 'Keep the change,' I added.

He guffawed. "S only ruddy sixpence, you generous b – bloke. Now see you bring it back lunchtime and all in one piece. That car's the apple of her uncle's eye.'

By the time I had got back to the office and changed into my theatrical police constable's uniform – it fitted and looked pretty well considering it had, no doubt, appeared in a thousand performances on other stages – PC had arrived, already dressed for the part. I was amazed how genuine he looked in a dowdy mac and trilby, and even his suit looked suitably non-descript. I asked him where he had got hold of it all, because I knew it could not possibly be his own.

'One of the clerks on the estate, old thing. Same figure as mine. Greased his palm with a couple of the readies. Only too happy. Good sport.'

I took him aside as we walked out to the Wolseley.

'Now, remember PC, when you're with Seagrave, it's not how you look or what you ask that may give you away half so much as how you speak. Inspectors of county forces just don't drop 'eh whats' and 'old boys' and 'old things' into every sentence, so just bear that in mind. And watch the accent. Act authoritatively, but always with that touch of humble civility public servants show – especially when they're interviewing someone with more money than they've ever dreamed of.'

He nodded sagely. 'Tally-ho, old bean. . .I mean, yes, I promise I will bear that in mind. . .sir.'

Even though I had parked the car some distance from the imposing front door of Seagrave's mansion, I felt distinctly nervous after PC had been shown inside by the housekeeper, despite my uniform, theatrical bushy eyebrows and Chester Conklin moustache.

I tried to look bored and uninterested whilst at the same time keeping my eyes peeled for any untoward happenings around the house. To my horror, at one point, an aged gardener trundled round the car with his barrow and I lowered my eyes and stared at the dashboard with its big oval dial that held all the instruments.

After quarter of an hour, I started to sweat in my thick, high-necked uniform and I dared to pull back the sliding roof which, of course, decided to stick in its runners. Some five minutes later, I could see from the sky that some pretty heavy showers were in the offing, so I endeavoured to close the cursed thing again, for the car's owner would hardly appreciate its return with the interior as soggy as a baby's nappy.

But move back, it would not. Despite my using considerable force, I could not get enough leverage somehow from the driving seat to budge it. As the first few heavy drops of rain pearled on the bonnet, I realized I would have to get out to see if some sharp knocks on its top might get it to shift. It was whilst I was still hammering away at it in the rain, that I heard the motor-cycle.

I only just got back in the car in time. While I sat there, trying to look nonchalant as the rain pit-patted onto my helmet, the bike swept up the drive from my rear to come to a stop directly outside the front door. From a surreptitious glance, it was clearly an Indian and I didn't need to look again to know who was riding it.

I held my breath as I heard the crunch of feet on the gravel. It seemed for a moment that they were coming nearer – maybe they did, for the sight of a copper sitting in a police car in the pouring rain with the roof open must have held a certain intrigue – but, to my relief, they eventually receded to be followed by a distant clang of a bell. I didn't dare move until I heard the front door open and close again. Then I quickly got out and gave the leatherette-covered roof frame an almighty thump which, heaven be praised, shifted it along its runners sufficiently for me to finish closing it from inside. Briggs, wife's uncle's heart attack was thus thankfully postponed.

That wasn't necessarily true of mine, however: Tom Dawlish's unexpected arrival worried me intensely. For whilst I was fairly certain PC wouldn't make too much of a fool of himself in a one to one interview, one to two was a very different kettle of fish. Every second that now went by seemed like an eternity and I expected our little subterfuge to be violently exploded at any moment. I even toyed with the idea of starting up the car and keeping it running, in case we needed to make a quick getaway, but decided – wisely – that running an engine for no apparent reason was quite as ridiculous as sitting in the rain with the sunshine roof open.

I tapped the steering wheel nervously for a further ten minutes before I again heard the click of the front door. Looking sideways through my chinstrap, I saw to my unbridled joy the lanky figure of PC being seen out by the housekeeper. And lo and behold, he was certainly taking my advice about humility to heart. He actually walked down the steps backwards, bowing his head to her slightly, until she finally closed the door on him.

I got out of the car, went round and opened the passenger door for him.

'Go all right?' I hissed between my clenched teeth.

'Hope so, sir,' he smiled back, 'but it was agony all the way.'

'Tough, was he?' I whispered, tucking the edge of his raincoat away from the door opening.

'I'm not talking about him,' he frowned. 'I just have never realized how many rotten times I normally say "old boy", old boy.'

I was as good as my word; I waited for the full story until Tracy turned up at half past twelve. In the meantime, after I had dropped PC off at my cottage, I doffed the police plates and bell and drove the Wolseley back to Briggs.

His only reaction, other than a look of immense relief, was, 'Heard a car. But didn't think it could be you, Johnny. No scream of brakes or rat, tat of gunfire.'

I let it pass and thanked him and his wife's uncle, profusely.

'Any time, old lad.' He pointed his stubby finger towards a huge black hearse at the back of his yard. 'Got an old Daimler here that would pass for Queen Mary's, if you took the coffin rails out. So, if next time, you want to pose as royalty. . .'

Bless him. It's guys like Briggs that keep the old world spinning.

Back at the cottage, Tracy had already arrived and was chomping at the bit for the latest. Once we were all armed with drinks, I got PC to put us in the full picture.

'Well, I hope it worked, old bean. Did me best. Asked all the questions you wanted. Was suitably civil and servile, yet I think stern enough to show I meant business.'

'So what were Seagrave's reactions?' I asked impatiently.

'Difficult to tell, old boy. Tell you one thing. Didn't like him. Not one bit. Not a man's man, if you get my meaning, old bean. Though, I suppose, I can see he could wow the odd lady or so. That is, if she goes for looks, rather than the old pedigree.'

'But he must have said something, PC. You can't more or less tell a man he's under suspicion for a girl's murder and not get some reaction.'

PC put his glass down. 'He just asked how we could be certain the body washed up on the beach in Guernsey was that of Miss Phipps. I had to tread carefully then, old boy. Like we rehearsed.'

'I know. I know, but did he rise to the story at all? I mean, do you think he accepted that Daphne Phipps' body could have been in the English Channel? Because if he murdered her, he would know, wouldn't he?'

'Couldn't see his eyes, old chap. More's the pity. Stood at the French windows with his back to me a lot of the time. So, I only had his old voice to go on.'

'Didn't his old voice give anything away?' I asked, slightly irritably and then instantly regretted my tone. For I had known before I'd started that PC's strength lay more in physical action than mental intuition.

'He didn't laugh the idea out of court, old boy, if that's what you mean.'

'How did you answer his question?' Tracy interceded.

'Oh that. Well, you see, old girl, Johnny and I realized we couldn't possibly know in what state this girl had been dumped in the sea. That

155

is, if she had been at all.'

'Clothed, unclothed. How she was killed. Was her body weighted down, etcetera?' I rapidly explained to help PC along.

'So I said,' PC continued, 'that though her body was legless – we concocted that bit, old girl, to try to cover how a body could wash ashore, if it had been weighted by the feet – her estimated age and physical characteristics more or less matched those of the missing Phipps girl. And we would be checking her old dental records, directly we had shipped her remains back to Plymouth.'

'How did he react to your connecting his name with hers, in the first place?'

'Didn't deny he knew her, old bean, if that's what you mean. Quite the contrary. Admitted he had seen her a few times recently. Said it was because he was thinking of going into the dance business himself. In a big way. Nationwide. Sort of "Fred Astaire" academies to cash in on the dance crazes. Said he'd always been fascinated with dancing. Been a hoofer once himself, he said. Knew a bit about it.'

I sipped my drink reflectively. 'Quite a smart cover,' Tracy commented. 'And all ready prepared to trot out in case the girl's body was ever found.'

'How did he react when you went on to the actor's disappearance?'

'Quite a different kettle of fish, old boy. Flatly denied knowing him, meeting him or having anything to do with him. Got quite cross at this point. Made me a bit nervous, I can tell you. And then, when that ginger moustache poked its face round the door!'

'Did he actually dare to come in?' I asked in some amazement. 'I thought he would hide away in the house somewhere, until what he thought were the police had vamoosed.'

'No, he didn't come right in. Seagrave sort of gave him a frown and he closed the door again. I think, old boy, he was just checking I wasn't slapping the old handcuffs on his friend.'

'Did you mention Tom Dawlish at all?'

'No. We agreed I wouldn't, remember, old bean? You said it was a bit too early for the police to have latched on to him.'

I downed the last of my drink. 'Maybe I was wrong,' I sighed. 'Anyway, go on. Tell us what else happened.'

'Nothing much. Oh, naturally, he asked right at the outset why on earth we, the police, had come to him at all. He said he doubted very much that the body would prove to be of Miss Phipps. And even if it did, what had the girl's drowning got to do with him? He has a point, old love. After all, it's only your guess that she might have been blackmailing him and you said even you were a bit unhappy about the old thought, because you couldn't see how she could possibly have known anything about the way his wife died.'

I suddenly got up. 'Yes, yes, I know. It's worried me from the start. But go back a bit, PC. Repeat the *exact* words Seagrave used after he had said, "Even if the body did turn out to be that of Miss Phipps". Now I want you to remember the precise wording. It's important.'

He uncrossed his long legs and thought for a moment. It seemed like hours.

'Now, as I recall it, old boy, it went like this. . . "Even if you discover . . .the body is Miss Phipps'. . .then what has a girl's drowning got to do with me?"'

I went to his chair. 'PC, are you certain he said "a girl's *drowning*" and not just "a girl's death" or "girl's accident", or – ?'

He cut me off. 'No, old bean, I distinctly remember he said "drowning".'

'Think it's significant?' Tracy asked. 'I mean, when a body is found in the water, it's pretty natural to assume it's drowned.'

'Yes, I know that. But if you're the person who caused the death. . .'

'. . .you know how they died,' Tracy completed my thought.

'Yes.' I threw up my hands. 'Oh, maybe I'm just clutching at straws. But somehow or other, if Daphne Phipps is dead and her body is ever found, it could be we'll discover drowning was the cause of death.'

PC frowned. 'What are you saying, old boy? That you now think the girl may have drowned accidentally?'

'No, not quite,' I smiled. 'Just that she may have been still alive when she hit the water.'

'You mean she was tipped in, bound and gagged, or what?' Tracy asked.

'Something like that. Maybe she was offered an evening trip in the seaplane by Tom Dawlish. Romantic idea to a girl like Daphne Phipps. He could feign having engine trouble and alight in mid channel. Ask her to get out of her cockpit and onto the floats to help him do something or other connected with the engine, then a smart shake and a quick take-off and she would not have a chance. Verdict: death by drowning.'

157

PC enquired, 'Couldn't we check, old boy, whether anybody saw her getting into that seaplane or – ?'

'I doubt if she was seen,' I cut in. 'Seagrave would have been too careful to risk that. And you've been over to his place now. His house is isolated and his land goes down to the sea. In all probability, he's got a jetty there. Most big houses on land bordering the sea have somewhere for their boats.'

'Seagrave's got a housekeeper. Couldn't we somehow ask her whether the girl was around that evening?'

'We could. But if you plan to murder someone, I guess you would first make sure your housekeeper isn't around. Like you'd give her the night off or you'd arrange for her to be away somewhere.'

'I'll do some checking,' Tracy offered.

I wagged my finger at her. 'Now don't you go taking any risks, Tracy. I feel bad enough letting old PC here go into the lion's den this morning.'

'Enjoyed it, old bean. Just hope my little attempt at acting will bear some fruit.'

'Well, that was the general idea,' I smiled weakly. 'If it doesn't, we're back to square one.'

'Which is where?' PC queried.

'God knows,' I replied. 'Or maybe, I should have said the Devil.'

Soon after we all repaired to the Cott Inn at Dartington for a dram or two and some ploughmans. Then PC roared off back to Brooklands in his Bugatti and Tracy and I La Salled back to the cottage.

There, we mulled over the whole Seagrave affair until we were almost blue in the face, but knew, in reality, all we could do now was wait. That is, except for one little detail. As PC had reminded us, we should not really let poor Miss Susan Prendergast continue in total ignorance of the kind of man on whose words she seemed to be hanging. For, as PC said, if he wasn't a murderer, we could at least prove he was a hell of a bounder.

Tracy and I tossed up who should make the call to Burgh Island Hotel. I won. A few minutes later, Mr Prendergast had been summoned from the Ganges bar to be warned by an anonymous caller with a theatrical cockney accent, that his daughter was in considerable moral danger through her contact with an ex- *thé dansant* hoofer and philanderer by the name of Michael Seagrave – and that he

158

should put a stop to it forthwith if he had his daughter's interest at heart. By the snorts of surprise and bellows of indignation from the other end of the line, I gathered dear Susan had told her father next to nothing of Seagrave's past history and background. Maybe she did not even know it herself.

I had only just put back the receiver on the hook when the phone rang. It was Tubby Trouncer and he sounded in a considerable tizzy.

'You must have heard the news, Johnny. It's dreadful. . .dreadful.'

'What news?' I asked. 'I've been out most of the day.'

'About poor Henry Swindon.'

I instantly glanced at Tracy. She got the message and bent her ear to the receiver.

'What about Henry Swindon?'

'Oh God, you haven't heard, then? He's been murdered. Least, that's what the police think.'

'Murdered? By whom?'

'By that convict fellow they recaptured yesterday. He was wearing old Henry's jacket, when they picked him up. And he had tried to pass a fiver from his wallet at a shop in Widdecombe. That's how the police got on his trail.'

I bit my lip. The reply was certainly not one I'd been expecting.

'Have they found Swindon's body?'

'Not yet. They're still combing the boggy parts of the moor – that's where the convict swears he found the jacket.'

'So the convict hasn't confessed to killing him?'

'Not as far as I could glean from Inspector Wyngarde. He was here ages this morning, interviewing the cast, going through Henry's things.'

'So the con claims he just found the jacket?'

'Yes, I know. Doesn't sound a likely story, does it? I mean, people don't just discard jackets and leave them on the moor, do they? Especially with wallets with a fiver inside.'

'Does it seem likely to you, Tubby, that Henry Swindon would carry a fiver in his wallet, anyway? Pound notes, maybe, but hardly a fiver.'

'Didn't occur to me, old chap. But now you mention it, not many people carry fivers around with them, do they? Unwieldy things. Don't suppose half the population have ever even seen one.'

159

'But they haven't found any other sign of Henry?' I asked, as my brain buzzed with wild imaginings.

'Not yet. But the Inspector reckons the body has probably sunk down into some bog up there. The convict's legs were covered in mud and mire up to his crutch, he said.'

I thought for a second. 'Does the Inspector have any idea as to how Henry Swindon got up onto Dartmoor? After all, he hadn't taken the Trojan that he shares.'

'He didn't say, old chap. But it's a hell of a point, now you mention it. Maybe he got a lift or something.'

'It's the "or something" that's worrying me,' I muttered.

'Of course, old Henry could have just taken off his jacket somewhere and left it by mistake, I suppose. And the con just had the luck to come across it.'

I didn't comment. I didn't want to upset old Tubby any more than he was already. But he went on, 'You got any guesses, Johnny? I mean, you're in the business, so to speak.'

'Let's wait a bit and see. Too early to jump to any conclusions.'

'Henry wouldn't have gone up on Dartmoor for nothing, old bean. Hardly a bird fancier or nature lover is our Henry Swindon. Hey, it wouldn't have anything to do with the case you're working on, would it? I mean – '

I had to cut him off. 'Look, Tubby, I've got to go. Sorry. Ring me if you hear any more and I'll do the same for you.' And that's how we left it.

Tracy took hold of my hand, as I hung the receiver back on the hook.

'Hell's bells, Johnny, you don't think – ?'

I nodded. 'Could be, couldn't it? One body dropped into the English Channel, another dropped into an English bog.'

'So you don't reckon the convict can have killed him?'

'Of course, it's possible. But it's not very probable that a man on the run would find a convenient lone actor wandering about on Dartmoor with fivers in his wallet, now is it? Especially as the actor lived miles away in Torquay and hadn't taken a car. I guess the Inspector will have to admit that sooner or later.'

'Just convenient, I suppose, to blame a multiple murderer on the loose for yet another killing.' She suddenly frowned. 'Hang on a minute, Johnny. If you're thinking Seagrave and Dawlish killed

160

Swindon and Dawlish tipped the body out of an aircraft into a bog, how is it that the convict found his jacket? Wouldn't that have sunk too?'

'That's exactly what makes me think Swindon could have been thrown from a plane.'

'How do you mean?'

'Ever parachuted?'

She shook her head.

'I have. Before the canopy opens, you're falling at about a hundred miles an hour. Now you know the effect of wind at that kind of speed from driving your SS with the windscreen folded. It tears at you like it's got claws. Anything not firmly fixed to you, will rip off. Your flying helmet would go if it wasn't firmly fastened. So a corpse might well shed some of its loose clothing in its hundred-mile-an-hour drop. Nowadays, young men tend to do up only the centre button of their jackets.'

Tracy sighed. 'If you're right, that means the jacket could have fallen to the ground quite a distance from the body and that poor Henry Swindon may never be found.'

'Could be. One of the things worrying me though, about my theory, is why Seagrave wouldn't have taken the precaution of removing anything and everything that might identify the body should it be found sometime. If he's been so successful at faking his wife's death, surely he would have thought of things like that.'

'Isn't there an old saying about murderers always making *one* slip?'

I grinned weakly. 'The saying about St Swithin's day doesn't always rain true.'

Tracy rose from her chair and came over to me. 'What are we going to do now, Johnny?' she asked, with a note of despair in her voice.

'I'm going to keep my eyes and ears peeled for any move Seagrave and his pal may make down here. After all, if they're guilty, PC's little visit must have unnerved them more than somewhat. And with the news of the finding of Henry Swindon's jacket, they must be as jumpy as grasshoppers.'

She put her arm affectionately round my waist. 'Well, I'll see whether I can make some kind of contact with Seagrave's house-keeper – '

'No, you don't, old girl,' I cut in rather sharply, then smiled. 'The grasshoppers might jump you right now. Besides I'd like you to go up to London, if you will.' She looked disappointed. 'London? What for?'

'To see that agent fellow, Trenchard.'

'Trenchard? We've seen him. Why see him again?'

I took her hand and, rather self-consciously, told her.

Thirteen

After Tracy had gone, I immediately rang Diana Travers, but could get no reply. I sat and communed with Groucho for a bit, over the problems of private eyes who couldn't afford to employ tails for all their suspects, but all I got as solace were a couple of 'Hello, baby's, a 'Drop 'em' and one 'Aren't I a pretty boy?'. Then I rang my employer once more, but the tring-trings just went on forever. It worried me a little that not even her maid was around, but we aren't living in Victorian times, so I supposed she had to have a half day off sometime or other. And what better day than when her mistress was going out?

I then rang Bobby Briggs to see if our little police impersonation had triggered any prowlings around his yard by the ginger moustache, but he reported all was quiet, indeed too quiet for him ever to make a crust. He asked about the shreds of cloth he had found in the Frazer-Nash. I had to admit to him I had not given them a moment's more thought. But directly I had put the phone down, I repaired the omission and took the grease-marked envelope out of a drawer of my desk. At least it would fill in some time until I rang Diana Travers' number once more.

The slivers of cloth looked even more insignificant in my cottage than they did in his yard. Just blackened, greasy strands chewed small by the Nash's chain drive. As they were making my fingers filthy, I took them to the kitchen sink and washed them in an old pudding basin with a little Oxydol. Through the suds, I soon began to see colours replacing the black, one set of strands appearing to be a mid-blue, like the Royal Dutch Airlines use, the other set as red as Swissair's tail fins. What's more, when they were washed, the threads were patently different from each other in both weave and texture.

I placed both sets to dry on the edge of one of Groucho's spare feeding bowls, then went to the phone and rang my Black Eye office. I had almost given up waiting, when Babs at last replied.

'Hello,' she piped. 'This is the Black Eye Detective Agency. Mr Black is out of the office on one of his most important cases, right now, but I am his assistant, Barbara Mason, and will be only too happy to take down your message or enquiry, your name, address and telephone number. Mr Black will then contact you immediately he's – '

'Babs,' I interrupted, 'this is me.'

'Me?' she queried. 'How do you spell that? M, double E?'

'No, M with one E.'

'I take it that's your surname, Mr Me? Now if you give me your address and telephone number. . .?'

'It's Rose Cottage, Dartington,' I sighed. 'Dartington 7003.'

'I'll just repeat that. Mr Me, Rose Cottage, Dartington. Telephone num – ' She stopped suddenly and gasped. 'Oh, I'm so sorry, Johnny. It's you, isn't it?'

I was tempted to say, 'No, it's me', but let it pass.

'That's okay, Babs. We all make mistakes. Now have you got a minute?'

'I think so. Mr Ling is stock-taking right now.'

'Well, listen carefully. Go to my filing cabinet and get out the Seagrave folder. Okay?'

She was gone but thirty seconds. 'Right, I've got it, Johnny.'

'About half-way through it, you'll find a couple of pages of press cuttings of the inquest on Seagrave's wife's death. . .Found them?'

'Yep. Think so. Do you want me to read them all out?'

I laughed. 'No thanks, Babs. I just want you to turn up the one that I think has a headline something like, "It's Isadora Duncan all over again, says husband in tears". When you've found it, read down until you come across the description of the scarf that caught in the sports car wheels. All I want to know is its colour. Okay?'

'Right. . .er. . .seven feet long. . .Handwoven in Scotland. . .Bought in Harrods. . .Ah, here goes. It was plain cer – u – lean blue.'

I hardly recognized the word, as she pronounced the 'c' of 'cerulean' hard. 'Is that all you want, Johnny?'

'That's all I want, Babs,' I smiled. 'You're an angel – from out of the cerulean sky.'

It was just the whiff of a clue, I well recognized, no more substantial than the red threads themselves. But it did show that some material other than the actual scarf had got itself caught in the Frazer-Nash's transmission. Whether that material had been fed in by Seagrave in some dress rehearsal for his wife's death, or whether it had been picked up from some other source accidentally, I had no means of knowing. My sliver of satisfaction came only from the fact that the red threads fitted with my preconceived notion that a man like Seagrave would definitely have tried out his Isadora Duncan type plan before relying on it as evidence of his innocence.

I rang Diana Travers once more, but to no avail. I tried unsuccessfully twice more before six o'clock, when I turned on the news on the wireless. As I had been expecting, the newsreader mentioned the recapture of the Dartmoor prisoner and his wearing of Henry Swindon's jacket. But no body, as yet, had been discovered, despite the combing of the area by some fifty members of the Devon Constabulary, working up to their knees and beyond in the boggy sections.

I wondered whether Seagrave and his pal were tuned into their respective wirelesses, waiting with bated breath for the news that might just undo them. I certainly hoped so. And I prayed that news would not be too long in coming. For without any bodies, there really wasn't any sustainable case against Seagrave, red threads or no red threads.

But, darn it, there was a good chance that the actor might never be found. Dartmoor tends to like to keep its secrets and thus, if Seagrave and Dawlish kept their heads after our subterfugue of the morning, then. . .

I eventually became more than a little depressed and switched the radio on again, hoping that *Monday Night at Seven* might cheer me up. But somehow, the light-hearted banter and badinage of the programme only emphasized the seriousness of my problems. I soon turned it off and rang my employer again. This time, to my huge relief, she answered.

I brought her up to date with the news, including that from Dartmoor, which she hadn't heard, and my discovery of the red threads. The latter she deemed interesting, but her evident distress at the thought that the actor had actually been murdered overshadowed everything – to the point where she reiterated her fears about continuing our investigations at all. I tried to buoy her up, but it was an uphill task, made steeper by the news she was now to tell me.

'Johnny, I think I was followed this afternoon.'

'How do you know? Where did you go?'

'I went into Dartmouth to do some shopping, take my mind off

165

things. You know how windy those roads are? Well, I didn't see it all the time in my mirror, but very often there seemed to be a small blue sports car behind me.'

'Recognize the make?'

'No. It seemed very modern. Not like Tracy's SS100, for instance. More streamlined, headlamps in the wings, no chrome radiator. Looked a bit foreign to me.'

I racked my brains. 'Do you remember if it had a "V" windscreen, instead of a flat one?'

'Yes, I think it did. Yes, it came to a "V". I remember the strip down the middle.'

'Could have been the new BMW sports car. All the rage with the Brooklands set right now. But I have yet to see one down here in Devon. Anyway, how far did it follow you?'

'I first noticed it just before Totnes. I thought it might turn off at Halwell, but it didn't. Kept on behind me all the way to Dartmouth.'

'See who was driving?'

'Not terribly clearly. He had the top down and was wearing a helmet and goggles.'

'Wouldn't have been a flying helmet, would it?'

'I don't know. It was brown, I think and sort of bulky. Why do you ask? Think it might have been that man Dawlish?'

'I don't know. He doesn't have a BMW though. Just an Indian motorbike. Anyway, did you see him at all while you were shopping or on the way back?'

'I didn't whilst I was in Dartmouth. But on the way back, I thought I saw a blue sports car on a couple of occasions. But it wasn't right behind me, so I couldn't be certain. Oh, Johnny, let's call the whole thing off. Please. It's all turning out to be much more terrible than I ever dreamed.'

I thought for a second and then said, 'You mean that Seagrave may have murdered more people than just your sister?'

'Well, even that – ' she began and then stopped.

'Even that what, Diana?' I asked firmly.

'Oh nothing. Really. I don't know what I'm saying. The experience this afternoon has really unnerved me. I even had to drop off to get a drink on my way back. Most unlike me, going into a pub on my own. Not very ladylike, is it? That's what made me late.'

I realized I would have to wait for Tracy to report before I probed her further.

'Don't let this sports car thing panic you, Diana. After all, he could have just been a guy going into Dartmouth for the afternoon, just like you.'

'But he had plenty of chances to pass me, though he didn't. And his car was obviously much faster than mine.'

'Maybe he's just bought it and he's running it in,' I offered, but without much conviction. 'So, don't lose your head. I'll give you a ring in the morning.'

'I still think we should call it off.'

'No you don't, Diana. Now is just the time when we may be heading for a breakthrough. Be in touch.'

I put the receiver back before she could protest further. Five minutes later, I was in the old La Salle and heading towards Teignmouth.

There's something about aerodromes at night. A kind of spookiness. Maybe it's the black silhouettes of aircraft against the dark grey of the sky. The spread of wings eager to feel the slipstream of the morning, the lift that will bring them back to life. Or it's the curious whispering of the wind as it plays with the planes' rigging, before coursing off again across the short mown grass of the landing field. Or maybe it's the stillness, a tranquillity so deep you could drop a pebble into it. A quiet that waits to be broken at dawn by a thousand horses from engine after engine, as they run up to start the day's work.

I parked the La Salle near the only place I could see lights – the main hangar. There were two other cars parked there but neither was a BMW. I made my way to the gap in the hangar doors from which the light was coming. Inside two men were working on one of the engines of a Railway Air Services Rapide. Both looked up as they heard my footfalls.

'Oh, hello,' the fatter of the two smiled. 'You from RAS? If you are, I'm afraid this one won't be ready until at least midday tomorrow; if then. We've got to wait for a new piston to be flown in.'

I explained I was not from Railway Air Services, but just looking for a friend of mine.

'Tom Dawlish? He hasn't been in today,' the thinner man answered. 'He told us on Saturday he would be taking the day off.'

'Say what he'd be doing?' I asked as nonchalantly as I could.

167

'Sure. Lucky blighter,' the fat one grinned. 'Wish I was in his shoes.'

I went in and rested back against the rear of the engine nacelle. 'Oh? What's old Tom got in his brogues then?'

'Hasn't he told you? Told everybody else. He took the day off to pick up a new sports car.'

'German job,' the thinner one piped up.

'Made by the same people who make aero-engines, BMW.'

I expressed both pleasure and surprise. 'Good for old Tom. Didn't know he had that kind of money, though. Last time I saw him he still had his Indian bike.'

'He did till today. But I don't blame him changing, now that his aunt's died and left him a tidy bit of money.'

I raised my eyebrows. 'So old auntie has at last kicked the bucket, eh? Well, she was seventy-two. Can't live for ever.'

The fat man put down his spanner. 'Coo, was she really only seventy-two? Tom told us she was ninety-eight.'

I grinned. 'Oh, you know Tom. Likes spinning a bit of a tale now and then. Never know when to take the old lad seriously.'

The fat man turned to his colleague with a laugh.

'Yeah. Don't we know it, eh Bert? You ought to hear the things Tom comes out with sometimes. They're absolute murder.'

Having found out what I wanted, I turned to leave.

'I bet they are,' I said. 'I bet they are.'

'Shall we say who called?' he shouted after me.

I thought for a moment, and then replied. 'Tell him Henry was asking after him. Henry Swindon – from the Drake Theatre.'

The next morning there was still no news on the wireless that the actor's body had been found. So after feeding Groucho and myself, I hightailed it in the La Salle down to Salcombe. There I hired a small boat with an inboard motor from a fisherman, who seemed thunder-struck that anyone like me would want to go out on such a cool, grey day.

It took about ten minutes to start it, but thereafter, it phutted well enough all the way round to the little cove which I guessed from the map must mark the marine edge of Seagrave's property.

As I rounded the headland, jacket collar up against the cold and hand numb on the tiller, I saw more or less what I had been expecting. A white painted boat-house and wooden jetty long enough for yachts of a considerable draught and, certainly, small floatplanes. But the only thing moored there that morning was a beautifully streamlined American Chris-Craft power boat that looked brand spanking new. Seagrave was, indeed, on a spending spree of some proportions, now that his wife's fortune was his. I mentally totted up the cost of the Lammas-Graham, the BMW and the Chris-Craft and whistled into the wind. It whistled back.

I kept in close by the headland for around quarter of an hour, just watching. Seagrave's mansion was only just visible, almost on the horizon of the hills and his land tumbled in richly green folds down to the grey-brown rocks and the long stretch of beach where he had exercised his Frazer-Nash, Isadora Duncan style. But there was no sign of life, just the bobbing Chris-Craft and swooping sea-gulls. Frozen to the old marrow, I at last turned back for Salcombe. For I had found out what I came for – that a seaplane could come and go from Seagrave's property more or less without being seen by anybody. And even if a passing fishing boat did see it, it would hardly venture sufficiently in shore to be able to spot the difference between a live plane passenger and a dead one. And that would be in daylight. Now in the dark. . .

After I had returned the boat, I raced back into Torquay, anxious not to miss any call Tracy might be making. Babs met me at my office door, all agog with excitement.

'Been *two* people on the phone for you, Johnny.' She announced the news as if there had been at least two hundred.

'The first one was a man. He wouldn't leave his name or number. Just said he'd ring back.'

I went over to my desk. 'The second one?'

'That was Tracy. I mean Miss Spencer-King.'

'Does she want me to ring her back?'

'No, Johnny. You'll find her message on the pad on your desk.'

I went over and read, in Babs' over-round but readable hand, 'Miss King rang at ten thirty-two a.m. Says she has seen Mr Trenchard and it was a success. News too difficult to tell over the phone, so motoring down. Be with you, she says, as soon after lunch as she can. Sends her love, Babs.'

'Make sense?' Babs asked nervously.

'Yes,' I said, thoughtfully. 'Thanks. But I wish I'd been back in time to take the call, all the same.'

'Her news important, Johnny?'

'Could be.'

'Miss Spencer-King sounded quite excited, so I thought it must be.'

She edged towards the door. 'Well, I had better be going. Got a lot of celluloid dolls to unpack.'

I waved my hand, as she hit the door knob. This time I had to say, 'Look, Babs, maybe we should wrap a cloth or something round that knob to save you getting black and blue every time you go out.'

Her face turned as red as a traffic light.

'Oh, no! Really, Johnny, it's my fault, not the door handle's. I'm always bumping into things.' She smiled sheepishly. 'My mother says she'll move heaven and earth to see I never learn to drive a car.'

'Be all right,' I grinned, 'as long as you wrap enough bandages round it.'

Quarter of an hour after I had made a call to Diana Travers to see that she was all right and to confirm I thought Seagrave's jetty could well accommodate a seaplane, the man from Babs' first message came through on the line. It turned out to be Mr Percival Prendergast, father of the pretty but naïve Susan of Burgh Island.

'Relieved to get hold of you at last, Mr Black. I'm sorry to bother you with a personal problem, but I would like to see you about – well, about my daughter, actually.'

'That's all right, Mr Prendergast. I'm glad you rang. I'd like to see you, too. And I have a feeling it's about the same matter. But tell me, how did you get hold of me? We don't know each other.'

'Oh, I do apologize, Mr Black. I should have told you. My daughter mentioned your name to me. You've met, I believe. I made a few enquiries around and soon found out you run a detective agency called Black Eye. Now a private detective is just the kind of person I need to see right now. So that's why I'm ringing.'

'Is it about your daughter and a man called Michael Seagrave?'

'The very same, Mr Black. I can see I'm talking to the right kind of man. Now, when can we meet? I'd like to make it as soon as possible.'

I looked at my watch. It was eleven twenty.

'How about twelve fifteen, today? I can just about get to Burgh Island at that time.'

'Oh, er I'd rather not meet at the hotel, if you don't mind. I don't want anybody to see us together really – especially my daughter.'

'Name a place,' I invited.

"Tell you what. I don't know many places round here, but I do know the Clipper Ship, just outside Salcombe. Yachting friend of mine took me there once. We could meet there and have a spot of lunch, maybe.'

I knew the place. It was at the top of the steep narrow hill that wound down into Salcombe.

'All right. Thank you, Mr Prendergast. I'll meet you there at the same time – twelve fifteen.'

'Twelve fifteen it is, Mr Black,' Prendergast confirmed, his surprisingly vigorous and youthful voice now sounding far less full of worry.

The Clipper Ship bar was starting to fill up by twelve thirty, yet there was still no sign of Prendergast. I wasn't yet worried, as I guessed that tycoons of the Prendergast scale might well have delaying business calls to make, even when on holiday. So I ordered myself another Scotch and was quite happy to wait awhile. For it helped fill in a bit of the time before Tracy was due later in the afternoon; and gave me a pause in which to consider whether I should own up to Prendergast that I had been the anonymous caller who had warned him about Seagrave some days before.

But by one o'clock, I was definitely starting to feel both edgy and rather annoyed at the high-handedness of those with business empires, and by quarter past, I was incensed enough to go to the hotel phone in the lobby and put in a call to Burgh Island. But the receptionist there coolly informed me that Mr Prendergast and his family had chartered a plane and flown to Jersey for two days and would not be back until tomorrow night.

I went back to the bar and ordered another Scotch to try to restore a modicum of self-confidence. For I kicked myself for not realizing that I had been duped. After all, Prendergast's voice had certainly sounded youthful for a man of his obvious age and, on reflection, the answer given to the question of how he found me had not exactly been a winner. I left the bar, feeling that I had certainly been paid back now for my own anonymous phone call to the real Mr Prendergast.

Unfortunately, the many Scotches I'd downed in the Clipper Ship, rather than buoying my spirits, inflamed my anger which, I'm afraid, I took out on my La Salle. Now normally, like most pilots, I am most considerate of machinery. But once in the car, a kind of demon seemed to grip me and I accelerated out of the car park like a Prince Bira off the starting grid, and with a scream of tyres, turned right onto the road towards Malborough. With all eight cylinders pushed to the limit, the speedometer soon showed eighty on the first short straight, which, to be frank, was about thirty miles an hour more than the road allowed in safety. I wound down the window. I needed the raw rush of air to the face, the sense of speed, the blur of the scenery flicking past to revive me, to remind me of who I was and, maybe, of who I had been. For a moment, it was almost like being back in the open cockpit, soaring across limitless landscapes, temporary king of the world around – only now the wind from outside was tearing at bare eyes, not the glass of goggles. Tears started to haze my vision. I took one hand off the wheel to wind my window back up. As I did so, I spotted the roof of a charabanc appearing above the hedgerows around the next corner.

To slow the La Salle down in time for both bus and bend, I, reluctantly, put my foot down on the brake pedal. Instantly, I knew something was wrong. The pedal, firm at first, progressively went soft. The big car came down to seventy, then stopped slowing. I pumped the pedal frantically, but it felt like jelly. Cursing new-fangled hydraulic brakes, of which I'd had no previous experience before the La Salle, I looked desperately for any possible escape route, like an open gate-way or a farm track. For at seventy miles an hour, I knew I had as much chance of missing the charabanc and rounding the bend, as beating Jesse Owens at the Berlin Olympics.

I clutched at the gear lever, but realized I was still going far too fast to change into second. After a quick glance in my mirror, I resorted to the only manoeuvre I could think of. I swung the wheel and started to swerve the La Salle from bank to bank. The tyres hit the grass verges with a series of deafening thuds. The whole car shuddered with each impact and the body creaked ominously, as the chassis flexed. But to my relief, the car was undoubtedly slowing. But as I glanced down at the speedometer, my door, against which I had been bracing myself, suddenly flew open.

My body slid across the slippery leather. I clung like a drowning man to the only thing that could now save me from falling out – the steering wheel rim. But now my head was no longer at a height or angle to see forward out of the windscreen.

The car veered alarmingly to the right as I pulled at the wheel to try to get myself back on the driving seat. It didn't take a genius to see I now had only a split second left before the open door was slammed against my body by the dry stone walling atop the grass verge. My right foot somehow found the running board and by pulling on the wheel and pivoting on my heel, I just made it before there was a sickening scream of tortured metal, as the door struck the wall, tore back on its hinges, then slammed back against the body and running board at a crazy angle.

I was now on the wrong side of the road and through the windscreen, I could see the charabanc's bluff bonnet nosing around the bend ahead. I banged my fist down on the horn button and kept it there, whilst the car careered along the grass verge at a thirty-degree angle, the mangled door catching every projecting stone in the wall. Each impact rocked the car sideways, as if it had been hit by a giant's fist and I had images of the La Salle turning turtle right in front of the charabanc that was now only a hundred yards or so ahead.

I held onto the wheel like grim death, for every collision with the wall tried to deflect the car back onto the road and towards the charabanc, which had now got the message and switched lanes. As the right hand tyres thudded and bumped over the uneven bank, I now saw I had a chance, if only the door did not rip back or fold, thus projecting the La Salle further across the road.

By now I could clearly see the look of sheer panic on the charabanc driver's face and I vaguely heard another horn join mine. At the very last moment, I closed my eyes – not through fear, I like to think, but through the agony of effort to keep the big car on a line-ahead course. When I opened them again, the charabanc was gone and all I had now was the bend with which to contend. I swung the wheel to the left. The car responded, but my speed was still far too high.

The last thing I remember was the sound of splintering wood, as the La Salle crashed through a five barred gate and yours truly struck his forehead on the windscreen, producing a star display worthy of a thousand galaxies, before all was blackness.

Fourteen

'You know, Mr Black, you should really stay in overnight,' the nursing sister admonished. 'It's what we always advise in concussion cases.'

I held onto Tracy's arm and let her do the talking.

'I agree with you, sister,' she smiled, 'but Johnny is more a mental case than a concussion one. He had a plane crash a year or two back that would have killed anyone else, but he discharged himself from hospital at least a fortnight too soon for any of the doctors.'

The sister shook her head, then gently shook my hand.

'Well, if the aches and pains in your head don't clear in the next day or two, you ought to come in again, or at the very least, see your doctor.'

'He will,' Tracy promised. 'I'll see to that.'

And so we left the quaint little hospital in Totnes and Tracy drove me back home at a funereal speed, the like of which I'm certain her SS100 had never experienced. Once back at the cottage, she fussed around me like a mother hen – about the most temptingly beautiful in the old coop, I must add – and insisted I went straight to bed. I was in no mood or condition to argue, so I obeyed. The hell was she wouldn't tell what she had discovered in London until I was snugly tucked up and had told her all the frustrating, infuriating and terrifying details of my morning.

'It could have been murder number four,' she sighed. 'Just before I came to collect you at the hospital, Bobby Briggs rang Black Eye to confirm he'd picked up your La Salle and has it back at the yard. Thinks he can patch it together, given a bit of time. But the main point is that he's discovered what caused your brakes to fail – the hydraulic pipes had been neatly cut, presumably whilst you were in the Clipper Ship.'

'I guessed as much. But I have a feeling that was just a warning, not a full-blooded attempt at murder.'

'You can't be sure.'

She came and sat down on the counterpane and took my hand. 'Johnny, if you had turned left and gone down that almost vertical hill into Salcombe. . .'

'But I didn't and there was no reason for them to suspect I might. No, I think if I'd been killed, that might have been less of a bonus to them than a danger. After all, if we're right and Seagrave and his chum are knee-high in three deaths, they would hardly want questions about a fourth. Dead private eyes might raise questions that dead actors and dancers do not.'

I turned in my bed and winced, as the movement sent a thousand little daggers into my brain.

'You all right, Johnny?'

'I've survived worse, old girl, don't fret.'

She extended a soft loving hand to my cheek. 'You know something, Johnny, you should always wear a bandage round your forehead. Suits you. Makes you look like some dashing bandit or a pirate on the Spanish Main.' She peered closely at me. 'Hey, I hate to tell you, but I think you're going to have a black eye in the morning.'

'Then I'll wear an eye patch to complete your pirate picture.'

'Johnny Black of Black Eye fame. It's all coming true,' she laughed, but I brought her back to hard reality by asking about what she had learned from Trenchard.

'All right,' she said, 'I'll tell you now. But only on one condition.'

'What's that?'

'That you don't go getting out of bed directly I've finished to follow up on what I got him to disclose.' She held up an elegant but wagging finger. 'Now, do you promise?'

I thought for a second, then chose the words of my reply rather carefully.

'I promise not to get out of bed until the morning.'

'All right then, here goes. But heaven help you, Johnny, if you break your promise.'

Tracy glowered at me, after I had made her make the phone call. In fact, she didn't speak to me again until Diana Travers actually arrived some thirty minutes or so later.

I didn't let Diana's outpouring of both sympathy and alarm go on too long, as my head was killing me and I wanted to get the whole thing over before I lost what little strength, tact and patience I had left. The trouble was, Diana now looked ashen and about as fit as I felt and I was nervous about how she would be able to take to my extremely direct and personal line of questioning. However, I just had to know, so, with a glance at Tracy, I began.

'Diana, what I'm going to ask you now may cause you embarrassment, even pain, and I guess you're not going to like me by the time I've finished. But things now have accelerated to such a point, I've got to clear these questions from my mind.'

As always, under tension, Diana Travers reached into her handbag for her cigarette case.

'All right if I smoke in your bedroom?' she asked.

I nodded from my bed and waited until she lit up before continuing.

'Today, Diana, we have received information about Michael Seagrave's past that may well have a bearing on this case and we need your help to evaluate its significance.'

Her eyelids flickered. 'Fire away, Johnny. I'll try and help where I can.'

'Thanks.' I took a deep breath. 'Question number one. You knew Michael Seagrave at one time pretty closely, didn't you? More than you've ever admitted to me.'

She stared at her scarlet finger-nails and didn't reply. I drew my own conclusions.

'Question number two. That was the reason you did not want me to extend my investigations to London, wasn't it? You didn't want me to know you and he were that close?'

The stare continued.

'I'm sorry, Diana, I have to go on.'

She inhaled long and deep on her Sobranie and gave an almost imperceptible nod.

'Does Seagrave have some hold over you?'

I saw her eyes flick toward Tracy. I tried another tack. 'I'd better tell you what we've discovered. Seagrave almost hanged a girl once. From a beam in her bedroom.'

I watched her face intently, as I went on. 'It seems that's how Seagrave gets some of his kicks. From mounting mock executions. Apparently, it's all very realistic, according to the girl who almost died. The right rope, the binding of the wrists, the hood. Only difference, he used a stool rather than a trap-door.'

Suddenly Diana gave way.

'Oh God, no, not any more...' she wailed. 'Don't say any more. You don't need to, Please...'

Tracy went over and put an arm round her shoulder.

'All right. I promise I've nearly finished.'

She looked up at me, her eyes now glazed with tears. 'What else do you want to know?'

'You knew all this about Seagrave, didn't you? That's what made you first suspect your sister's death wasn't an accident, wasn't it?'

There was a pause, then, staring into space, she replied, as if talking to herself.

'My sister liked being dominated. Always did, right from a child. I could never understand it. She used to fantasize about being taken prisoner ... didn't really matter who it was. Early on it was Zulus and African tribes. Then it became Arab slave dealers, sheiks and all that Valentino-type nonsense.'

She took the Sobranie from her holder and looked for somewhere to stub it out. Tracy went out to the landing and got an ashtray.

'I'm sorry, Johnny, I should have told you about all this, I suppose, but I felt too ashamed somehow. I felt ashamed when I went along with it all, when I was with Seagrave, the tying up, the submission, the debasement of his weird fantasies. I hated doing it, but I thought I was in love with him, you see. If I didn't go along, I'd lose him to another girl who would.'

'What happened?' Tracy asked softly.

'He ran off to another girl, anyway. All my pretence, my patience . ..my abasement was in vain. I hated him after that. Not for leaving me, but for making me go through all that for nothing...nothing.'

She sat slumped in her chair, her body limp and her eyes wide but seeing nothing.

I waited for a moment, then said, 'You think he played hangman with your sister that day and it went wrong or he took it too far, don't you?'

She nodded.

'So he covered up the accident with that Isadora Duncan stunt?'

She pressed her eyes tightly shut. 'She was always daring him. To do this, to do that. Right from the start. She loved the power her money gave her.'

Tracy moved back to sit on my bed. 'What did you feel when you first heard your sister had met him down here? Couldn't you have warned her about him?'

She hesitated for a moment, then replied, 'Oh, surprise, but nothing more really. I didn't feel envy, if that's what you're thinking. And I had no wish to punish my sister for having him, you must believe me. I just felt, well, he might be just the kind of man who could supply my poor sister's crazy needs. She'd had quite a few boyfriends before, you see, and she ended up despising every one of them.'

She sighed and turned away. 'She was never really a happy person, my sister. Never. I've wondered at times whether she would ever have been really content with anyone. She was more like two people than one – loved the power her money and beauty gave her, yet craved somehow to be at the mercy of others.'

My head suddenly began throbbing like a Junkers Jumo Diesel and I put a hand to my bandage, anxious now to get to my last two questions.

'That morning we first met, Diana, over at your house. Seagrave was leaving just as I arrived, remember?'

'I remember.'

'He didn't come just to give you some of your sister's effects, did he?

She suddenly sat up straight in her chair and became a little more the Diana Travers I knew. Maybe she was just glad she no longer needed to feel guilty about what she had kept from us.

'He came to warn me.'

'About what?' I asked, but I really knew the answer.

'About going to the police about my suspicions. You see, the evening before, I had plucked up courage to tackle him about my sister's death and he had denied everything. He said, if I went to the police, he would say I was just a jealous woman, who was trying to take revenge for his preference for my sister.'

'That all?' Tracy asked, echoing my own thoughts.

She shook her head. 'All right. He said he would tell them that I was weird. That I loved being tied up and forced him to carry out all those things, when we were together years ago. He said he would drag my name so deep in the mire that I'd – these were his very words – drown in the spit of society'.

'So you didn't call the police, but a private...' I pointed to my bruised optic '...Black Eye.'

178

Diana Travers got up from her chair and stood with her back to me at the window.

'I have another confession to make, Johnny.'

'Go ahead, but you don't need to make any more, Diana. I've more or less got the picture now.'

'Not quite,' she went on, talking to the garden outside. 'Of course I wanted to see justice done – for my sister's sake. But at the same time, I was desperately afraid of what Michael might do if he heard I had got in some high-powered private detective from London.'

I forced a smile. 'I guess I was ideal for you. Just starting out. No track record, no experience, no clients, no reputation, no London base – and maybe no talent.'

She immediately turned round and came over to my bedside.

'No, Johnny, it wasn't like that. It wasn't just a sop to my – '

' – conscience. Okay, Diana, sorry to raise it.'

She took my hand. 'No, I did and do want to find out the truth. I just didn't want Michael to drag my name in the gutter. So I thought using an unknown like you. . .' She looked at me with a half-smile. 'Now I've confessed it all to you two, I somehow don't mind so much any more. Funny, isn't it? The thing you dread most sometimes turns out to be not so dreadful after all.'

'It's not dreadful at all, Diana,' Tracy sympathized. 'Now how about my going downstairs and getting us all a stiff drink? I have a feeling we could all do with one.'

Nobody demurred, but after she had left the room, Diana said urgently, 'Johnny. He tried to kill you today. My God, I would never have got you involved in all this if I'd known. You see, I never dreamt Michael would turn out to be a *real* killer – I mean, as opposed to . . .sort of accidental. But if he and that terrible friend of his *have* done away with that dancer girl and Henry Swindon, then Michael has traded in play-acting executions for the real thing.'

She squeezed my hand hard and I saw her eyes were moist once again.

'And now you, Johnny. Is he ever going to stop? It could be me next – any of us. You've go to pull out, Johnny. Now. Before it's too late. I'll ring Michael and tell him you've dropped the case. Then I'll go away somewhere. We'll leave all the rest to the police.'

I thought for a moment, then said, 'I agree with one thing: you should go away until this whole thing is over. I hate to tell you, but you

179

were right about that blue sports car yesterday. It was following you. I've discovered who owns it – Tom Dawlish. Have you got somewhere to go?'

'I suppose so. An old school chum of mine, who now lives in France, has been badgering me for ages to visit her. I said I might go this year, and I could probably put the visit forward.'

'Whereabouts in France?'

'Near Le Touquet.'

'Great,' I said. 'Ring her and ask if you can come right away. Le Touquet has got an aerodrome, so you could even fly over.'

She looked a little surprised at my suggestion.

'You think it's that urgent?'

'I think it's that urgent.'

'But that still leaves you, Johnny. And look at you. You're not well enough to – '

'Don't be fooled by the forehead, Diana. By the morning, I'll be right as rain and raring to go.'

I smiled to myself at my optimism. Right then, I felt like the burnt out hulk of the Hindenberg at Lakehurst, New Jersey.

Luckily, it was at this point that Tracy returned with a tray full of Dutch courage. My own battered senses were shouting 'Enough, enough', and I guessed, after our inquisition, Diana's feelings were not so very different.

Tracy handed me a Scotch. 'Hair of the dog,' she grinned.

I could have done without her reminder. For the same mangey cur had contributed to my almost getting killed that afternoon. It was a mistake I have never made when flying. And from then on, I was never to repeat it when at the wheel of a motor.

After Diana Travers had gone, I insisted we chew the Seagrave cud for a bit, before I obeyed Tracy's strict instructions to get some sleep. For there were quite a few things worrying me since Trenchard's and my employer's revelations and I couldn't rest until I had explored them. In essence, they boiled down to two main questions, as I explained to Tracy.

'One, I can't quite believe, old thing, that Diana's sister died because one of Seagrave's hangman games went wrong. It doesn't feel right, somehow. What's more, if the different coloured shreds from the Frazer-Nash transmission are anything to go by and we are interpreting them rightly, Seagrave wouldn't need to carry out a dress rehearsal of the scarf trick, if his wife's death was accidental. Nor would he really have the time between her death and the drive along the beach in the car.'

'Yes, that occurred to me as well,' Tracy agreed, curling up at the end of my bed like a very luxurious cat. 'Tell me your other worries. I may share those too.'

'Well, I also don't imagine that anyone would go to the lengths of murdering two other people just to cover what was, in reality, an accident, albeit an embarrassing and sordid one. Nor can I see that Tom Dawlish would be willing to risk his neck – quite literally – for that kind of cover-up.'

'I agree. But we've no proof that the Phipps girl and the actor have been murdered, have we? If they're still alive and kicking somewhere, then that objection goes out the old window.'

'All right,' I went on, 'let's turn to Daphne Phipps, for a moment. She was pretty obviously black-mailing somebody and that somebody really has to be Seagrave. Now what could she know about the sister's death that could pull that many fivers out of him? After all, the drive on the beach in the car took place very early in the morning. She can hardly have witnessed it, can she? She's not the type to be up and out at the crack of dawn, let alone miles away from where she lives and works.'

Tracy shrugged. 'So what are you saying, Johnny?'

I put a hand to my bandage. 'I don't really know. The old brains are still a bit addled.'

'I told you to take a rest.'

I smiled and went on. 'Yet the actor must have thought it was all something to do with the Frazer-Nash, mustn't he? After all, he'd sent for the catalogue.'

'Maybe he wrong-guessed what Daphne Phipps was up to. Tried to get in on the act with what he supposed was the trigger for her sudden flush of funds.'

'Maybe. Hell, it's all too damned confusing.'

'Not just too confusing, my darling, too damned dangerous. We should go to the police and tell them all we know and – '

'We still don't know anything, Tracy. They're not going to take the slightest notice of anything we say until we've got a shred of evidence of something.'

'How about your coloured shreds?' From her mischievous grin, I knew I didn't need to answer.

She tried again. 'Your car's brakes?'

'Anybody could have done that. The police would put it down to a vandal or someone with a grudge against me or big showy cars. How can we prove Seagrave, or more probably, Dawlish, did it?'

She sighed and curled up once more.

'What we need is at least a body,' I ruminated. 'And not that of Diana's sister. Even then, we'll be lucky if either of the bodies can be connected with Seagrave or Dawlish.'

On that pessimistic note, we left it. A moment later, Tracy left me to 'get some sleep, or else'.

Little did I imagine that whilst I was in the old Land of Nod, one of the bodies would, indeed, be turned up.

Fifteen

That night, Tracy insisted on staying and slept on the camp bed. We didn't need the blanket curtain. Least, I didn't. My mind was too busy repairing itself from the bang on the windshield to wander up any other avenues.

Next morning, she got up early and brought me breakfast in bed. I could hear Groucho complaining downstairs the whole time I ate my bacon and eggs. For he usually likes to share the odd breakfast titbit with me. I had hardly downed the last forkful, when I heard a car pull up outside, quickly followed by the sound of another. I instantly put down my tray and leapt out of bed, much to Tracy's surprise.

'What on earth – ?' she began, then got the message.

We both went to the window and peered out from behind a curtain. To our immense relief, it wasn't Seagrave or Dawlish come to teach us both a violent lesson. We saw, surprise, surprise, Mrs Briggs getting out of the first car, a big black 1934 Buick and Bobby Briggs getting out of the second, the infamous Frazer-Nash. Tracy, being fully dressed, went downstairs to let them in.

To cut a long story short, dear Mrs Briggs – I guess to somewhat repay my favour to her over the phantom lover affair – had convinced her husband that, in my line of work, I needed a car. So she had persuaded him to lend me one of the better motors from his stock of restored wrecks, whilst my La Salle was being patched up.

'Saw to it he gave you a nice big powerful job, so you wouldn't miss your own swanky one too much,' she had smiled.

'Don't you go gate-crashing with this one, Johnny boy,' was her husband's only comment. 'It'll fetch a good hundred and seventy-five pounds in a week or two's time, when I've got your La Salle back on the road.'

I was overwhelmed by their generosity and could only stutter a few lame words of thanks before Bobby sped off back to his scrapyard in the Frazer-Nash, his wife clinging onto the old sides of the car's seat, as if her life depended on it. The way Bobby drove that thing, I guessed it might, at that.

After they had gone, I turned on the wireless for the nine o'clock news. The first report was of a speech by a bombastic Herr Hitler, pretending yet again he wasn't really after an Anschluss with his native country, Austria. I'd almost lost interest by the time the second item came up, but luckily, not quite. For it was what we had been waiting for. The discovery of a body. That of Henry Swindon, recovered from a bog on Dartmoor. Apparently in a hell of a state and with a multitude of broken bones, which were attributed to a frenzied attack by his assailant. The report ended with a quote from the police that a man who had been detained some days ago would be charged with the murder at the Crown Court at midday.

'Hell,' I swore. 'That ruddy convict would go and muddy the water by stealing poor Swindon's jacket. It's too convenient for the police to sew it all up by adding just one more murder to the old convict's list.'

Tracy got up from my bed, a determined look on her face. 'Well, that does it, my darling. You stay here. I'm just going out for a bit. Shouldn't be long.'

I swung out of bed and grabbed her hand.

'Now, hang on, Tracy. I'm going out myself now. I've been in bed far too long already.'

'You shouldn't get up. Just look at your eye. It looks like a black balloon.'

I stripped off my pyjama jacket and started to dress.

'You've got to be careful, Tracy. Tell me where you're going. If it's just shopping, then – '

She looked up and smiled, but her eyes weren't saying what her mouth was. 'It's just food shopping. You've got almost nothing left in the house.'

'Don't try and fool old Johnny,' I said rather crossly, as I turned away from her to don my trousers. 'You're up to something and it stands out a mile.'

'I'm not up to anything. And you shouldn't be dressing.'

She made for the door but I crossed over to it just in time, my trousers only held up by one hand.

'You're not going anywhere, Tracy, until you tell me the truth. You're going to try to do a Myrna Loy act, aren't you? Solve the old

184

case while dear old William Powell stays home with Aster and rests up in his silk pyjamas.'

'Jealous?' she grinned.

I'm afraid I lost my temper.

'Tracy, this isn't a bloody game. We're not actors where the worst that can happen to us is to get covered in ketchup. This is deadly serious, with the whole ruddy emphasis on the "dead" bit.'

She put her hands on her hips and glowered back at me.

'I'm not a child, Johnny. I know it's bloody serious, just as well as you do. But that doesn't mean to say I can't make my own decisions about what I should and should not do. You've made all the running so far. I've never tried to horn in ever. Just be around to help out now and then when you want me. Well now, after yesterday's little drama, you have to admit, you're a marked man. Whatever you say, if you go on like this, you'll end up like poor Henry Swindon.'

'So you admit you're not going shopping?'

'I admit nothing.' She tried to prise me from the door. 'Now come on, Johnny. Let me go. You don't own me, you know. I'm a free spirit. I can do what I please.'

I stood my ground. 'Tracy, I forbid you to get any further involved with – '

But I never got any further than that. For she suddenly reached out and yanked my trousers down to my knees. Whilst I was trying to cover my embarrassment, she made her escape. A moment later, I heard the growl of her SS100 as it accelerated off down the lane. And I knew by the time I got to the Buick, I would never be able to catch her.

The big, black car seemed like a hearse after the low and racier La Salle, but uncannily, its sombre and funereal appearance seemed apt for the occasion and my mental and physical condition. But the big straight eight that powered it was renowned for its silky power and it certainly was no geriatric on the road.

All the way into Torquay, my mind was alternately taken up with Tracy and what I'd been brooding over since fitfully waking in the night. And the latter was concerned with the now only remaining missing person – Daphne Phipps. For somehow or other, I felt she must be the key to unlocking the Seagrave cause. I cursed the fact I really knew so little about her.

I felt certain that if I could only discover what lever she was using to prise those fancy white fivers out of Seagrave, then I would be close to solving the riddle. For if my theories were correct, Henry Swindon had only tried to carry on where his old girlfriend had left off, or correction, where he assumed she had left off. I realized now that I should have given him far more of a grilling than I did – whilst he was still alive. Maybe that way, I could have prevented his death.

So if Daphne Phipps was the key, how the hell was I going to find out anything more about her, now she'd disappeared? By the time I'd had the row with Tracy, I had realized my only way was through the dancer's friends or relations. I doubted I would learn very much more from her parents in Plymouth, though I was quite prepared to try if my first bet failed. And my first – and perhaps last – resort was the nervous girl who had, seemingly, put hair-washing ahead of lunch with me the previous Saturday.

I had been waiting in the Buick, just up from the dancing school, for almost half an hour before she appeared. At first, I didn't recognize her, for despite the gayness of her little pillbox hat, she looked nigh on ten years older, her face gaunt and her walk slow and ponderous.

I slipped out of the car and caught up with her. She looked round and her cherry-red mouth gaped open at my battered appearance.

'Oh, it's you, Mr Conway.' She pointed to my face. 'Have you been in an accident?'

'Sort of,' I said. 'And remember my name is not really Conway. It's Black. Johnny Black.'

'Yes, I'm sorry, Mr, er, Black. I remember now.'

Her face suddenly perked up.

'Have you come to tell me Daphne has turned up? That's it, isn't it? Daphne's turned up, alive and well.'

I shook my head, I shouldn't have. I still had lead balls inside my skull.

'No, Dolly, I'm sorry, she hasn't. That's why it's urgent I see you.'

She looked around nervously, as if she was somehow afraid of the springtime shoppers bustling along past us.

'I'm just going for a bite to eat, Mr Black. I don't know how I can help you anyway – '

I took her arm. 'Look, Dolly. It may be a matter of life or death. I have to talk to you. And right away. I'll buy you lunch while we're chatting.'

I did not wait for a reply, but almost frog-marched her back to the Buick.

'Where are you taking me? This isn't your car.'

She looked really frightened now, as if I was kidnapping her.

'My La Salle was in a smash.' I pointed to my eye. 'That's how I got this. Now please, get in. We're only going up to the Imperial. I'll drop you back in time so that Mr Feather doesn't *"Gott in Himmel"* all over you. I promise.'

Her face twitched with indecision, making the powder on her face seem to almost separate from her skin.

'I can't help you, Mr Black. I really can't,' she pleaded.

'You don't know unless you try,' I said, then tried the sucker punch. 'You owe it to Daphne.'

It worked. She hesitated, then got in. As I drove on up to the Imperial, she seemed to be very close to tears.

Ted Shilling just did not believe my eye when I walked in – I had to admit myself it was more of a crowd stopper than the bandage. But I tipped him the wink to cool his comments, for I had no wish to further frighten Dolly Randan with a run-down of my previous day's misadventures. So, wearing a somewhat frustrated and querying look on his face, Ted poured us our drinks, a Scotch for me and a sweet sherry for my companion. Then promised to bring us over a plate of fresh crab sandwiches when they were ready; Dolly's lunch break quite clearly not extending to a full four-course luncheon in the Imperial restaurant.

I showed Dolly to a table in the corner – the same one, in fact, at which I had sat with Daphne Phipps. Her hand shook as she raised her sherry to her lips.

'I shouldn't be doing this,' she said in a voice hardly above a whisper. 'Mr Feather doesn't like us drinking lunch time. Says if he ever gets a complaint about our breath from our dancing partner – '

'I'll square you with Mr Feather, don't worry.'

She put down her glass and dabbed her mouth delicately with her finger. Even so, the lipstick smeared a trifle on her bottom lip, the red feathering like a graze against her powder-white and worried face.

'You've got to tell me about Daphne,' I began. 'Everything you know . . . anything she may have done or said recently that may give us a clue as to what has happened to her.'

She shook her head. 'I told you I don't know anything more. Really.

You must believe me. You know about the money she suddenly seemed to have. That's all there is.'

She picked up her glass and shakily took another sip. I could hardly believe she was the same girl I had met the first time I visited the dancing school.

'What's the matter, Dolly?' I asked softly. 'There's something the matter, isn't there?'

She didn't reply, but fumbled in her handbag for a handkerchief. 'No, nothing,' she sniffed. 'It's nothing. I just don't feel very well, that's all.'

She held her handkerchief to her nose, but I knew once I looked away, she would move it up to her eyes.

'Maybe the sherry will buck me up,' she added, with a weak smile.

'Are you frightened of something, Dolly?' I persisted. 'If you are, now's the time to tell me. Has someone been getting at you . . . threatening you?'

She shook her head and her hatpin loosened in her hair. Reaching up to fix it, she said, 'No, nobody's threatening me. I'm allright really.'

I reached across the table and took her hand.

'Dolly, I'm here to help you. You've got to tell me what's worrying you. It could be the very thing that will help us save Daphne.'

She looked up and now I could see a tear in the corner of her eye. 'Save?' she whispered.

'Yes. Save. I have reason to believe Daphne has put herself in the most terrible danger.' I did not add that it was probably far too late, for then she would have little, if any, reason to come clean.

'You think she might still be all right?'

I changed course. 'Look, Dolly, I think you know who Daphne was blackmailing. It was Michael Seagrave, wasn't it? The man whose wife was strangled by a scarf.'

She closed her eyes and hid them behind her handkerchief.

I went on. 'What did Daphne know that Seagrave was afraid of? Was it about his wife's death?'

She didn't reply, or move a muscle.

'You know, don't you, Dolly? That's what is tearing you apart, isn't it? You feel guilty about something. Is it because you've kept silent?'

She suddenly looked up, her face now a mask of anguish.

'No, no,' she uttered, under her breath. 'No, that's the trouble. If I had kept silent, none of this would have happened.'

I quickly looked round the bar again. To my relief, it was still pretty empty. I leaned forward across the table.

'If you'd kept silent about what, Dolly? Tell me. You must tell me. It's the only way.'

She closed her eyes once more. 'About my friend. In Croydon. She was a dancer too. Very good she was – caught Cochrane's eye. He put her in the chorus.'

I suddenly remembered something the agent Trenchard had said when Tracy and I had visited him. 'She was a friend of Seagrave's, wasn't she?'

She gave a slight nod. 'She loved him. She'd have done anything for him, except. . .'

'Except what, Dolly?'

She burst into tears and hid her face in her hands. The pillbox hat tilted at a perilous angle.

'I shouldn't be telling you this. Any more than I should have told Daphne. Oh God. . .'

I pushed her sherry glass towards her. 'Here, finish your drink. It might buck you up a bit.'

She blew her nose, then downed the rest of her sherry.

'Now, what did you tell Daphne? Please. I must know.'

She took a breath, then went on, 'Maudie – that was my friend – she was always a bit of a scream. The things she used to do and say. You never knew whether to believe her or not. Still, she was a good friend, until she. . .'

Tears again began coursing down her cheeks, leaving furrows in the powder.

'She's dead, isn't she?' I said quietly.

'Yes. She took her own life. Because of him, I think. He left her when she wouldn't do what he wanted.'

'What did he want her to do? Was it about. . .hanging?'

She blushed with incomprehension. 'Hanging? What do you mean hanging?'

'Forget it, Dolly. Just go on. What did he want her to do?'

'Well, I didn't know at the time whether to believe it or not – Maudie lived in a kind of dream world of her own. Full of fantasies, she was – but she told me he had asked her to go abroad and take some girls with her.'

I frowned. 'Go abroad? What for?

'The way she told it, he said she could earn a fortune in no time and then come back to England a rich woman.'

The penny was gradually starting to drop. 'You mean, help ship girls out to – ?'

'His brother,' she interrupted. 'He said he had a brother. I think she said he was in Marseilles.' (She pronounced it 'Marsails'.) 'And he'd arrange what happened to them after that. Some, she said, would work in France. Others would be shipped over to North Africa. It all sounded like out of some film to me. I didn't really take it seriously. But Maudie was full of tales like that. She said some of Cochrane's young ladies were no better than they ought to be. You know – '

'On the game, as well as on the stage?'

She nodded once more. 'You don't earn enough as a dancer, you see, Mr Black. And it's all so expensive if you have to live near London. It's different in Devon. That's why I moved down here.'

I downed the last of my Scotch, then asked, 'And you mentioned all this to Daphne. Why?'

'She became fascinated with Seagrave after she saw his picture in the paper. You know, after his wife had died in that car accident. Kept talking about him. Said now his wife was dead, he'd make a good catch for someone. Good-looking, well-off, and that. So I mentioned about Maudie – just in passing, like. Told her I didn't know whether there was anything in the story, on account of Maudie being such a fibber sometimes.'

Suddenly I saw the whole picture. It was only too easy for someone with Seagrave's matinée idol looks. Pretty young girls earning a pittance as dancers, whether in hotels, restaurants, clubs or chorus lines would fall for his charm and patter hook, line and sinker. And the next thing they knew, he'd got them seemingly profitable engagements in clubs and theatres abroad. They would only learn the truth when it was too late. When they were stranded penniless in a foreign country, with starvation or jail the only alternatives to prostitution.

'This brother Maudie mentioned,' I picked up. 'Did she ever mention meeting him?'

'No. Never did. Never thought to ask, neither.'

I wasn't too disappointed. I was pretty sure I could describe him almost as well as a camera lens.

'Dolly, you mustn't go on feeling guilty about all this. You couldn't ever, in your wildest dreams, imagine that. . .'

But I never finished. For, suddenly, I was interrupted by the sound of breaking glass. I spun my head round expecting to see I know not what. Over at the bar, Ted Shilling was making frantic signs to me, whilst picking up the pieces of two glasses he had quite obviously broken just to attract my attention.

I glanced over to the door at which he was pointing. Just moving to a table were two figures I knew only too well. As I hesitated, trying to plot my next move, Dolly Randan got up and ran past me. I tried to restrain her, but too late. She was out the door, before I could reach it.

'Having trouble with your women, Mr Black?' Seagrave asked with a malicious grin across his too-good-to-be-true face. I ignored him, and ran past and out of the hotel. Way down the hill, I could just see Dolly Randan's pillbox hat bobbing about as she ran. I was tempted to go after her, but then realized with some horror what I had already unwittingly done – drawn too much undesirable attention to an already very vulnerable girl.

I strode back into the bar and said in a loud voice to Ted Shilling, 'That'll teach me to go out with nurses. She seemed fun when I was in the hospital, but outside. . .'

Good old Ted. He got the message and indicated with a nod that the couple at the nearby table had too. Pushing a giant plate of crab sandwiches towards me, he said with a smile that almost unseated his spectacles, 'You've got a lot on your plate for just one.'

I put my hands to my bandaged forehead and sighed. 'You can say that again – whenever you like.'

Taking a circuitous route to try to avoid being followed, I was at the dancing school by the time I thought Dolly would have returned. When I asked for her all I got was the guttural Adrian Feather who looked most annoyed at anyone coming into his place with a bandage and a black eye.

'Miss Randan has no wish to see you, Mr Black, or vatever your real name.'

'But I must see her,' I insisted. 'It's vitally important.'

'Ze only thing zat is vitally important is zat you stop bothering my girls. I have told you vat she says – she von't see you. So go avay.'

'She must have said something else. She's got to see me.'

I made to go through the door at the back of the small dance floor,

191

but he barred the way.

'You can't go in there. Miss Randan is busy with a client.' He moved closer to me. 'Now if you von't go, I'll call the police.'

I toyed with the idea that it might not be such a bad thing, then realized that if I got detained at some police station for hours on end, then I would be no ruddy good to Dolly Randan or the headstrong Tracy. And time was the very essence.

'Look,' I suggested, tearing out a page from the notebook I always carried, 'if I write her a message, will you give it to her? Tell her she must follow my instructions to the letter. She'll understand why.'

He shrugged. 'All right. But then, get out of here. I don't vish to see you round here again – ever. Do you understand?'

I scribbled my message, folded the paper over and gave it to him. 'Don't bother to read it,' I smiled. 'You von't understand vone vord.'

I went back to the office. It took at least ten minutes to calm Babs down when she saw the effect closed gates tend to have on people's faces. I didn't tell her about the cut brake lines – I think she'd have had a seizure. Instead she started to berate me about what I had said the other day – about any car she might drive needing bandages wrapped around it.

'See, Johnny? You're no better, are you?' Smiling her peek-a-boo smile, she added, 'You should have me around with you. I wouldn't let you drive as fast, I wouldn't.'

Her last remark gave me an idea.

'Babs, would you really like to help me? I mean not just minding the phone and taking messages. But real. . .' I screwed my eyelids close together, '. . .detective stuff?'

She lit upon my enthusiasm, like a starving sparrow on a crumb. 'You mean it, Johnny? You really mean it? You want *me* to help *you*?'

'Yes. Really.'

She started to jump up and down like a schoolgirl. 'What do I have to do, Johnny? Tell me.'

I told her. It was a job for Tracy, really. She would have been perfect for it. But I had rung the cottage, both before I left the hotel and before Babs had found me in the office and there had been no reply. So I still had no idea where she was and it was worrying me.

So dear Babs was all I had. I briefed her like a Dutch uncle, going countless times over what I wanted her to do. She seemed to take it all in and repeated everything back to me parrot fashion – well, better actually, if Groucho is anything to go by. To my amazement and relief, she seemed to understand that she mustn't ask too many questions as to the whys and wherefores of her mission, but just accept it as a vital necessity.

The test run-through was interrupted by a ding-dong of Chinese swear words coming down the corridor outside. Babs immediately fled and hit the door knob with an almighty bang. She didn't even wince – I guess she felt detectives don't.

'See you spot on five past five,' she blinked and then was gone.

I sat for a while looking out at the gulls swooping on a dead fish on the quay and cursing myself for not having grilled Dolly Randan at length before, and secondly, for now, perhaps, having put her in some danger from Seagrave and what I had to assume could be his ginger-moustached brother.

Her white-slavery revelations, however, did not exactly help me in nailing Seagrave. I still had no proof of anything that would impress a half-witted constable, let alone the tubercular Inspector Wyngarde. The latter, I reckoned, would need a hell of a lot of concrete facts before he changed his mind about the multiple-murdering convict, let alone about Seagrave's wife's death.

I rang the cottage twice more, but still there was no reply. And Tracy hadn't rung in. I was now more than a little disturbed about where she could be and what she was doing. But I took a crumb of comfort that at least she wasn't with Seagrave and co. For I had seen them in Torquay at lunchtime and it would take them some time to get back to what I was now convinced was Murder Mansion.

In the end, I couldn't stand the waiting. I began having terrible visions of Tracy, having been followed back to Rose Cottage, lying in a pool of blood under Groucho's cage, all his 'Stick 'em, ups' and 'Drop 'ems' having been of no avail. I looked at my watch. I had time to get there and back before I picked Babs up. I went out to the car. As I did so, a white bomb fell from a swooping seagull and splattered onto the Buick's bonnet. I followed the bird's flight, as it thermalled up and away. Its deposit had summed up my thoughts exactly.

But it was a fool's errand. When I arrived, there was no sign of her SS at my cottage or anywhere around. The front door was still locked and inside Groucho was quite alone. I asked him if he had seen Tracy, but all I got was 'Hello, baby', followed by what I took to be parrot swear words. I gave him my finger to peck, then left.

All the way there and all the way back, I kept my old eyes peeled for any blue cars. For I had spotted Seagrave's new Lammas-Graham in the Imperial car park. Parked next to Ginger's BMW. They looked like mother and son, both being an almost identical pale-ish blue. But no blue cars did I see tailing me. If I was being followed, then they were being more than clever about it.

Back at the office, the notepad on my desk was still blank. So Tracy still hadn't phoned in. I tried the cottage again and let the phone ring for ever, but no go. Either Tracy was punishing me for my obstinate refusal to let her get too involved, or . . .

It was the 'or' bit that was now putting yours truly into a worse spin than any aircraft had given me. The worst part was that there was really nothing I could do – and certainly not until Babs and I had returned from our expedition. So I brought the Seagrave file up to date, but even so, the next quarter of an hour was purgatory. And it was sheer relief when the watch on the wrist said five past five.

Sixteen

I pulled up just down from the house.

'Now, you know what to do, don't you, Babs?'

She nodded, her goo-goo eyes glistening with excitement.

'Take as long as necessary to convince her to come. I'll still be here. Remember, don't take "no" for an answer.' I smiled encouragement. '"No" isn't a word in the detective's dictionary.'

'Right,' she grinned, then tidied her bubbly hair-do in the rear view mirror. ' 'Do I look all right?'

'A million dollars,' I winked.

She blushed, and let herself out. She kept looking back all the way to the front door of the neat little boarding-house where Dolly Randan had lodgings. Thirty seconds later, with a tiny wave, she disappeared inside.

Whilst I sat there, tapping the steering wheel nervously, I prayed that Dolly would take to heart what Babs had to say and realize the danger she might now be in. After all, I wasn't asking her to do too much – just move in with Babs' parents for a day or two until everything was resolved one way or the other. The arguments I had rehearsed with Babs were, to me, pretty fire-proof, if alarming. I just hoped they weren't so alarming that they scared her into paralysed immobility.

My heart missed a beat every time a blue car went past me down the road, one blue drop-head Bentley (whose body style the Lammas-Graham aped) actually having prompted me to grab for my door handle. I even scrutinized every passer-by on the pavement, much to the consternation of one ginger-haired man in a pork pie hat who didn't understand my stare at all.

Nearly half an hour had gone by before I, at last, saw the boarding-house door slowly open. Gradually a bobbly head emerged and peered around in all directions. Babs was certainly taking her sleuthing seriously. Then the door opened fully and Babs came running out, clutching at the arm of Dolly Randan, who, in turn, was clutching at her hat.

I got out and opened the back door of the car. Babs and Dolly were now half-way across the road. I extended my arm in greeting and as I did so, a shot rang out. Its deadly echo shattered the suburban stillness. Instantly, I ducked down by the side of the Buick and looked back in the direction the shot seemed to have come from. There was no one to be seen and no blue cars.

I looked back towards Babs and Dolly. They were no longer running. Babs was kneeling on the ground beside a supine body and trying to cradle its head in her hands. A pillbox hat was still rolling towards the gutter.

I ran up to them.

'Johnny!' Babs cried. 'She's been shot. Oh, my God, she's been shot.'

I knelt down. To my intense relief, Dolly Randan was still alive, her eyes open, but staring out in shocked disbelief.

'You were right,' she stammered. 'I should have. . .' Her voice tailed away and I saw blood oozing through an obscenely neat hole in the shoulder of her coat.

The sound of running footsteps alarmed me and I spun round. But it was only a man with a small dog, coming to see what had happened. As I was about to turn back to Dolly, I heard the roar of an engine and out of a small side turning came a blue BMW. It turned right, kicking gravel towards us, then sped off down the road towards Torquay.

I grabbed the man's coat. 'Look, this lady's been shot. Go and ring for an ambulance. And the police. Quickly.'

I ran back to the car. I heard Babs shout, 'Where are you going, Johnny?' as I climbed in and performed a faster U-turn than General Motors ever thought possible when they designed that Buick.

It was on the outskirts of Paignton that I lost sight of him. And all because of those newfangled beacons Mr Hore-Belisha is installing across the land. An old lady took her life in her hands by challenging my Buick to stop. I slammed on the anchors and the car only missed her by a whisker of the Pekinese she was carrying.

As I roared away up the road, a policeman on the pavement waved his arm in a 'softly, softly' gesture, I guess to remind me of another of our Transport Minister's new motorist millstones – the thirty m.p.h. town speed limit. I slowed, but once out of his sight, gave the old straight eight its head once more.

By the time I reached the Brixham-Totnes crossroads, there was no sign of the BMW. I had to stop to let an old steam lorry chug past, then took a right to Totnes on the hunch that the gun-happy driver would be on his way back to Murder Mansion. I was amazed how well old Briggs' Buick coped with the multitude of bends on the undulating road, its knee-action suspension working like a Dervish. Except for a waggon that soon pulled into a field, its horses no doubt glad to be off the metalled road, I had no real obstructions until Totnes.

To my intense relief, as I drove down into the town and across the old toll bridge, I spotted the blue of the BMW at the very top of Fore Street. Even though I kept my fist on the horn, it took an age to get up the High Street and by the time I was out of the town once more, the sports car was nowhere to be seen.

Cursing worse than any Mr Ling, I had no option but to follow my original instincts and turn left towards Kingsbridge. Once again, the Buick belied its stately appearance and must have appeared to the odd farm labourers toiling in the fields alongside the road, like a big, black bat out of hell.

Despite the frenzy of my driving, there was still no sign of my quarry by Halwell, but having gone so far, I really had no option but to go on towards Kingsbridge. Besides, my dander was well and truly up and I was damned if I was going to fail now. It was my one chance to nail something on Seagrave and his blood relative but only if I could get to them in time – before they could get rid of the gun or concoct an elaborate alibi.

It was just before the Churstow turn off that I saw it again, way ahead of me, glinting like the sea in the setting sun. But it had gained considerably on me now and as it turned off the Kingsbridge road and disappeared, I realized that once we were in the maze of narrow, wiggling roads that eventually run down to the sea, it would be only too easy to lose it for good.

But curiously, just after West Alvington, when I had almost given up hope of ever sighting it again, I saw the BMW on the crest of the next incline. I could hardly believe my eyes, for it seemed to be almost stationary. But as I too began to climb, using every last ounce of the

Buick's acceleration, it disappeared again and I guessed I'd been wishful thinking.

About a mile further, however, I came across a wheel lying on the verge beside the road – a distinctive centre lock wheel identical to the ones I knew were on the BMW. Whilst I was still puzzling over that problem, over the next rise I saw what could be its explanation. Way ahead, the rear of the blue sports car was sticking out from a small group of trees. And I fancied it was leaning at a bit of an angle.

I slowed cautiously and pulled up about a hundred feet from the BMW, right by the edge of the copse. I waited for about a minute, but there was no sign of movement and when I wound down my window, the only car's engine I could hear was mine.

Taking a deep breath, I got out of the car, but kept the door open as some kind of shield, in case a bullet came winging my way. But the only sound I could hear was that of a crow bemoaning his lot. Thirty seconds later and I was running, crouched as low as my lengthy old frame would allow, through the trees that edged the road. Very soon, I could see the smooth slope of the front of the car through the silhouettes of the tree trunks. A few more paces and I could see the cockpit. It was empty.

As I dropped down on one knee to wait for any sounds that might give away the whereabouts of the driver, I heard a twig snap behind me. I whipped round just in time to see the strobe of an arm as it crashed a pistol butt onto my cranium. For the second time in no time at all, I joined the stars in the sky.

My head lolled forward and I tried to support it with my hand. But somehow, I couldn't move. Then the pain in my skull hit me, like a thousand hammers. My head jerked upright and I tried to open my eyes. Each eyelid seemed as heavy as the Queen Mary in dry dock, but a slice of light did manage to glimmer through one.

I blinked at the shock and it activated the mechanism of the other. Through a kind of mist, I could just make out a mass of grey which I took to be a wall. I cranked my head to the right. Just more grey. Then I cranked to the left. Here the grey seemed to have a soft pink pattern decorating it. I blinked a few more times, then once more tried to move my hands. I was no more successful than the first time, but, at least, now I knew where they were. Behind my back. With something holding them there. And it felt like rope.

As my eyes now felt for focus, the pink decoration on the grey wall opposite seemed to move. And a voice came out of nowhere.

'Johnny,' it whispered.

I blinked some more and the pink on the wall started to take on a definite form.

'Johnny. Thank God, you've come round,' the voice went on. I tried to still the hammers in my head long enough to identify the speaker. I shut my eyes.

'Oh hell, I'm so sorry, Johnny. It's all my fault.'

By the time I peered out once more, both brain and power of vision had improved enough to identify both the speaker and pink form.

'That you, Tracy?'

'Yes, Johnny.'

I was suddenly aware that I was mostly pink too All my instincts urged my hands to whip round to cover my groin, but firmly behind my back they remained.

'Where on earth are we, Tracy? And our ruddy clothes. Where the blazes have they gone?'

Two more blinks and I saw the scene only too clearly. We were in a small stone building of some sort and trussed like chickens to bolts in the walls. But, as if that weren't enough, we were both stripped down to–well, yours truly to his underpants and the beautiful Tracy to her scanties, for want of a better word. And now my memory had returned with a sickening thump. And I realized how I, at least, had got there.

'Our clothes have gone for a ride in your Buick,' she grimaced.

I was still a trifle befuddled.

'Ride in a Buick. What? What. . .?'

'That's where they've gone, Johnny. You see, they're faking we had an accident.'

'Accident?' I repeated with horror, thinking not only of ourselves, but of the poor owner of the car, Bobby Briggs.

"Fraid so, my darling. We were very silly people. We drove too near to the edge of a cliff – '

'What cliff?'

'Johnny, does it really matter? I don't know what cliff, do I?'

I'm afraid I came out with an expletive I wouldn't say in front of a clothed lady, let alone one dressed, or should I say undressed, like dear old Jane of the *Daily Mirror* strip.

199

'And the clothes?'

'They're going to take them right out to sea tomorrow or sometime, so they're not washed in too soon.'

I tried to get myself more upright and winced as the ropes burned my wrists.

'How do you know all this?'

'Oh, Johnny, it was terrible when they brought you in. They've been crowing ever since, telling me how clever they were to trap you.'

'They didn't trap me. They tried to kill Dolly Randan and I –'

She shook her head.

'No, they didn't Johnny. They intended you to think they were after Dolly, but they weren't.'

'But the bullet hit her. In the shoulder, thank God, but it could have killed her.'

'A mistake, my darling. Seagrave was very cross with Dawlish about that. Apparently, the shot was intended to get close, but not actually hit anyone. Dawlish only fired to get you to follow him, you see. He laughed like a drain that the whole thing worked so easily. He said the most difficult part was not to lose you for too long. He said he even had to wait at the top of one hill for you.'

The expletive surfaced again, I'm afraid. If I had been able to move a muscle, I'd have kicked myself.

'They had got you. So all they needed was me. Correct?'

'Correct.'

I sighed like a dying whale. 'And what little ploy did they use to get you, Tracy?'

'Didn't need one.' She wriggled in her bonds. I tried – rather unsuccessfully – to avert my gaze from her slim and beauteous form that a silk brassiere and frilly panties did little to conceal. 'I...er...sort of walked into it. I can't tell you how sorry I am.'

I'd have waved my hand, if I'd had a hand handy to wave. 'Forget it, Tracy. Just tell me what happened.'

She lowered her eyes. 'Well, I was a bit annoyed with you this morning, as you know. Otherwise, perhaps I'd have had more sense –'

She was interrupted by the sudden scream of a seagull that seemed to come from right above us. For the first time, I took a good look at our surroundings. It was plain as a pikestaff where we were, just from the assorted fishing tackle, lifebelts and sou'westers, let alone the drums of what I took to be petrol and oil, and the distant sound of lapping water.

'Is this part of his boat-house?' I interrupted.

She nodded. "Fraid so.' Then she went on, 'Oh Johnny, I shouldn't have done it, but... anyway, I drove over here on the off-chance I might be able to see his housekeeper alone. I left the car some way from the drive,' she smiled weakly, 'thinking that's what a good detective would do, then climbed into the grounds through a hedge and did a quick recce of the premises. I couldn't believe my luck. There were no cars in the drive and I even went round the back and checked out the coachhouses. No cars there either.'

She eased herself round on the stone flags as far as her bonds would allow. 'Hell, the floor's hard and cold,' she smiled. 'If I'm not careful, I'll get piles before I die. What a way to go.'

I closed my eyes to hide my feelings. Wow, Tracy was one hell of a girl. If I had to be tied up, then there was nobody I'd rather be tied up with in the whole wide world.

'Nobody's going,' I said firmly. 'Least, not that way.'

She blew me a kiss, then went on, 'So, coast being clear, I went round to the back of the house to try the tradesman's entrance. Just as I was about to knock, Mrs Sayers – turned out to be her name –'

'Like Dorothy L.?'

'The very same. She came out with a wicker basketful of washing to hang on the line.'

'Seagrave's old dirty linen,' I smirked. She ignored me, rightly.

'I quickly explained who I was and that I wanted to speak to her about Mrs Seagrave's death. At first, she told me to go away and that there was nothing to tell about the tragedy that the papers hadn't already covered. But then, as I helped her peg out the washing on the line, I started to take her through our theories with the speed of light. I had just got to the bit about Daphne Phipps and the blackmailing, when I heard a car coming up the drive. Like a fool, instead of running, I tried to rattle on about her actor boyfriend and all that. But I don't think she was really listening after she'd heard the car. Anyway, by the time I'd decided discretion was the better part of valour, Seagrave was standing at the back door with a gun in his hand. To my amazement, Mrs Sayers didn't seem to turn a hair. What's more, as he came towards me, she went up to him and said something like, "She has been trying to pump me, Mr Seagrave, but I didn't say nothing."

201

She shrugged. 'So what could yours truly do, but surrender?'

'So the housekeeper is in it in some way too. That would explain how they've been able to get away with – '

'Murder,' she smiled. 'Sorry, Johnny, murders.'

I gave an almighty heave of my bonds, but got nothing for my pains but more pain. A quick glance behind me confirmed that no amount of jerking and heaving was ever going to free me. The ring bolt was mediaeval in its thickness and firmly fixed in the stone of the wall. The ropes were marine-best and strong enough to hold a yacht in a Cape Horn gale.

'Save your energy,' Tracy urged. 'If you're tied like I am, then all the straining in the world won't free you. I've been trying since they left and all I've managed to get is a ladder in my silk stockings.'

I looked across at her legs. At least they had been kind enough not to take her suspender belt when they stripped her. Suddenly, I wished they hadn't. She was just too damned seductive to be tied up opposite, for my battered mind to function as sharply as it must if we were to stand any chance of survival.

I looked around the boathouse once more, in case there was anything useful on the wall or floor that I could wriggle myself towards. But Seagrave and his brother had obviously thought of that one. Everything was neatly piled or hung miles out of reach.

I looked out of the window at the end of the boat-house. I could see nothing but a greyish sky and that I wouldn't be able to see much longer, as it was getting dark.

'Got any ideas?' I asked.

'Not helpful ones,' she smiled weakly, as her eyes scanned my all but unclothed frame. So she had the same little problem I did. If we were tied up much longer like this, Seagrave and his henchman wouldn't need to kill us when they got back. We'd be already dead from sheer frustration.

I suddenly had a thought. 'Where's your SS? Still down the road from here?'

'No, more's the pity,' Tracy replied. 'That's the first thing they did when Dawlish turned up. Take my car keys and drive my SS over to park it at your place.'

'To make it look as if you called round and we both went for a fatal ride in the Buick.'

'I guess so.'

I groaned.

'Head hurting?' Tracy asked anxiously.

'Yes, but it's not that. I'm just regretting that I didn't tell Babs the whole ruddy story. Then she could have told the police and they might add two and two together and, at least, make a call on Seagrave if nothing else.'

'So Babs doesn't know about any blue BMW and who was driving it?'

I shook what was left of my head. 'No. And what with her fretting over poor wounded Dolly, and not knowing one car from another. . .'

'So we'll have to rely on Dolly Randan?'

'She doesn't know about blue BMWs either.'

'But she might come clean about what she knows about Seagrave.'

'And she might not. She was scared to death before she was shot, remember? Imagine what she feels like now. She may just clam up like a – '

'Now let me guess.' Tracy smiled. 'Would it be another clam?'

'Tracy, how can you joke at a time like this?' I pulled again at the bolt in the wall.

'With difficulty, my darling. With difficulty.'

I relaxed. I was wrong and Tracy was right. We had to keep our spirits up. After all, that was just about all we could shift about.

'Sorry,' I muttered. Neither of us spoke for a minute or two. I spent the time staring at the bulb hanging from the ceiling, Tracy appraising her long, silk covered legs.

After a while, I asked, 'Any idea what they plan for us both? I mean they can hardly leave us tied here for ever – or can they?'

'Seagrave is capable of anything, Johnny. Anything. I'm glad you didn't see him when Dawlish stripped me. He seemed to have more hands than a cartoon octopus. And when it came to tying me up, he made a noose with one of the ropes and suggested it might be better just to hang me.'

'God, Tracy. Don't say any more. Please.'

'All right, darling. Don't worry. I've survived. Anyway, rope marks around a neck don't really go with drowned bodies, do they? Not that we'll probably be found, unless the concrete blocks rot before we do.'

I looked at her. 'That's what you reckon they plan for us? Concrete shoes?'

She nodded reluctantly. 'That's what I gather.'

I thought for a minute. 'How are they going to manage it? Toss us out of old Seagrave's Chris-Craft or drop us from a seaplane?'

Tracy did not respond. I persisted. 'Come on, Tracy, tell me. You know, don't you.'

'You tell me first why you were seeing Dolly Randan. It's been puzzling me ever since Seagrave told me you'd been with her.'

So I told her. And recounted what Dolly Randan had told me. When I'd finished, Tracy leant her head back against the wall and shut her eyes.

'Hell, Johnny, if only we had known about all that before. Think of all the blind alleys we've been up.'

'I'd rather not,' I said. 'But Dolly's revelation might well explain what hold Daphne Phipps had over Seagrave.'

'But surely, couldn't he just deny it all? After all, she had no proof of anything. Just Dolly's chat.'

'Yes, you're right.' I shrugged. 'Maybe he was rattled by a girl down in sleepy old Devon knowing anything about his goings-on in naughty old London.'

'And even naughtier Marseilles and downright degenerate North Africa,' Tracy muttered and then suddenly looked up at me. 'Hey, it's all starting to fit.'

'Fit what?'

'Well, I heard Seagrave say to Dawlish, as they were leaving after tying me up, something about, "It will soon all be over," and that he – that's Dawlish – would be back sunning himself on the best beaches in the world in no time.'

'South of France?'

'Could be, couldn't it?' She smiled, 'Devon beaches are good, but not that good.'

'So, maybe old Massey-mouth has chucked in his job hauling advertising signs across the sky and is going back to his old game – hauling young girls across continents.'

'Sounds more than a bit like it. Dawlish wouldn't want his brother to be the only one up to his shifty eyes in money, would he?'

I looked up at the window again. The light was fading fast now and the little bulb hanging from the rafters was having a hard job substituting for the sun.

Out of the gloom, Tracy asked, 'Which do you think it'll be, Johnny?'

204

'Which what?' I retorted dumbly.

'By boat or seaplane?' She went on, almost as if talking to herself: 'If it has to be one or the other, I would prefer an aircraft. At least, for a short while, you and I would be together in the fresh clean air, kind of lord and lady of all we survey. . .like when we first met.'

I wasn't so unkind as to interrupt. As for me, I had no preference for either. After all, corpses don't actually care what hearse they ride in, do they?

Seventeen

We had our answer about an hour later. It was just after our fourth concerted effort to draw attention to our plight by frantically shouting for help. However, only seagulls seemed to hear us, by the way their shrill cries and mewing receded into the distance, away from the now decibel filled building.

We heard it circling long before it landed. We didn't need to see it to know precisely what it was – a bright red and yellow Fox Moth. The noise of the Gypsy Major engine, as the seaplane taxied over to tie up at the jetty, would have been sweet music at any other time but this. Now it just sounded like the Death March from *Saul*.

'So now we know,' Tracy sighed.

I didn't comment. My bludgeoned head was too busy trying to remember every feature of the one and only Fox Moth I had ever flown – a landplane version, registration G-ABT.

'What are you thinking?' she asked.

'Probably the same as you, old girl. How the hell we can out-fox them in the Fox Moth. It'll be our only chance.'

She was about to respond, when the engine was cut and I heard the clunk of the floats hitting the wooden jetty. A moment later, we heard footsteps which proved to be Seagrave's, as he came down to greet his brother-in-crime.

More clunking and footfalls ensued, which were obviously the pilot climbing down from the cockpit onto the floats and Seagrave tethering the aircraft to the jetty. Then a muffled, indecipherable conversation, more footfalls, followed by the dull scrape of bolts, as the wooden door of our section of the boat-house was opened.

The pilot came in first, doffing his flying helmet. His Raymond Massey mouth slanted a smile in our direction.

'My, my,' he leered. 'I hope you two love-birds haven't been getting up to anything naughty-naughty whilst we've been away.'

Seagrave followed and rather brusquely brushed past his brother. I saw his eyes follow every contour of Tracy's exposed body and I pulled savagely away from the wall to distract his attention.

Seagrave chuckled. 'You never give up, do you, Mr Black? Still, I'm not surprised. It's always the mark of the unintelligent man – not to know when it's time to call it a day.'

I didn't give him the pleasure of a reply. He turned to his brother, and pointed at Tracy.

'You know something, Tom, we may be making a hell of a mistake getting rid of her.'

The ginger moustache quivered with incomprehension. 'What do you mean?'

'What I say. Just look at her sitting there. Isn't she delectable?' He grinned. 'Can you imagine what she would fetch over in Morocco or Tunisia? They love long, lithe white bodies over there. Such a change from their usual diet of short, stumpy, hairy women, I suppose. You could make a fortune out of her before she – '

'Shut up, Seagrave,' I shouted, my one good eye blazing. 'You're finished. Don't you know that? You and your brother will never make another buck out of your loathsome trade.'

'Buck?' he laughed. 'I love it, Mr Black. You're starting to talk like you're out of a cheap American detective magazine. Buck, indeed!'

He stood over me, his hands on his hips.

'Anyway, my pathetic friend, you won't be in a position to influence anything I do, from the bottom of the ocean, will you?'

I stared up at him. 'Haven't you got enough money, Seagrave? Or wasn't what your wife left you really worth murdering for, after all?'

He looked across at his brother and both laughed out loud.

'Oh dear, oh dear, Mr Black. You're a worse private eye than even I imagined.' He knelt down in front of me, but too far away for me to lash out at him with my fettered feet. He went on, 'I didn't murder dear Deborah for her money. Least, not directly. You see, I was quite willing to let her live a while longer. After all, we made a perfect couple – in every way. Especially in and around the bedroom. Let us say – ' he pursed his lips '– we shared the same kind of tastes. I find lots of women aren't quite so keen on some of my little games, you see.'

'They don't want to *hang* around with you. Is that it?'

He looked surprised. 'So you did find out something, Mr Black.

Congratulations. I wonder who told you that little snippet.'

'It doesn't matter,' I snapped. 'But very soon, Seagrave, you'll be meeting a hangman's noose again. But this time it'll be you on the receiving end. Anyway, do go on. Dim detectives love to know where they went wrong.'

He uncurled from his crouch. 'I will humour you, Mr Black. I wouldn't have considered murdering Deborah just then, had it not been for her finding out about one of the little ladies I sometimes dally with. Saw me pick her up and take her to the hotel. Hey ho, I should have been more careful, I suppose.' He looked down at me. 'Like you, Mr Black. Anyway, she said she would divorce me. And she meant it. She was going to her lawyer the very next morning. Silly girl. That statement was her death warrant.'

'So you spent the evening thinking of a way of killing your wife that would look like an accident?'

'Not just thinking. The idea of replicating the Isadora Duncan death came quite quickly. The rest of the evening I was out in the Frazer-Nash.'

'Feeding a red scarf into its wheels and transmission.'

'Well, well, well, Mr Black. Full marks, for once.'

His brother suddenly interrupted. 'That man who bought the car must have found some of the other scarf.'

'So he must,' Seagrave smiled. 'Well, there we are, Mr Black. You know it all now.'

'Not quite,' I said. 'We know about the actor you murdered and dropped into a Dartmoor bog, all because he was blackmailing you. But what about the poor girl from whom he learnt his blackmailing tricks – Daphne Phipps? What have you done with her?'

Seagrave looked round at his brother with a scowl. 'Ah, I must confess. We made a little mistake there, didn't we, dear brother?'

'Don't blame me, Mike – ' Massey-mouth began, but his brother persisted.

'But I do, Tom. If you hadn't been with me when the poor girl first came to the house, two deaths could have been avoided.'

He looked back at me.

'Unfortunately, my brother panicked somewhat, when he heard the Phipps girl's then totally unsupported story about our activities of some years ago. And instead of categorically denying her accusations, as I would have done had I been alone with her, he turned to me and blurted out something along the lines of "How the hell did she find out?"' He patted his brother on the shoulder.

'It's all right, Tom. We've repaired the mistake now. With the help of the English Channel.'

Turning back to me, he continued. 'Takes after our mother, does our Tom. All emotion. She never learned to restrain her emotions. Never. Not until her dying day, poor soul.'

The brother came towards me. 'Let's get on with it, for Christ's sake, Mike,' he said, irritably. 'Your bloody trouble is you're never happy unless you can crow over somebody or dominate them.'

Having no other real plan, I opted for all I could think of – delay.

'So when you've got rid of us, what then? You, Tom, go back to living off girls in the South of France. Why did you ever leave and come over here? Did you think you could live off your brother now that he's got his wife's money? Can't see him allowing that for long.'

I saw a flash of anger flick across his face. I went on, 'What did he say, Tom? "Get your own rich wife to murder?"'

Seagrave came across and slapped me hard across the face – twice. It was all my black eye needed, but I smiled. For it proved I had pricked a nerve of his too. I kept going.

'You missed an opportunity whilst you were over, Tom. Did you know that? It's you who should have been after that Susan Prendergast over at Burgh Island, not Michael here. Then you'd have your own heiress. After all, your brother doesn't need two.'

Seagrave rocked with laughter.' That's enough now, Black. I know what you're up to. Trying to needle my brother, so you can try to set him against me, even at this eleventh hour.'

I smirked across at Tracy and shrugged. I think she got my point. For she shrugged too. Setting brother against brother hadn't really been in our minds at all.

But I let it go and said instead, 'Well, Seagrave, dumb detectives will try any old thing, won't they?'

Seagrave looked down at me. 'Not any longer, my friend. Your time is up.'

He took a sharp looking little revolver out of his pocket – it looked like a Beretta to me. Not that it mattered. Every make fires bullets. He wagged it in my direction.

'Tom, you'd better be getting these two onto the plane. Black first. I'll keep him covered whilst you untie him from the wall.'

Dawlish came round behind me. I tried one last ploy. 'Don't you see, you two? The game's already up. Any moment now you'll hear the ding-a-ling of police cars. Why add two more deaths to your list, when you should be making a run for it while there's still a ha'p'orth of time?'

'Johnny's right,' Tracy added in her 'you've got to believe me' voice. 'He told me all about it whilst you two were away.'

I could feel Tom's hands hesitate behind me. I gave a slight tug, but he obviously had not yet loosened the knots sufficiently.

'What did he tell you?' he asked nervously.

I decided to cut in. It would have been caddish to leave it all to Tracy.

'About the call I put in to the police, before I left to pick up Dolly Randan.'

Seagrave gave out with a mocking laugh. 'And what did this mythical telephone call say, pray?'

I quickly glanced across at the window. By the darkness outside, I guessed it must be at least nine thirty or so. 'It said that if I did not report back to them by nine, they were to go to my office and consult a file of mine titled "Seagrave".'

'Don't talk rubbish,' the man of the title snapped. 'You're making it all up. Anyway, your office will have been closed hours by now.'

'My landlord, Mr Ling, lives over the premises. I told them he would let them in.'

'Don't believe him, Tom. Go ahead and get them both on the plane.'

But Tom's hands didn't move.

'What does the file say?' he asked, coming out in front of me.

'Very simple,' I smiled. 'It details how you and your brother are responsible for three deaths and that I, and Tracy here, feel in danger of our lives too. So now you can see why I'm surprised we haven't heard those ding-a-lings already.'

'You're out of your mind,' Seagrave retorted, 'if you expect us to believe all that boloney. Now hurry up, Tom. Get them on the plane.'

I smiled up at Dawlish. 'You taking us on your own, Tom?'

His eyes flickered as he tried to fathom what I was getting at.

'You're taking a bit of a risk, aren't you?'

'I can manage you two, no trouble,' he affirmed and went round the back of me once more.

'I didn't really mean that, Tom.'

I felt him starting to loosen the rope.

'What did you mean then?'

'That you won't be here when the police come. That'll leave your precious little brother scope to explain it all away exactly as he chooses.'

'What?' he grunted. But Seagrave cut in, 'Don't be thick, Tom. He's trying to divide us again. He means that I might blame it all on you.' He came across and kicked my bare leg, charming fellow. 'Now hurry up. Get them on board. You won't be gone any time and the quicker you're back, the better.'

I could feel that Tom had now got me untied from the wall but the Beretta was pointing straight between my eyes. I got up slowly, every joint aching. Dawlish tried to pull me over by the wrists towards his brother but my feet, being tied, wouldn't follow.

'You're coming with me, Mike.'

Seagrave's eyes flared with surprise and anger. 'You're kidding. Are you taking what this dummy says seriously? He's just trying a last wild throw of the dice. That's all.'

'Maybe,' he grunted, fingering his ginger moustache with a freckled hand. 'But all the same – '

Seagrave gestured impatiently with his Beretta. 'All the same nothing. Let's get 'em onto the plane and stop arguing.'

Dawlish (it would confuse to now call him Seagrave) hesitated once more. 'But supposing I have trouble getting them out when I land on the water. It would be easier with two of us.'

'With two of us, we'd just get in each other's way. You know how narrow those floats are. Anyway, I'll give you this gun when you go. This should persuade them to do exactly what you say. Besides, they'll both still be trussed like chickens. All you have got to do is release them one at a time from their seats, give their ropes a yank and they're in the water. They will go to the bottom in no time with those concrete blocks we've got on the jetty.'

The pilot tried one last time. I had to marvel at his persistence. 'But do we need to use the plane? We could take the boat. We wouldn't trip over each other in that.'

'And we wouldn't get to mid-Channel and back until ruddy Christmas, either,' Seagrave retorted. 'Now come on, don't be so damned foolish,'

He suddenly lashed out with an almighty punch to my stomach. As I doubled up, his colleague gave my wrists a tug and I fell to the floor. Almost immediately, I felt him start pulling my feet towards the door. I didn't even have time to blow a kiss to Tracy, before I was outside and could both see and smell the dear old briny which they planned to be our double grave.

As the noise from the spray from the floats suddenly ceased, I turned my head to Tracy, who was tied securely into the seat next to mine.

'Thank God, it's a Fox Moth,' I shouted above the sound of the engine.

'Why?' she shouted back.

I nodded towards our rear. 'We haven't got *him* in the cabin with us.'

I'd better explain to the uninitiated that in the Fox Moth, the pilot sits in an open cockpit, quite separate from the enclosed passenger cabin, which is below and forward of his elevated position.

'So what?' she grimaced. 'Tied up like this, we don't really need privacy, do we?'

I nodded and cast my eyes down to my feet. She looked across.

'I noticed it when they were putting me aboard.'

'Noticed what?'

I strained and moved my bound ankles as far rear-ward as I could. To my relief, I felt the rope contact something hard.

'The frame of my seat. It's got a ragged weld on the tubing.'

She raised her lovely eyebrows. 'Ragged enough?'

'We'll see,' I said. 'It's about our only chance.'

I started to move my feet up and down against the tubular bar, but, curses, the bands across my thighs holding me to the seat cushion prevented the movement being more than an inch and a half, a couple of inches at most. Then I had to stop, as the plane banked steeply to climb out of the bay. For a brief moment, I had a perfect view out of the side window of the black curving landscape and the lights from widely scattered houses twinkling in the dark. Then suddenly, in the split second before we resumed level flight, I seemed to see a mass of headlights coming down what I took to be the sea road that led down to Murder Mansion. But in a blink of an eye, the vision was gone and I was back to the painful inching of my ankle ropes up and down against the seat support.

I looked across at Tracy and saw, in the light of the moon, that she was attempting the same old trick on her own seat.

But when she caught me looking at her, she shouted, 'Not much cop, darling. Mine feels as smooth as a baby's bottom. How's yours doing?'

'Goodness knows,' I said. 'Let's just hope the file in my baby's nappy is rough enough.'

Despite my almost naked condition, I could feel the sweat beading on my forehead with the effort and the heat from the engine just ahead of us. Soon it had formed a rivulet into my black eye, and I cursed that my hands were not free to wipe my face dry.

Soon I saw in the dim light that Tracy had given up her efforts.

'Sorry, darling,' she mouthed. 'Too smooth.'

I cursed the welder at Rumbold who had made her seat. Didn't he realize that jagged welds can save lives?

My ankles now were hot with the friction of the fretted ropes and I began to wonder whether the ropes or my ankles would be the first to drop off – that is, if either did, before Massey-mouth landed us in deep water. The pain caused more rivulets to flood into my eyes and my vision became intermittently blurred. The whole agony would have been much more sustainable, if only I had a way of seeing whether my efforts were having any effect. For the friction alone told me nothing, except that I was fast losing all of the skin off my ankles.

It seemed an eternity before I at last felt the first strand give, but at least I now had encouragement to redouble my agonized efforts. With my eyes tightly closed against the pain and sweat, I increased the tempo of my fretting to the very maximum, short of causing a heart attack or seizure, that is. I didn't really want to die trying not to die and the crazy thought somehow enlivened my spirits.

Tracy said nothing, knowing, I guess, I needed all my strength for action, not words. Not that I was exactly silent. The pain now was causing me to gasp and groan in roughly equal measures, but, luckily, the noise of the motor absorbed most of them.

At long last, I felt more strands go and then, as they say in penny dreadfuls, with a bound, I was free. Well, my ankles were, at least. Nothing else. I kicked my legs out in front of me and stubbed my foot on one of the concrete blocks on the floor ahead of me, that were ready and waiting to be tied to us at the last minute.

I let out with an unprintable expletive. Tracy let out with a whoop of joy.

'Don't celebrate yet, Tracy,' I shouted. 'My hands are still tied and I'm still trussed to this seat.'

The plane banked slightly and moonlight flooded into the cabin. Outside the window, the sea looked like a huge sheet of rippled glass, as the waves bounced the light from one to another.

I looked down at the ropes binding my thighs to the seat cushion. It soon became obvious that the only way I could be free of them was to wriggle my bottom as far forward on the seat as possible, in the hope that they would slide off the end and give me sufficient room to lift my legs, one at a time, out of their embrace. But there was one hell of a snag. I was also tied to the backrest, which made wriggling forward a kind of ridiculous challenge. However, Johnny Black is nothing if he is not ridiculous.

I suddenly heard what I had been dreading. The engine being throttled back. I gave one last desperate push down on the seat cushion, at the same time mightily heaving my body up and against the seat back, to try to slip the ropes off the base of the seat, when I heard a crack like a rifle shot.

For a split second, I though someone must have fired at me, then to my amazement, I fell backwards and slightly sideways and struck my head on the side of the cabin.

Somewhat dazed, I heard Tracy emit another whoop of joy. The next second, the whole cabin tilted downwards, as the plane began its descent.

I wriggled myself semi-upright and discovered immediately what had happened. My straining against the backrest had snapped it off where it joined the seat. (Thank you, Rumbold, for employing that lousy welder.)

With Tracy looking on excitedly, I now wriggled backwards from the ropes across the seat and was soon free of them. I could now move about the cabin, the only restrictions being no hands and the cursed seat back still roped to me like a Sherpa's load.

'What about my teeth?' Tracy shouted and gnashed them once or twice to try to show their effectiveness as rope demolishers.

I shook my head, as I suddenly realized there was only one way I could fool our executioner when he came down to the door. And that was to appear to be still tied up. Besides, I doubted if I'd have enough time to free myself, teeth or no teeth, before we landed on the water, for the angle of descent was now quite steep.

The ropes that should have been over my thighs, I could do nothing about – I just hoped the window in the door was too high for him to see down that far. I explained my plans quickly to Tracy, then sat back on the now crooked cushion, my body holding up the backrest, rather than the other way about.

In under thirty seconds, we heard the floats kick up the first spray. The plane lifted momentarily, then settled back on the water, the cacophony of metal hitting waves filling the aircraft and drowning the note of the now throttled back engine.

Before we actually came to a stop, the plane executed a hundred-and-eighty-degree turn, presumably, so that the pilot could make an instant take-off into the wind directly we had been dumped overboard. I was expecting to hear the motor being cut, but, instead, we heard the slight thuds of Massey-mouth getting down from the cockpit and onto the wing outside our cabin door.

I put my foot on the door catch, then glanced at Tracy. 'Hold onto your hat, old girl.'

'I'm not wearing a hat,' she grinned bravely. 'I'm three-quarters naked or haven't you noticed?'

I had no time to reply, before a face appeared at the door window. I waited until the eyes started to relax and a smile to lift the ginger moustache, then I pressed my foot down on the catch and pushed with all my might at the flimsy door.

There was a scream, followed by a horrendous scratching sound. Then an almighty splash.

I edged my way cautiously out of the door. But there was no sign of Seagrave's brother. I got onto the lower wing, then heard more screams. This time they weren't of surprise, but of supplication. Still encumbered with the backrest and my hands tied behind me, I felt very unsteady on the wing, as the plane bobbed about with every wave. The cries were now receding, as I peered out across the black water, trying to spot any sign of the pilot. As the moon came out from behind a cloud, I saw the white of some disturbed water. But it was a good two hundred feet away. My immediate instinct was to jump in and try to rescue what was obviously a man who couldn't swim well

215

enough to survive in that swell. But I remembered in time that my hands were tied – quite literally. All I could do was watch helplessly until an arm came vertically out of the water for the last time.

Eighteen

Removing the backrest was comparatively simple, if time consuming. For the now broken structure of my seat provided ample chafing points. Once unfettered, I released Tracy, who then insisted on embracing me for a further ten minutes. Still, that part couldn't be reckoned a hardship in anybody's old book.

And taking the controls of an aeroplane (by necessity, please note) would have been the greatest lift in the world after our gruesome experiences, had I possessed such things as a flying helmet and goggles. And, what's more, had I ever flown a seaplane before in my life. Correction – *taken off* and *landed* a seaplane before. The flying along part, I could do blindfold with any aircraft.

However, with the luck of a novice who had read just enough about floatplanes in his life to know about such things as 'porpoising' and 'getting up on the step' and the like, I just about got us unstuck from the water without destroying the whole flimsy structure, and by dint of a little primitive celestial navigation, flew us to the bright lights of Torquay.

The sight of a Fox Moth calmly cruising into the harbour at that hour of the night caused more than a few old salts' mouths to gape, as they strolled around on the quayside, having a last pipe in the balmy spring air. But what made then stop and salivate was the sight of the two occupants, nude except for underpants and the scantiest of scanties, and shivering with cold from the freezing flight.

In fact, word of our arrival got round so fast that we didn't have to seek out the police ourselves at all. And no more than ten minutes after tying up at the quay, we were getting into a black Wolseley, blankets around our shoulders like a couple of Peruvian peasants and on our way to join the other Wolseleys that they told us had been at Seagrave's place since around nine thirty. So it hadn't been just wishful thinking about the headlights I had seen from the plane's window, as

Seagrave's brother had taken off on his murder mission. But what I dearly wanted to know was how they'd got there.

I was soon to learn. For as our car pulled up in front of the mansion, I was amazed to see Babs coming down the steps and getting into one of the Wolseleys parked in the drive.

I got out of the car before it had totally stopped, and ran over to her, before the policeman could close her door. In my hurry, my blanket had parted somewhat and I saw her baby-blue eyes go from my face to my underpants and back again with blank astonishment.

'Johnny,' she eventually cried out, 'thank heaven you're safe.' By the time she was out of the car and embracing me, she was crying her eyes out.

'It was you, Babs, wasn't it?' I exclaimed. 'What on earth did you do to get the police here? I've never really told you anything about the case.'

She stood back from me, tears coursing down the powder on her cheeks.

'I know, Johnny. That's why, after the ambulance had come and taken poor Dolly Randan away, I took the policemen back to your office and I found your file and made them read it. You see, I guessed you would be in some kind of trouble, Johnny, chasing that gunman. I hope you don't mind.'

I clasped her to me. 'Mind, Babs? Are you kidding? You couldn't have done better. You know something? You have got the makings of a real professional.'

She looked up at me, her eyes now brimming with tears *and* excitement. 'Do you mean it, Johnny? Can I leave Mr Ling and come and work for you? Say yes, oh, please, Johnny.'

She had really caught me on the hop, but what could I say to a girl who must have only escaped Dolly Randan's bullet by a flutter of an eyelash?

'All right, Babs, directly I get another big case, you're on.'

The next moment she gave me a hug of which a jolly old grizzly could have been proud. By this time, Tracy was at my side and she quickly disengaged and immediately asked, as you might expect, what on earth had happened to us both and, as she said to Tracy, 'your lovely clothes'?

I was about to reply, when a skeletal hand descended on my shoulder. I looked round and into the face of Inspector Wyngarde.

'Excuse me, Mr Black, but I gather from my colleagues that you and I', he turned to Tracy, 'and your friend, here, Miss King – have I got your name right? – '

'More or less,' Tracy smiled and he went on – 'have quite a lot to say to each other. Would you care to come in? I can have a constable drive over to your home to get some clothes.'

I stopped him. 'Before that, Inspector, you've got to tell me – is Seagrave still here? Did you catch him?'

He gave a thin smile. 'He's still here, Mr Black, don't worry.'

'And has he confessed to killing his wife and Henry Swindon and. . .?'

'Uncle Tom Cobley,' he grinned. 'Well, he didn't right away. Denied everything, of course. And I began to think you and Miss Morgan here had led me up the garden path.'

I put my arm around Babs' shoulder. 'I'd never do that, Inspector, honest, I'd never. . .' she began, but Tracy calmed her down.

'But he's come clean now?' I pressed on.

He nodded. 'Wonderful thing, wireless,' he said. 'Wish we'd had the benefit of it in our cars years ago.'

'What's that got to do –?' I began, but he raised his hand to silence me.

'That's how we heard about your and Miss King's arrival in Torquay. One of our Wolseleys is equipped with a wireless unit. I naturally imparted the gist of your news to Mr Seagrave, who, after a final bluster, confessed, with a performance that was quite worthy of the London stage. Half-way through, we all started to feel the whole thing was unreal, Mr Black, and that we were just an audience in the stalls of some theatre.' He nodded in the direction of the house. 'He's only just finished. It's a pity you and Miss King missed it. It was a quite extraordinary experience.'

I raised my eyebrows. 'Once a ham actor, always a ham actor, Inspector.'

Tracy pinched my arm. 'You should know,' she grinned.

So that, more or less, is how Black Eye's first significant case ended. Seagrave confessed to killing both his wife and Daphne Phipps. In court later, he described, in graphic detail, the macabre method of the latter's death. He had hung her from the rafters in one of his barns. 'I had always wanted to hang a woman for real. And that was my chance.

After all, no one would see the rope marks on her neck at the bottom of the English Channel.'

However, he categorically denied killing Henry Swindon and attributed that death to his over-hasty and emotional brother. 'There was no need to kill him. He could prove nothing. This time my dear brother had not made the mistake of panicking in front of him. But he panicked the next day. I should have known he would. He phoned Swindon and made a late night appointment, as if he was going to hand over money. He drove him in his car to a place near the aerodrome. There he battered him to death, then put his body aboard a plane and inverted the craft over the bogs on Dartmoor. He was too much of a coward, you see, to fly out over the sea in a land plane, which was all he could lay his hands on that week.'

Michael Seagrave was hanged in Pentonville on a raw and blizzard swept December dawn. It seemed somehow inappropriate to disturb the virgin white of the snow to hide him six feet under. No trace of Daphne Phipps was ever found. As for poor Dolly Randan, she recovered well from her shoulder wound and was back on the dance floor within two months. But not that belonging to Herr Adrian Feather. She moved to Exeter to the Stardust School of Dancing, a much larger and more sophisticated academy. Last thing I heard, she was engaged to be married to an ex-airship rigger from Cardington.

And Diana Travers? We were in time to stop her flight to Le Touquet the morning after Seagrave's arrest. When the police had finished with us, we spent most of the next day with her. For the final revelations, I think, had shaken her to the core, especially the terrible end of the over-ambitious Daphne Phipps. I guess guilt was eating away at her soul for having loved such a man once and then having more or less given her blessing to his pursuit of her tragic sister. Whatever the reasons, they were enough to persuade her eventually to sell up and move away. But not before she had presented me with a most handsome cheque and a beautiful silver box from Aspreys, on which is mounted a stunningly accurate model of a Hawker Hart.

At present, she is living near Dover and now frequently crosses the Channel to visit a man she met at her friend's house in Le Touquet. (Yes, she did at last visit her.) I hope they make something of it. Diana Travers deserves some happiness while she is still young enough to revel in it.

Which brings me to dear old Buick-less Bobby Briggs. Naturally enough, he didn't take too kindly to the idea of his car now being a jolly old submarine, but a generous cheque from my client soon turned his dismay into delight and he at once resumed talking to me, if not lending cars. However, he did do a wonderful job on my La Salle, which was back with me by the end of June, bright and shiny and rarin' to go. And Mrs Briggs, I'm sure, had worked on him about the bill. It totted up to only a pony, bless her.

Diana Travers' cheque naturally did wonders for my ego and my cottage. The latter is now much more shipshape and Bristol fashion and even sports a decent bathroom, with one of those modern panelled baths. The tiles on the old walls reflect my singing well too.

And from that moment on, to my intense relief, Black Eye began to take off and soon I no longer needed those little adverts in the local rag.

Last, but not least, of course, there's Tracy. Not was, but is. She's still around and I'm mighty proud she is. What she sees in me, really, I don't know. But I do know what I see in her. The list begins with . . . a jolly fine pilot when I feel like flying, a jolly fine chauffeur when I'm taking a back seat, a jolly fine cheerer-upper when I'm down in the dumps, a jolly fine friend when I'm lonely, a jolly fine ally when things gang up, and a jolly fine . . . . Well, she's coming round in a few minutes and if she finds me still writing, she'll kill me – and that's without reading what I've written!